Jagged Grass
Book I

James Tindall

Look for the following books from this author in the future:

Sun God's Treasure (Book I)
Alas Omega (Book II)
The Transparency (Book II Seminole Trilogy)
Indian Law (Book III Seminole Trilogy)

Authors Note:

A fully developed screenplay is available for this novel, i.e., Jagged Grass. Please contact author for information.

JAGGED GRASS
Book I

James Tindall

Library of Congress Cataloging-in-Publication Data
Tindall, James
  Jagged Grass/James Tindall
    p. 277

ISBN: 0-9817037-5-5
ISBN: 978-0-9817037-5-6

Cover: Oil painting by Guy LaBree, Hollywood, Florida. All rights reserved. Font: Palatino Linotype; 10.5 point.

Published by DTP Publishing, Denver, Colorado

Printed in the United States of America

10 9 8 7 6 5 4 3 2 1

ISBN: 0-9817037-5-5
ISBN:978-0-9817037-5

#1 Bestseller from the author of "Sun God's Treasure." His most compelling Native American saga taking you to an unforgettable place, the Florida Everglades, where the traditions of the past collide with corruption, greed, and politics. A magnificent novel about Billie Panther, Tribal Councilman of the Panther clan, who is pitted against modern challenges and a mafia adversary to preserve his dignity, the heritage of his people, and the love of Christina.

The Post
A fast paced, fun read that enlightens us about a people, our hearts, and the environment of a dying ecosystem where prehistoric creatures coexist with nature and man's greed...

Sun Times
An extraordinary new novel of man's struggle with himself...

The Herald
... a natural born storyteller..., he taps into the roots we call home...

Jacob Osceola
... weave of excitement, fascination, and conflict..., renews memories of the long struggle of obstacles placed before the Indian..., if you like Hillerman, you will love Tindall.

Seminole Tribune
Colorful, captivating, riveting... You cannot put it down...

Authors Note:
Big Cypress Reservation is just north of Big Cypress National Preserve. Other Reservations that are part of the sovereign nation of the Seminole Tribe of Florida are in Immokalee, Brighton, Tampa, Ft. Pierce, and Hollywood. The latter is located about 20 miles north of Miami along Interstate 95.

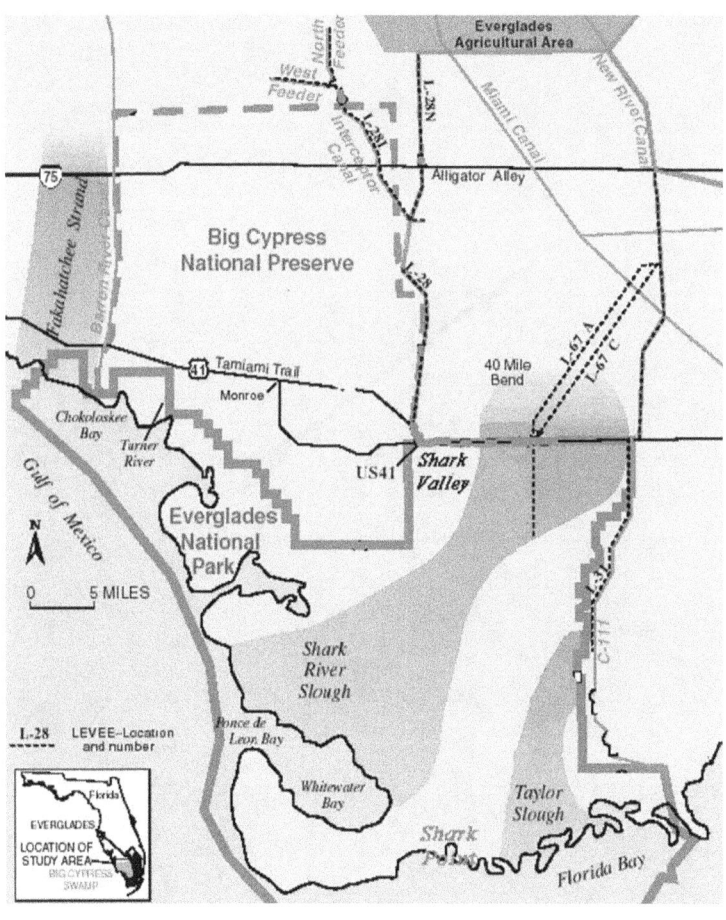

CHAPTER 1

It was humid, sweltering as the orange glow of the rising sun bleached the eastern horizon. Billie Panther, sitting on the tail gate of his pickup, glanced at his watch, 6:00 a.m.; the day promised to be a long one. Billie and his crew were about to attempt the capture of a large alligator to use in the wrestling pit of the Seminole Tribe of Florida's Hollywood Reservation. Usually docile, gators', as the natives were fond of calling them, can be extremely aggressive and quite unpredictable.

As Billie sat waiting for his crew, at the community store and diner on Big Cypress Reservation, located in the middle of the Florida Everglades, he thought about some of the struggles in his past and how he had ended up here. He was an important man in the tribe. As a Big Cypress Council Representative, he had paid his dues. Having worked hard to obtain his council position, especially since he was a half breed, he bristled with confidence. Although many were quick to remind him of his half-breed status, he had shown them all. Billie had spent time in the military receiving an honorable discharge and then, he had attended Yale University obtaining degrees in hydrology and law. Smart as a whip, he was constantly alert to the needs of the Seminole Tribe, his people.

Billie was a handsome man possessing an easy, contagious smile that relaxed everyone with whom he came in contact. His thoughts were interrupted as tribal constable Genesis Motlow pulled up with Timmy Jumper and Jacob Cypress. They were a motley crew. Genesis, with severe, weather-beaten features, looked like the meanest man alive, but underneath his stoic and foreboding features was a kindness that knew no bounds, to which many could attest. He smiled at Billie as he jumped out of his truck. "It's going to be a hot one today," Genesis said.

"Yeah, it's already 85 degrees and climbing," Billie said. "The weather report calls for about 100 with 95 percent humidity."

"August in the Everglades," chimed Timmy.

"Well, let's get this over with," Jacob said. "I've got too much to do today and I don't want to be wrestling an alligator at three this afternoon."

"Alright then," Billie said. "Let's make like a bakery truck and get our buns a rollin'."

They climbed into Billie's truck and headed south toward the airboat docks. The morning was calm. Not a soul was stirring, which wasn't surprising since the constant heat and humidity created a lethargic attitude that was hard to shake off. It just seemed to suck the life out of you. Even with the best of intentions, it was difficult to climb out of bed to face another hot August day in the Glades. Already sweating from the humidity, their strength was sapped before the day began.

They had the mood of men returning from work, not going. No one talked as the truck wove its way down Snake Road. Occasionally, a Whippoorwill could be heard calling as they passed willow heads along the highway. Across the pastures were small herds of wild pigs and an infrequent flock of turkeys, mingled here and there with White Ibis and Egrets. The humidity had created a thick haze, not yet burned off by the sun. It hung like a heavy blanket over the cypress and Sawgrass swamp. Genesis was thinking it would be the perfect backdrop for a horror movie of a "Jack the Ripper" type.

After a few minutes, the truck turned east and headed down a muddy dirt road that slowly changed from pressed shell rock to black muck submerged beneath coffee-colored water. Billie slowed the truck as he slipped it into four-wheel drive. "It'll be a great day if we can just keep from getting stuck," Billie said. "Somehow, I don't think we'll have the energy to get out after wrestling this gator."

"How big is it anyway?" Jacob asked.

"You don't want to know," Genesis replied.

"It's so big you're going to wish you had stayed in bed, its nickname is Goliath; that should give you an idea." Timmy said.

"I'm regretting this already; Billie always manages to recruit me for some fool thing that no one else wants to do," Jacob muttered.

They all smiled at him.

The truck bounced back and forth and up and down as they made their way to the airboat docks at road's end. By the time they reached their destination, both truck and gear were covered with syrupy muck that dripped like black ooze from every piece of gear and metal. The sun, a rising orange globe, was now clearly visible above the tops of the cypress. As it climbed, so did the temperature. Billie coasted to a stop as they reached the docks. Everyone piled out and began collecting equipment: ropes, snare, noose, gloves, various tools, and a couple of cell phones, mostly used for emergencies. Timmy walked over to the two airboats pulled up to the dock and began checking their 180 horsepower, Lycoming airplane engines for proper oil levels, spark, and fuel.

Billie approached with a canvas tote bag that carried his lunch, a water bottle, cell phone and first aid kit. "How are the boats?" Billie asked.

"Everything looks good," Timmy said. "They shouldn't give us any problems."

"Good to hear it," Billie said. "Hey Jacob, let's go before the sun bakes our ass."

"Your chauffeur will be right there," Jacob yelled.

"C'mon, I don't have all day," Genesis quipped. "Someone might get mugged and then where would I be?"

"Based on what you said about this gator, it's likely the only ones who will get mugged today are we wild Injun's," Jacob joked.

Laughing, they loaded into the two airboats: Jacob and Billie in one, Timmy and Genesis in the other. "If we somehow manage to catch this monster, who is going to transport it to Hollywood?" Genesis asked.

"I have another crew coming in about one o'clock," Billie said. They'll be ready at the diner when you get back."

"Cast away then, shall we," Timmy said.

They started the air boats and pulled away from the docks. For a few minutes they were in the open water of a large pond, but shortly entered the nine-foot-high sawgrass of the Florida Everglades. The boats left a depressed trail of grass behind them as they slipped effortlessly through the swamp. Riding high in the seats, they could not help noticing the shimmering heat waves rising above the sawgrass. As they passed nearby hammocks, Anhinga birds, commonly called water turkeys by the locals, could be seen perched on overhanging branches. Each time they passed one, it would dive into the water, like a seal performing a trick.

Billie was thinking hard about a business deal he had been working on. It would be good for his people, although it involved going into business with a New York firm installing a landfill on Big Cypress in return for a long-term lease and a large share of the revenues. The people of Big Cypress would benefit through added jobs. Being more than forty miles distant from the nearest town did not seem like much of a hardship, but when you didn't have a car to seek employment off the reservation, you might as well be as far away as China. The biggest drawback Billie could think of concerning the deal was potential environmental damage. However, as a qualified hydrologist, he knew that landfills were safe when installed properly. Still, it worried him. Big Cypress was home, and he couldn't bear to see such a pristine ecosystem harmed. There was no doubt the Everglades had evolved into one of the most unique ecosystems in the world, to which the white man, tourists, and even some of his own people had caused irreversible damage. Protecting it was a high priority.

As a boy growing up on Big Cypress and going to school in nearby Clewiston, he had watched the farmers ditch and dike the surrounding swamps to plant sugar cane, citrus, sod, vegetable crops, and raise cattle. The once pristine wilderness had sprouted ugly patches of endless farms and ranches, cut into numerous sections like a patchwork quilt by the canals that ran through them. Without the canals, there could be no water control and no crops. Although a necessary evil, they were unsightly and damaging to the environment in Billie's opinion. He had seen Alligator Alley, later called State Road 84, then Everglades Parkway, and finally renamed I-75, cross the glades south of the reservation, stretching from Naples on the Gulf of Mexico to Hollywood on the eastern Atlantic seaboard. The population of Broward County, which comprised Ft. Lauderdale and Hollywood, was growing at the rate of a thousand families per week with no indications of stopping. A great burden was being placed on the Key Biscayne aquifer system that runs beneath the swamp southward to Florida Bay. The Glades and Lake Okeechobee were also taxed and now served as primary water storage areas for the population of south Florida.

All this disturbed Billie. He didn't know what to do, or if anything could be done to curb the growing population. With the current growth rate alone requiring an additional half million gallons of water per day by the families moving into just Broward and Dade Counties, plus the millions more for residents and businesses who were already here, it was no wonder there had been droughts and fires for several years. Perhaps one day he thought, the population growth could be managed and brought more in line with current land and water resources, but the more people there were, the more trash they would generate. This would create a thriving business environment, ideal for landfill revenues. However, there was another dilemma, the Seminoles had water rights on Big Cypress reservation and the surrounding farmers were continually clamoring for more water from them. Now that water was in short supply, Billie didn't know how much longer they could maintain good relations with their farm and ranch neighbors. The new landfill could tax an already strained relationship.

Time had passed quickly as the two-hour trek seemed like a few short minutes, interrupting Billie's thoughts as the two teams reached their destination, a cypress head in the middle of the vast expanse of sawgrass. The airboats glided to a stop as Timmy and Jacob cut their motors. The four men jumped off the boats into waist deep water, then waded through the sawgrass along a narrow trail into the head. Deeper inside the head, sawgrass gradually gave way to more open water and cypress knees, a favored tourist item at the local Seminole shops. Seminole collectors would dry them, saw the wood into more aesthetically appealing shapes and coat them with varnish, then fashion clocks and other specialty items from them.

In the middle of the cypress head was a gator hole. There was no telling how deep it was. Some have been measured to depths of sixty feet by local game biologists of the Florida Game and Fish Commission. Many swamp animals owed their lives to the alligator. In times of drought, the gator holes throughout the swamp become the main supply of water. Many animals die at the grasp of death from their swift, vice-like jaws, but most of them would have died from drought and starvation anyway. Although alligators' prey upon their share of the local wildlife, they kill only what they need and save more lives than they take because of their water engineering feats in creating gator holes. Although such a task would require the use of a dragline by man, gators had learned the engineering feat through eons of evolution. All in all, the alligator does a great deal for the wildlife and overall balance of the ecosystem.

Timmy put his equipment down and began attaching a snare to the end of a long pole. He had years of experience snaring gators and was a good man for the job. Once the snare was attached, Timmy made a large loop in it so it could be submerged in the water and easily moved over the alligator's head, when and if they could call it up. All four men gathered around Timmy. Genesis cupped his hands over his mouth as Timmy lowered the snare into the water. With the snare lowered, Genesis began calling the alligator. "Aaargh, aaargh, aargh," over and over, pausing between every two or three calls.

Suddenly, the gator's eyes emerged above the surface of the water, a few feet in front of Genesis. As their mouths fell open and their eyes widened, it was evident they were astonished at its size. Swallowing hard, with no time for words, Timmy maneuvered the snare and slipped the noose quickly over the gator's head. With a quick yank, the gator exploded into a fury of whipping tail and swaying head. It was over twelve feet long, and judging from the size of it, probably a thousand pounds. Adrenaline began to rush through their veins as the life of the party made its attendance noticed. All four men strained mightily as Timmy pulled the gator back into the cypress head away from the hole so that they could surround and subdue it. Thrashing wildly about, the gator made the process a slow one. After a few minutes, they had managed to get the gator about fifty feet into the cypress head toward the direction of the airboats.

Billie, having helped Timmy on previous occasions, approached the gator's head while Genesis and Jacob carefully approached the thrashing tail. Billie was trying to get his arm around the gator's neck. In the blink of an eye, the gator snapped its head back and its mouth closed like a steel trap. Fast as lightening, the head twisted back the other way with Billie's shirt sleeve and a piece of skin in its mouth; the reptile had narrowly missed ripping Billie's arm off at the elbow.

"Damn it, hang onto the son-of-a-bitch before he kills me, Jacob," Billie screamed.

"So, sue me, he's like a greased pig," Jacob screamed back. "Maybe we should shoot the bastard and find a smaller one."

All four men were gasping for breath as they tried to control the gator. It was difficult to maintain footing as the alligator tossed them like salad.

"Genesis, help Jacob," Timmy yelled. "I'll tighten the snare and maybe Billie can get a noose around its mouth."

Billie had gotten the gator in a head lock. He relaxed his left hand and slid it behind his waist, returning with a noose, which he quickly slipped over the gator's mouth. Genesis and Jacob were holding onto the gator's tail by a thread, getting slung back and forth, above the water one minute and below it the next, barely able to breathe.

"Hold him a minute longer," Billie yelled. "There, got the slick son-of-a-bitch."

The four men held the gator down as Timmy adjusted the snare around its neck and Billie made sure the mouth was securely tied. Each man grabbed the gator by one of its four legs as they began hauling and dragging it back through the cypress head to the waiting airboats. Passing through the cypress knees into the sawgrass, the trail narrowed. They were forced to walk on either side, right through the sawgrass. It began tearing at their clothes and the flesh of their hands and arms. By the time the group had reached the boats, their clothes were ripped to shreds; blood mixed with sweat as everything they wore slowly turned crimson, blood flowing from too many small cuts.

Using the boat as a lever, they managed to push, pull and drag the alligator into the front; it took almost an hour and was all they could do to stand. Billie could not remember being so tired. The sun was almost straight up as sweat poured from their hot bodies, dripping off their foreheads and into their eyes, stinging their cut skin. Constantly trying to wipe the burning sweat away with sweaty arms was a losing proposition. The four of them were panting like racehorses, examining their torn clothes and bloody hands. Almost unconsciously, they began washing their face, hands, and arms, cupping their hands to collect small amounts of water from the swamp. After a few minutes they were able to function and climbed back aboard their respective airboats. Atop the boats, a gentle breeze cooled their sweat-soaked bodies.

"Damn, that breeze feels great," Timmy remarked.

"It'll feel a lot better once we get underway," Jacob said.

"This gator will be great for the wrestling pit down in Hollywood," Genesis said. "It should help us earn some much-needed money."

"I'd rather make a pair of boots out of the old bastard," Timmy gasped.

"Well, next time they can come get old Al E. Gator themselves," Jacob said.

"Thanks for the help everyone," Billie said. "Genesis, you and Timmy take Goliath to Big Cypress so the other guys can transport it down to Hollywood for us."

"No problem," Genesis said. "By the way, I'm surely grateful for the opportunity to get out of the office Billie, but next time, let's do something else. Somewhere the sawgrass doesn't rip me and my clothes to shreds."

"Jagged grass is a bitch ain't it," Jacob smiled.

"Yeah," Timmy replied, "But, what you gonna do?"

"We'll catch you later Billie," Genesis said. "Let's go Timmy."

Timmy cranked the airboat and roared off toward the docks. Billie and Jacob sat watching for a few minutes until they were out of sight. They just didn't have the energy to move.

"Where to Billie?" Jacob asked.

"Shark Key," Billie replied. "I need to go by the hammock and see mom."

They literally flew across the swamp, Billie sitting in front, Jacob at the controls. There was nothing but sawgrass and a few hammocks as far as the eye could see: the terrain flat as a tabletop. Nearing Alligator Alley, Timmy slowed down as he ran the boat under an overpass that supposedly allowed the swamp to flow from the north to the south without interruption. Once through, he opened the throttle again and sped quickly away. Now a toll road, in the back of his mind, Jacob wondered how much money the state received for tolls each day.

The airboat was gliding effortlessly, mist thrown in its wake, leaving its characteristic trail. Abruptly, the engine sputtered several times and conked out, bringing the boat to a stop.

"What's wrong?" Billie asked.

"The fuel filter is a little clogged," Jacob said. "I need to clean it. By the way, did you ever call that guy in New York about the landfill project? You told me to remind you."

"Damn!" Billie exclaimed. "I forgot; I'm so tired I can't even think straight. Thanks for reminding me."

Jacob began checking the engine. Looking at the fuel filter, he could see a big wad of crud in it. He pulled out a few tools and greasy rag, then patiently sat down and began working with the filter, a not unfamiliar site in the swamp. Billie watched him for a minute, entranced at his aptitude for equipment. Snapping out of it, he reached into the canvas tote bag and retrieved his cell phone. He climbed into the driver's seat for an unobstructed view of the Everglades as he dialed a New York number. While the phone on the other end was ringing, Billie cast his gaze over the vast expanse of the glades, reveling in its pristine beauty, inhaling the aroma of it.

Paul Lorio was sitting at his desk sorting through budgets for the proposed landfill project with the Seminole Tribe. Unknown to the Tribe, he was a mafia boss, a man to be reckoned with. He always got his way and when he didn't, people usually didn't live to talk about it. He was ruthless and cunning, yet suavely friendly and charming. Unlike most bosses in his position, he believed in using proper language most of the time and thus, refrained from swearing. He believed it was pointless and often remarked there were better ways to express one's ideas.

The intercom on Paul's desk suddenly crackled to life. "You have a telephone call on line two Mr. Lorio," the secretary said.

"Who is it?" Paul asked.

"It's a Mr. Billie Panther with the Seminole Tribe of Florida sir," she replied.

"Excellent," Paul said. "Put him through and hold all other calls. Also, call Ms. Sandow and tell her that we need to talk immediately."

"I'll take care of it," the secretary said.

As Paul picked up the telephone, he swiveled a half circle in his chair and stared out the large plate-glass window in front of him. His view was filled with the ugliness of an unsightly landfill. Fortunately, the glass kept out the stench that went with it. Bulldozers were pushing heaps of trash; trucks rushing to and fro, dumped even more trash. Here and there, flocks of frenzied sea gulls fought each other for choice morsels of New York's finest garbage. The view was in stark contrast to that of the primeval beauty of the Florida Everglades. None of this mattered to Paul. He was a businessman; the only thing that mattered was the money he could make on this venture. The amount promised to be substantial.

"Billie, it's great to hear from you," Paul said. "Have you and the tribal government made a decision about the landfill operation?"

"It looks like it'll be a go," Billie said. "However, I have two council members who want additional information."

"What can I do to help?" Paul asked.

"Send down several more copies of the environmental impact studies and arrange a presentation between your people, the state, and our council officials," Billie said. "That should convince them."

"That will take some doing on this end," Paul said. "Are you sure it's necessary?"

"There is absolutely no way to sway these two men if you don't," Billie replied. "If you do, the project is in the bag. Don't let me down Paul; I have a lot riding on this."

"Likewise, my friend," Paul said. "We both have a lot to lose."

At that moment, two of Paul's associates, wise guys of the darkest order, Mike Crandell and Blayde Incitti, dragged a man into the office and placed him in a chair directly in front of Paul's desk. The man was in great pain, having already been nearly half beaten to death. Paul glanced over his shoulder at the trio and held up one finger for silence. Waiting, Mike and Blayde positioned themselves on either side of the man who was handcuffed, slumping forward in the chair.

"Consider it done," Paul said. "I'll have my associates get to work on it right away and make the necessary arrangements. Don't worry my friend."

As Paul talked, he leaned over to the windowsill in front of him, grasped a small box and placed it in his lap. Opening the lid revealed a 9 mm Beretta pistol and silencer. He casually screwed the silencer onto the barrel.

"Alright," Billie said, "I'll continue to discuss the operation with the council and arrange a meeting. Keep in touch."

"I'll contact you as soon as I've made the necessary arrangements," Paul said. "Ciao." Paul hung up the phone and signaled to Blayde to close and lock the door behind them.

"Here's the scum bag boss," Mike said. "Do you want us to waste him for you?"

Paul still had his back to them as he spoke, not answering Mike's question.

"I don't like traitors," Paul said. "You stole money from me and my clients. What you did tarnished my reputation. My boss found out and has asked me to correct the problem. I have repaid him, but one small matter remains—Paul paused as he spoke. What do you have to say for yourself?"

"I needed the money," the man replied. "My wife and kid need to eat."

"To hell with your wife and your bastard kid," Paul said. This has nothing to do with them; it's business. Your explanation is unacceptable."

"I promise I won't do it again," the man said. "Give me another ch..."

The man stopped in mid-sentence as Paul swiveled in his chair to face him, gun in hand.

"If I give you another chance, I lose," Paul said. "I never lose. I've already lost money, but this will repay the debt."

Paul squeezed the trigger and put a bullet through the man's forehead. The lifeless body jolted backward into the chair from the force of the bullet penetrating hard bone. Only a trickle of blood ran down the man's forehead onto the front of his shirt.

"Blayde, dispose of that trash," Paul said. "Put him in the usual place. I do not want any traces. Mike, go with him. When you're finished, get rid of the wife and kid. There is no telling what he's told them and that could be a liability we shouldn't have to deal with. When you're through, the secretary has some plane tickets for you. I want you to go to Miami and check out Panther. I want to know everything about him and the other council members that make up the tribal council. There are millions at stake here. If you screw this up, you'll be joining your friend there."

"No problem boss," Mike said nervously, glancing at Blayde. "We'll make sure everything's taken care of."

Mike and Blayde took the corpse out the back entrance and loaded it into the trunk of their car.

"Do you want to do the dirty work this time?" Mike asked.

"Yeah, it'll be good practice," Blayde said.

They got in the car and headed east. Near the end of the landfill, they pulled onto a small, barely visible dirt road. From the undergrowth, it was apparent the road was seldom used. Driving to the end, they deftly unloaded the body and carried it into the woods. After a few minutes they entered a small, tree-covered clearing that had mounds of dirt beneath a carpet of leaves, a graveyard for those who became enemies of Lorio. Mike uncovered a shovel from beneath the branches of a tree and began digging a hole. It was all too obvious they had done this many times before. They were both sweating by the time they finished the hole and dragged the body to the edge. For a few seconds, it was as if they had forgotten what they were doing, or perhaps they were in their own way paying last respects to the corpse as they stared blankly at it. Almost in unison, they kicked the body into the hole. Mike walked beneath a large tree with low overhanging branches, rustled through the leaves and pulled out a half empty bag of lime. Blayde poured it over the body, threw the empty bag into the hole and shoveled dirt on top. Once finished, they carefully covered the area with a thick layer of dead leaves. It was one more mound in their private cemetery.

"There," Blayde said. "No one will ever know. The lime will feed the bacteria and they'll do a number on Mr. Scum Bag. Let's go take care of the wife and kid, got to tie up all the loose ends."

A large black limousine pulled slowly to the curb outside Paul Lorio's office. A professionally dressed chauffeur makes his way to the passenger side and opens the rear door. From the back seat stepped Monique Sandow, one of the most beautiful women in New York. Wearing a black knit dress of mid-thigh length, with a double stranded pearl necklace draped provocatively about her neck, heads turned to look her way. Without realizing it, she was a real traffic hazard. Bending over, she spoke a few unheard words to the passenger she had been sitting next to, breasts struggling to escape her dress, the nipples protruding provocatively. As her auburn hair, ruby lips and flashing green eyes confront the passenger, it is obvious they are more than friends.

"Thank you for the beautiful day Don Cilatro," Monique said. "I had a wonderful time. Call me again soon."

"Count on it," Cilatro said. "Next time, we'll meet at my home."

He motions to the driver to close the door. As the limo pulled away from the curb, Cilatro was thinking that he couldn't remember the last time he had met or been with such a sexy woman. He made a mental note to congratulate Lorio.

As the car slid away, Monique stared after it; hesitating for a moment she turned and entered the building, walking across the lobby and up the stairs to the second floor.

"I must be careful with Cilatro," Monique thought. "I won't see another sunrise if I displease him."

At the top of the stairs, she turned left down the hallway. Men and women were busy scurrying from one office to the next. As Monique passed, the men couldn't keep their eyes off her. It was as if they were looking at the Playboy playmate of the month. One man, staring intensely, was oblivious to his surroundings. Turning to retreat into his office, he bumped into a female coworker. The contents of the coffee cup he held spilling all over the front of her white blouse.

"Bastard," she screamed, "Watch where the hell you're going!" She slapped him hard across the face and stomped off.

A small smile upon her face, Monique entered Paul's office. A secretary was sitting behind a large mahogany desk that stood as a guardian to the door just beyond. An older lady, she was impeccably dressed.

"Is Mr. Lorio in, Susan?" Monique asked.

"Go right in," Susan said. "He's expecting you."

Monique passed by Susan's desk and entered Paul's private office. Elaborately furnished with fine, dark-grained tables and desks, leather furniture and expensive paintings, it had the trappings of a successful man. Monique always thought how the office seemed out of place with the surroundings of the landfill.

"Monique!" Paul exclaimed. "It's good to see you. I have a special job for you." Paul walked to the door.

"Susan," Paul said. "Hold all my calls for the remainder of the day and cancel my appointments. Ms. Sandow and I have work to do."

"Yes sir," Susan said. "I'll take care of it."

Paul closed the door.

Without saying it, Susan thought, "Yeah, I can imagine what kind of work, especially with Ms. Centerfold."

"You mean you want my feminine charm for another client," Monique said. "That's the job isn't it?"

"That's one way to put it," Paul said as he walked up behind her, kissed her on the cheek and pinched her butt. Monique turned and they embraced; a sensual embrace that denoted more than casual friendship. They kissed long and hard.

"How come you don't treat me like this around your friends and associates?" Monique asked.

"You know they wouldn't understand," Paul said.

"Hah!" Monique hissed. "You mean I'm not good enough for you because of the work I do. Which, I might add, I do only for you. I've never done it for another. Besides, no self-respecting woman would have you. They always buzz off like flies when they find out you're involved with the mob."

"Alright," Paul said, "Enough already. Let's not get into this again."

"So, who's the mark this time?" Monique asked.

"His name is Billie Panther," Paul said, "A leader of the Seminole Tribe in the Florida Everglades. Actually, he's a great looking guy and smart."

"God," Monique said. "You mean I have to go to the swamp and get eaten by mosquitoes and chiggers? That could only mean you're up to no good again. What kind of deal are you pushing this time?"

"The installation of a landfill," Paul said. "Mr. Panther wants the jobs and money for his people, and I want the extra-curricular dividends."

"Damn," Monique said. You're going to pull the same stunt you did in Washington, aren't you? You almost got caught there. I can't believe you want to dump that toxic crap again."

"Look," Paul said, his voice rising. "I warned you to never talk of that. If Don Cilatro finds out I told you, he'll make sure you disappear. I wouldn't want that to happen."

"In that case," Monique said. "I want five percent of the deal instead of my usual hundred grand or no deal. It'll be dangerous."

"You know who I am, what I can do to you, and you're trying to screw me," Paul said icily. "Hmmmm (softer). I'll tell you what, three percent and you do it my way." Paul walks up and pulls her close. Monique dropped to her knees as she began undressing him. "I'll think about it," Monique said, unbuckling his trousers.

Paul hastily removed her clothes and threw her onto the sofa. She had such a hard sexy body, and yet so supple and soft. He began caressing her nipples with his tongue. It was driving her crazy. She grabbed Paul, kissing him, pulling him inside. He was in heaven as afternoon waned to night.

Mike pulled to the curb in front of a rundown Bronx apartment building. Blayde got out of the car, picked up a box from the back seat, and walked up the stairs into the main entrance on his way to the third floor. Walking nonchalantly down the hallway, he located apartment 306. Standing quietly outside the door, Blayde carefully checked the hallway. Sure no one was watching, he pulled a silencer out of his pocket and screwed it onto his pistol, which he re-holstered and then softly knocked on the door. The wife of the scum bag answered.

"Compliments of Mr. Lorio," Blayde said, holding up a package as a ruse to enter the apartment.

"What a pleasant surprise," she said. "Put it on the table." She closed the door behind him as Blayde walked over to the table and deposited the box. Blayde looked around the apartment. It was a dump. The 20-year-old son was watching TV with his back to them. A few minutes later, he reappeared on the street below, cautiously looking each way as he strolled to the car.

"That should tie up all the loose ends," Blayde said to Mike as he opened the door. "Nice and neat; just the way Mr. Lorio likes it."

He fumbled around in his coat pocket, extracted a lighter and lit a cigarette, thinking about what he had just done. Mike saw a small smile crease Blayde's lips and instinctively knew what he was thinking about. "Blayde is a very sick bastard," Mike thought. As they drove across the river, Blayde wiped the gun down and tossed it out the window. He was thinking he should have carved two more notches on it.

CHAPTER 2

Billie was sitting in his office studying projected revenue estimations from the anticipated landfill. They were impressive. If business went well, they could earn eight figures per year. It was a substantial sum of money for the Tribe and an excellent source of employment for residents on Big Cypress. Billie was so wrapped up in the figures that he didn't notice Christina Jumper walk in.

Christina was a woman to be reckoned with. She was all most men would ever want and likely couldn't handle, as intelligent as she was beautiful. At five feet, one inch, she had a perfect figure, athletic and demure. Her thick black mane framed a strikingly beautiful face with piercing dark brown eyes. She edged her way around the desk and put her arms around his neck.

"Got time for me, handsome?" Christina asked.

"I could probably pull away for a minute or so," Billie said. "What's up?"

"I was wondering if you'd like to go fishing at the lake this afternoon?" Christina asked. "We could take James along and have a good time."

"That would be great, but I have a meeting with two associates Mr. Lorio is sending down from New York," Billie said. "I imagine our meeting will last quite a while."

"I swear Billie, you never have time for me anymore," Christina said. "Correct me if I'm wrong, but I thought we had something going. All you ever think of anymore is that damn landfill project."

"It's important Christina," Billie said. "You know how much it means to our people."

"To our people or to you?" Christina asked.

"That's not fair," Billie replied, a terseness creeping into his voice. "You know how much this will help us. Without these jobs, our people will go on languishing in their own misery, with nothing productive to do."

"I'm sorry Billie, it's just that I want to spend time with you and there never seems to be a spare moment anymore," Christina said. "When will you find time for me? I just want to be with you."

"Soon," Billie said. "I promise. When this landfill deal is passed, we can spend some quality time together; deal?" Billie held out his arms and they embraced. She kissed him softly on the cheek.

"Deal," Christina said. "You know I'll hold you to it."

"Believe me, I know," Billie said.

As Christina left, Billie couldn't help but think how lovely she was. He needed to get his problem under control. Focus on life more so that he could deal fairly with her. More than anything, he wanted to take her in his arms and tell her how much he loved her, ask her to marry him. But he was afraid he couldn't handle the emotional commitment after what had happened with his first wife.

Blayde and Mike were tired from their long flight as they arrived at Miami International Airport. After retrieving their bags, they proceeded to the rental car counter and obtained a large sedan for their trip to Big Cypress. Mike decided to drive while Blayde used the map to help negotiate the route. They were near the Sawgrass Expressway on a frontage road when they had to stop at a major intersection. A street bum walked up and began to clean their windshield. Blayde reached into his pocket. Anticipating payment, the bum came around to the passenger side window and leaned down, holding out his hand. Blayde pulled his hand the rest of the way out of his pocket and coldly shot pepper spray in the bum's eyes, who screamed in pain as he fell back from the car. Mike, seeing what happened, gunned the car, leaving tread marks on the asphalt.

"What the hell did you do that for?" Mike screamed. "We're supposed to keep a low profile. Lorio will be pissed." "Fuck Lorio," Blayde said. "I do what I please when the hell I please. The bum's lucky I didn't cut his damn throat." Mike turned and shook his head, muttering under his breath, "asshole."

For a while, Blayde and Mike rode in silence. They headed west on the Sawgrass Expressway and drove through the toll booths at the east end of State Road 84, now I-75, near the intersection of I-27, heading toward Naples. Blayde was looking at the map and then out the window, back and forth. There was nothing but sawgrass as far as he could see. It was like being in the middle of the Nevada desert, except it was flat as a table and green. The weather seemed hotter. The humidity was suffocating. Blayde, sweat trickling down his face, was clearly irritated.

"Would you look at this fucking place," Blayde said. "Hot as hell and in the middle of nowhere, and look at this," impatiently tapping the map, "name for the road we're on-- Alligator Alley. What a screwball name. Why in hell would someone name it that?"

"Maybe because of him," Mike said, pointing to a large alligator lying alongside the canal directly north of the road.

They continued west on Alligator Alley until they reached mile marker 56, then turned north onto Snake Road, the turn off for the junction to state road 833. It was now early afternoon. They passed a large sign along the road, which read "Seminole Tribe of Florida". They had been wondering if they were in the right place, now it was confirmed. A brief thundershower ensued. As it subsided the sun peaked through showing white cumulus clouds in the distance surrounded by almost blue thunder clouds while creating a golden hue atop the sawgrass plain. Steam rose from the highway. Blayde noticed several cotton-mouth moccasins crawling across the road in front of them. It gave him the creeps.

"Look at this place!" Blayde exclaimed.

The steam rising from the road and the visible heat waves gave the landscape a surreal appearance.

"It's like the fucking twilight zone."

Mike and Blayde exchanged glances.

"What a hell hole," Mike said.

About 15 miles farther, they entered the main community on Big Cypress Reservation. On the north end was Big Cypress Seminole Headquarters. Mike pulled the car into the parking lot.

"Let me do the talking," Mike said. "If we screw this up, our next pair of shoes will be concrete."

"Whatever," Blayde said. "Let's just get it over with and get the hell out of this backwoods shit hole."

As they stepped out of the car, Mike retrieved his briefcase. Upon entering the main doors, Blayde looked up and noticed a surveillance camera. He nudged Mike who also saw it. They walked to the receptionist's desk who sat directly across the large lobby they had entered. "Excuse me Ms., we have an appointment with Mr. Panther," Mike said. "Could you show us the way to his office?"

"I'm Robbie," she said, shaking their hands. "Mr. Panther's not in right now but should be back soon. You can wait in his office. This way please."

She led them down a short hallway to Billie's office, which was adorned with several pictures hanging on each wall depicting scenes of the Florida Everglades and modestly decorated with Indian artifacts. Directly in the middle of the room sat a large conference table.

"Get comfortable gentlemen," she said. "There's coffee and refreshments on the table and drinks in the small fridge under the counter. Let me know if you need anything."

Mike and Blayde watched the receptionist walk back down the hall.

"Blayde, keep an eye out while I snoop around," Mike said.

Blayde sauntered over near the door, casually looking about as Mike began to plunder through desk drawers and a nearby file cabinet. He was sorting through various papers and looking at miscellaneous certificates, diplomas and pictures on the wall.

"Hey, look at this," Mike said, "Two degrees from Yale. Panther's no dummy. I wonder if Mr. Lorio knows about this."

"Pssss," Blayde said. "Someone's coming!"

Mike quickly walked to the sofa and sat down. At the same moment, Billie Panther walked into the office.

"Good afternoon gentlemen," Billie said. "You're Mr. Lorio's associates?"

"Yes," Mike said as they shook hands. "It's good to finally meet you sir. I'm Mike Crandell and this is Blayde Incitti. Mr. Lorio sent us down to see what you need in regard to the landfill project."

"It's a pleasure to meet both of you," Billie said. You are aware of Mr. Lorio's goals. My goal is to bring in an influx of money via employment for my people. This is important due to our remote location."

"Remote ain't the word for it," Blayde said. "It's like the land from hell."

"Yeah," Mike said. "Your roads smoke and there's too many snakes."

"Welcome to Big Cypress," Billie said, laughing. "The locals call this place and the surrounding area Devil's Garden. Hell, I remember as a kid when I attended Clewiston High School being a member of the Devil's Garden Rodeo Club. It was lots of fun. For training, we used to tie a fifty-five-gallon drum between two trees. The drum was positioned above a blackberry briar patch. Other club members would grab the ropes on each end and shake the drum to try to throw us off. The briars beneath it were quite an incentive to hang on."

"Sounds like a fun childhood," Blayde said. "Devil's Garden is a perfect name for this place."

"Anyway, before I wander too much, many of our people have no jobs and no transportation to the nearest town," Billie said. "So, the landfill is a great opportunity for us. I intend on doing everything in my power to make it a reality."

"Well," Mike said. "We're here to help you. Oh! Before I forget, here are the studies you wanted."

Mike handed Billie several packages of bound documents. They were the environmental impact studies Billie had requested. The studies would help Billie prove his point to other council members, that the installation of the landfill was environmentally safe. And, as an expert hydrologist, his recommendation would carry significant weight with council and tribal members.

Billie clicked on the intercom. "Robbie, hold all my calls until we're done here," he said. "Shall we get down to business gentlemen?"

Billie got up and closed the door. The trio settled themselves around the conference table. The meeting continued for several hours as they discussed the current environmental studies and how to present them so all parties would be assured that installation of the landfill would not be deleterious to the environment. They also discussed scheduling and construction problems and costs. Every piece of information that had any bearing on the project was discussed in detail. At the end of the meeting, Billie was certain he had reached a critical juncture in the landfill project and that he now had more than adequate information to convince all stakeholders it would be a great deal for Big Cypress.

"I'll relay our plans and progress to Mr. Lorio," Mike said. "I'm sure he'll be pleased with what we've accomplished."

"Tell him that I will call him next week to confirm the planned meeting and my progress with the last two council members," Billie said.

"Well," Blayde said. "It's been a pleasure working with you. I'm sure we'll be in touch soon."

"Right," Billie said. "Please give my regards to Paul."

As they left, Billie couldn't help thinking how competent they seemed, so wrapped up in getting the project complete for the jobs it would bring to Big Cypress, he never suspected their true nature.

Mike and Blayde were glad the meeting was over. They didn't appreciate the hot and humid environment of the swamp or their surroundings. Bright lights and city streets were much more to their liking. As they left the office, they headed back down Snake Road south, through the community. Mike was so wrapped in thought and conversation with Blayde that he didn't notice he was passing through a school zone. Several children were walking alongside the road as the car passed a blinking yellow caution light and sign, indicating a speed limit of fifteen miles per hour. Blayde was the first to notice the police cruiser behind them.

"Damn!" Blayde exclaimed. "You've got a cop in a 4x4 on your ass."

Mike glanced in his rear-view mirror to confirm Blayde's observation, slowed the car and eased onto the shoulder of the road. Mike watched a large Indian get out of the vehicle and walk toward him. It was Genesis Motlow, tribal constable. As Genesis reached Mike's window, he leaned down until he was face to face with him. His severe features and penetrating eyes sent shivers up Mike's spine. Mike couldn't remember having ever seen such an intimidating face.

"Is there a problem officer?" Mike asked politely.

"Didn't you notice the school zone back there?" Genesis asked, nodding.

"No sir," Mike said. "I guess I was daydreaming. Please accept my apologies, officer."

"I'll need to see your license and registration," Genesis said. As Mike handed them over, Genesis began writing his name down on his violation log.

"Oh, come on," Blayde blurted out. "It's not like we were drag racing. Couldn't you give us a break?"

Genesis stooped lower to look directly at Blayde. The expression on his face made it clear that Blayde would be better off with a tight lip.

"I apologize for my friend, officer," Mike said. "Guess we were a little preoccupied after our meeting with Mr. Panther. We didn't see the school zone."

"You know Mr. Panther?" Genesis asked.

"Yes," Mike said. "We're working with him on the installation of a landfill project here on Big Cypress."

"I've heard him mention it," Genesis said. "Tell you what, I'll let you off with a warning this time, next time it'll cost you our normal fine of one hundred dollars."

"Don't worry officer," Mike said. "There won't be a next time. We'll be more alert."

Genesis handed Mike his license and registration and walked back to his car. As they pulled off, he looked at the name he had written down, ripped the violation sheet off, and stuffed it into his shirt pocket. He made a mental note to discuss this episode with Billie the next time they talked. Something about Mike and Blayde gave him an uneasy feeling, a feeling Genesis had learned to trust. It had helped him, and his squads survive in Afghanistan.

Mike and Blayde, having returned from Miami, were informing Paul about their trip. They were in conference in Paul's office, seated around his desk.

"Let's have it," Paul said. "What did you find out for me?"

"Panther is no dummy Mr. Lorio," Mike said. "He has two degrees from Yale; one in hydrology and one in law. There were no interesting documents lying around, but he also served in an LRRP (Long Range Recon Patrol) unit in the U.S. Army based out of Ft. Bragg. He spent only a couple of months in Afghanistan and served with others who were long-time veterans. It appears several of them are also Seminole Indian. Genesis Motlow was one of their sergeants over there. He taught knife fighting and won a silver star disrupting the enemy during darkness. They all served at a combat outpost named Lowell. From what I could find out from my military buddies, it was a small stone castle, sandbagged and bristling with weapons and American soldiers, rising from a rock spur beside the Landai River. Mountains lean overhead. Apparently, these guys served in a deadly contest for Afghanistan's borderlands. The castle lies exposed near the bottom of a natural amphitheater deep within territory and out of government control. Afghanistan and Taliban insurgents would hide in caves surrounding it and in villages nearby, operating unhindered almost to the castle's concertina wire. These insurgents would lob mortar shells toward it at will. Their mission was to disrupt the Taliban and foreign fighters on supply paths from Pakistan's tribal areas. I'm not certain I have all my facts straight, but the current tribal President was their commanding officer of a larger task force in the region and distilled how the mission often worked. Their presence at the outpost served as a Taliban magnet, drawing insurgents from more populated areas. Essentially, these guys were a bullet sponge."

"I had assumed he was uneducated, and I certainly did not consider that he and the others had this type of background," Paul said. "This could cause serious problems. With his knowledge in hydrology, it would be much easier for him to discover our illegal dumping. We'll have to make certain he doesn't get too suspicious. What else did you find out?"

"Well," Mike said sarcastically, "It just keeps getting better. My source told me these guys were part of an elite LRRP unit assigned to Special Operations Command called Apache Troop. The U.S. Army had avowed that no such units served in Afghanistan. They are a tough bunch. Hell, for one four-month period they took fire on at least 70 days. The attacks came by rocket, mortar, machine gun and rifle fire. The troop's patrols were continually ambushed, and its observation posts hit by rocket fire. On one day alone, the outpost was attacked four times. The fighting was so frequent and the terrain so rugged and heavily populated by insurgent spotters, that the outpost's patrols dared not venture far, excepting Sergeant Motlow. He used Vietnam style tunnel rat techniques and guerrilla warfare tactics to carry the war to the Taliban; Billie Panther assisted him for several months. He'd sneak up on the enemy and kill them hand to hand. Sometimes, he would only wound some of them so they would go back and tell their cohorts. The Taliban had a nickname for him, 'Silver Fang', because of his long knife."

"Holy cow," Paul said, "I had not counted on any of this. I will need to carefully rethink our entrance and exit strategies."

"It's not all gloom and doom. I did find something that may help us," Mike said. "One of the other councilmen Billie is trying to convince is a mortal enemy. Apparently, they trade off in the council seat Billie has every couple of years. Right now, Billie has it and this other guy, Solomon Osceola, wants it back. As a result, he's deliberately delaying his decision so that Billie is in a vise."

"Hmmmm," Paul remarked. "That could be good news for us. Set up a meeting with Mr. Osceola when we go down to

Florida. I'd like to see if we can get him on our side long enough to pass this resolution. After that, he and Billie can squabble over politics all they want. It would even make it easier for us. In any case, let's not underestimate these people. It could have grave consequences. What do you have on the other council members?

"It appears most of them are just your average working stiffs," Mike said. "For the most part they are involved in cattle ranching and farming. They are respected; active in the community, but what they say carries weight. Since most of them are on our side already, their support will help us. They are backing Billie in his decision so far. We got the impression that if the environmental impact study was favorable, their votes would be in the bag."

"Excellent," Paul said. "The impact study is very favorable and shows only a very remote chance of contaminating the ecosystem. That will make them and us, very happy. I want you to stay on this. Contact all concerned parties and set up the meeting Billie requested. Once that's been done, we should be able to breathe a little easier."

Later that night in an upscale New York restaurant, Paul found himself waiting for Monique. The waiter was pouring a glass of wine as Monique was escorted to the table.

"Here's your guest Mr. Lorio," the maître-de said. "Will there be anything else?"

"No, leave us," Paul said. "We'll order shortly."

Turning to Monique, Paul said, "You look gorgeous tonight."

"Why don't you cut the crap, Paul," Monique said. "Let's just get right to the point. You know I have a soft spot for you, but don't try to sweet talk me."

"Very well," Paul said. "As it turns out, I will need your special talents. We're trying to schedule a meeting with the

Seminole Tribal Council soon and I want you to go to Miami with us. Here's the client."

Paul handed her a picture of Billie.

"He's cute," Monique said. "What do you want me to do with him?"

"The usual," Paul said. "I want him to fall in love with you."

"Don't they all?" Monique queried.

"Just make sure of it," Paul said. "He's smart as a whip and could be a significant threat to our operation. If you want your three percent, you'll need to earn it. He apparently has a girl he's been seeing, but they are not engaged. Her name is Christina. It's likely she'll be stiff competition."

"Just leave everything to me," Monique said. "One look at my hard, sexy body and irresistible charm and this Panther hunk won't even know he has another girl."

At that moment, the waiter interrupts, handing a cell phone to Paul.

"Yes," Paul said.

"What's the news on your Florida project?" a voice asked.

"It looks like a go Don Cilatro," Paul said. "We'll know for sure in another day or so."

"When can we expect to receive shipments of chemicals?" Cilatro asked.

"Don't make plans yet," Paul said. "I'll let you know as soon as we're ready."

"A delay could cost us," Cilatro said.

"I realize that," Paul said. "But these people aren't dummies. They are more educated and savvier than we expected. We must use caution."

"Alright Paul," Cilatro said. "I understand. By the way, you've been doing an exceptional job on this. If you bring in the kind of money we anticipate, I'll be giving you control of all east coast operations. You'll answer directly to me. If you don't, well..."

"Don't worry Mr. Cilatro," Paul said, the blood draining from his face. "Everything is proceeding according to schedule. I'll let you know our progress within the week."

"See to it," Cilatro stated.

As Paul hung up the phone, Monique said, "The big boss is in a hurry." Without answering, Paul dialed another number.

"Mike," Paul said. "Press Mr. Panther to hurry the meeting along as quickly as possible. Do whatever it takes but be cordial. Get that meeting set. We must convince the other council members of the benefits of our mutual collaboration."

"Yes sir, Mr. Lorio," Mike said. "I'll get on it first thing in the morning."

After completing their meal, Monique and Paul left the restaurant. They climbed into a limousine outside and headed for Monique's apartment. As they rode up on the elevator, Paul couldn't help thinking how sexy and beautiful she was. If it weren't for Cilatro, who also thought much of her and used her as a sex toy, he would already have made a commitment. They got off the elevator and walked to her door. As Monique fumbled with her keys, Paul was almost touching her. The sweet fragrance of the perfume she was wearing excited him. As soon as they were in the apartment, Paul closed and locked the door, then began unbuttoning his shirt as he pulled Monique close.

"What do you think you're doing?" Monique asked.

"You're mine," Paul said. "I own you. Don't forget that."

"You don't own me," Monique said. "Neither does Cilatro."

"Don't kid yourself," Paul said. "What he says is law. If he decides he doesn't like you, you'll be history. Besides, he only uses you for sex. I on the other hand have a deeper interest.

One day he'll be gone, and I'll be in control. So, don't get any bright ideas about leaving. There is no place you could ever hide where I wouldn't find you."

Deep in the Florida Everglades, Billie, Jacob, Genesis, Timmy, and several others had gathered for a friendly airboat race. The Jagged Grass Challenge would soon be held, and they wanted to get their boats in good shape before the big day. All of them were lined up on the starting line in their respective boats. The idling engines and attached airplane props going round and round caused an air of anticipation. One airboat had pulled out several yards in front of the rest; its motor was off. Standing atop the seat was the race announcer.

"Attention please," the announcer said. "The race will commence in ten minutes. The finish line will be Mabel's Hammock. Ready your boats."

"Hey Timmy," Billie said. "I've got my boat souped up this year, so watch out."

"I don't care what you did to it," Timmy yelled over the roaring engines. "Nothings' gonna help you. Check this baby out." Timmy gunned his engine, the sound drowning out the other boats.

"Sounds pretty sick to me," Genesis said. "Like a baby gator. You better hope it's faster than one."

"I don't care what any of you say," Billie said. "You better hang onto your ass if you want to keep up with me."

"Put your boats on the line," the race announcer yelled. There were a few minutes pause as the racers complied.

"Ready, mark, go."

The race announcer dropped his flag, and they were off.

Each boat began jockeying for the lead as they made their way through the sawgrass and mud flats. Timmy tried to cut

Genesis off; another racer bumped into both of them. For a brief moment, all three were at a standstill, like bumper cars in a carnival. Billie, slightly behind the rest, caught up. The lead began changing back and forth. Large, misty sheets of water were thrown into the air as the wind generated by the props ricocheted off the surface of the swamp. The boats had veered close to a cypress head; a risky maneuver because of the danger of striking a submerged cypress knee.

Suddenly, one of the airboats did; the cypress knee protruded just above the water line, hidden by the sawgrass. The boat careened off the knee on one side as it was lifted and rolled into the air landing upside down in the swamp. The driver was thrown away from the wreck unhurt. In an instant, Billie passed the now-wrecked boat and Jacob, who had begun having fuel problems. Just as Billie passed, he had to corner sharply to the right to avoid missing a submerged log. Before he could react, Genesis was struck across the bow by Billie's boat and sent fish tailing out of control.

The only boats in contention for the lead were Billie and Timmy. Timmy rammed Billie on the right side trying to maneuver him into some thicker sawgrass so he could get by. He was unsuccessful.

"Giddy up", Billie yelled, as he passed Timmy.

"You're mine now," Timmy yelled as both boats neared the finish line.

Mabel, Billie's mother was standing outside her chickee watching the two boats approach. She was silently wondering to herself if the boats would stop in time.

"What fool stunts these men are always pulling, just like a bunch of kids," she thought.

Billie was first to cross the finish line, marked with a small red buoy. He eased up on the throttle pedal to slow the boat.

Nothing happened. He tried to steer the boat around the hammock where Mabel's chickee stood, again, no response. Both the throttle and the rudder were locked. Realizing there was no time to try anything more, Billie stood up and desperately began waving his arms back and forth to warn his mother as he jumped from the airboat into the swamp.

Mabel saw the predicament Billie was in. As the boat roared toward her, she dove to her left into the water as the airboat hit the hammock's edge and hurtled through the air like a missile, crashing into the chickee. The high-octane fuel quickly caught fire causing the fuel tank to explode. A huge fireball erupted and within seconds, the chickee, which consisted only of four posts and a thatched palm roof, was incinerated. By now the other racers had come up and couldn't believe what they were seeing. Nothing like this had ever happened before. They were taunting Billie, laughing at his racing skills. Timmy pulled up beside Billie in his airboat and fished him out of the water.

"Congratulations chief," Timmy said, grinning. "Your win is gonna cost you, in more ways than one."

By now the other racers were bent over with laughter.

"I don't suppose you'd trade the trophy for rebuilding mom's chickee?" Billie asked.

"Not on your life," Timmy said. "Right now, I don't even know you. What did you say your name was?"

"Damn it Billie," Mabel yelled angrily from the hammock, water dripping from her drenched body, "If I were white, I'd scalp you myself. You've ruined my business. I have tourists coming out tomorrow. How can I run my business now?"

The excitement and pandemonium of the other racers were dying down as Timmy dropped Billie off at the docks. Timmy pulled away, glancing back over his shoulder and laughing. Mabel was hurrying down the docks toward him.

"Just tell me where I'm supposed to sleep tonight," Mabel said. "You've totally wrecked my chickee, not to mention destroying most of my bead work and other artifacts."

"I'm sorry mom," Billie said. "The controls locked up on the boat. I promise to have a crew here this afternoon. They'll have it fixed by morning. You can stay with me if you like."

"I swear Billie," Mabel said. "I thought I was out of this kind of stuff when you went off to college, seems like the Medicine Man was right, parenting never, never ends."

"Oh mom," Billie said, hugging her. "Life isn't that bad. There's always going to be a few rough places."

"Rough places I expect," Mabel said. "What I don't expect is my chickee run over and destroyed by an airboat."

The two began walking, their dripping wet clothes leaving a trail of water puddles behind them, down the docks to the cat walks that traversed the hammock so tourists could watch the wildlife, which included alligators, fish, deer, birds of all kinds, snakes, armadillo's, an occasional bobcat, and sometimes a rare Florida panther. Mabel had built most of the cat walks and chickee herself. She was a very self-reliant, strong-willed woman. Attributes that made Billie proud and that he spoke highly of to others.

Mabel, now graying, was a beautiful woman with a regal walk and gracious attitude. Her long dark hair hung thick and loose about her shoulders, a light breeze wafting the ends into the air. Although often stern with Billie, she was very compassionate and loving. Her high cheek bones and noble appearance made her look like an aristocrat. Today as most days, she wore traditional Seminole garments. A red ribbon was tied to her waist-length hair, which hung over a patterned, gold blouse. She wore a colorful patchwork, full-length skirt. The main color was red, bordered on top and bottom with white, with an occasional gold band. The skirt was completed with a border of pale blue. The only jewelry Mabel wore was a pearl necklace and a gold ring on her left middle finger. Billie was watching her closely. She was still so beautiful he thought. It made him wonder why his dad had left.

"Has Christina talked to you lately?" Billie asked.

"She was out yesterday," Mabel said. "She loves you Billie. You need to tell her how you feel. You've told everybody but her. Don't you think it's about time?"

"Yes," Billie replied. "I should but haven't been able to."

"Mary's been gone a long time now," Mabel said. "You can't keep blaming yourself for the accident. What's done is done. You need to get on with the rest of your life."

"I've been on the wagon," Billie said. "Trying to get things back on track hasn't been easy. I just don't want to hurry things too much."

"Three years is not too much Billie," Mabel said. "If you don't tell her how you feel soon, she may not wait for you. I don't know how you feel about that, but I like her Billie. She's like the daughter I never had. Promise me you'll talk to her."

Walking along the cat walks they had made a complete circle of the hammock and were approaching the boat docks again.

"I promise I'll talk to her mom," Billie said. "And don't worry; I'll have a crew out right away to fix your place."

"Don't forget Christina now," Mabel pleaded.

"I won't," Billie said as he kissed her on the cheek. "I'll talk to her soon."

Genesis had pulled his boat up to the docks. As Billie reached the boat, Genesis was picking up a ringing cell phone. "It's for you," Genesis said, handing Billie the phone. "It's Paul Lorio."

Billie covered the mouthpiece on the phone. "Genesis," Billie said. "Would you get a crew out here right away to fix the mess I made? Make sure they're here today."

"Hello Paul."

"Billie," Paul said. "I have the meeting you wanted set between your people and mine. It's next Monday. Can you have everyone there?"

"I'll take care of it," Billie said. "Why don't you bring your people down a few days early and we'll break the ice with an airboat and swamp buggy tour."

"That sounds great," Paul said. "I'll look forward to seeing you on Thursday."

Billy Osceola was staring unconsciously out the window; Chairman of the Seminole Tribe of Florida, also known as the Chief. Staring unblinkingly, he reminisced about when he and Billie Panther had first met. In the hot, arid mountains of Afghanistan, he had the responsibility of giving last minute training to newly arrived personnel in the LRRP unit. Normally, due to his rank the role he was playing on this day would be performed by a sergeant, but as ranking he officer there was someone he wanted to observe in person. On this day, his specific assignment was to teach the LRRP (Long Range Recon Platoon) members how to deploy out of a helicopter at full battle ready while repelling from a Huey to the desert floor.

As the instructor in charge, he was standing in the door of the chopper giving instructions. The unit had done this many times before, but today was different, it was going to be a live fire exercise. An exercise that always gave Colonel Osceola a thrill because it was an adrenaline rush and each squad member always reacted differently. He was particularly interested in how Billie Panther would react. He had been told that Panther was sharp, always learning to do things a little better than he had been instructed. Having talked to other instructors, they all confessed at having learned little tricks by watching Billie. Thus, it was with great interest that Colonel Osceola observed Billie today. Besides, he was proud that a Seminole Indian had made the brass notice and, as regional officer in charge of LLRP for Special Operations Command, it was always helpful to have highly qualified personnel.

The noise of the engine and the rotor blades slapping the air was deafening as the chopper hovered about seventy feet above the ground. The squad could barely hear the instructor as they attached their individual, olive drab nylon ropes to the deployment rail in preparation to exit each side of the chopper. On the desert floor below, makeshift targets had been set up. Each squad member would concentrate on targets in his quadrant. Feeling they were about to get the word to descend, the chopper suddenly flew forward and began banking sharply to the right, making a circle. The squad hung on tight as they looked toward the Colonel.

"Forgot to tell you, today is going to be like the real thing. The pilot will make a circle and then return to the hover position above the deployment area. As soon as we begin to hover, you will immediately descend toward the targets and disperse as per operational orders." Colonel Osceola yelled. "Got it?"

All squad members nodded in understanding. The chopper had finished its turn and was making its final approach. Colonel Osceola watched Billie closely to see how he would prepare for his descent. Billie hooked his rope into his rappelling harness and then left a few feet of slack. This aroused the instructor's attention, who was watching him closely. Billie took the slack and seemed to wrap the rope around his leg and then between his feet and around one toe of his boot. Colonel Osceola couldn't believe what he was seeing. The kid was going to lose a leg; he began to approach to stop him as the chopper came to a hover. Osceola had scarcely moved when Billie and the rest of the squad jumped out the doors and began their descent. Colonel Osceola quickly ran to the chopper door and looked down.

Billie was flying down the rope headfirst, like a bolt of lightning. He had already managed to destroy every target in his quadrant with his M4, set on full auto. Incredulously, Billie was on the ground before the others made it halfway down. He twisted in his harness, with both feet landing in the dirt. As he did so, he methodically covered a full circle, firing on each target before his squad reached him. At first, Colonel Osceola was afraid Billie would kill several of his squad members, but then he could see the whites of Billie's eyes as he glanced frequently up. This kid had real potential. Billie was like poetry in motion. He never exaggerated, never made an unnecessary move, but coolly assessed the situation and did what was required. Colonel Osceola liked that. He had actually thought about chewing him out, but when he descended the rope and the chopper had cleared the area, Osceola could see the respect of the other men for Billie and how they were drawn to him as a natural leader. Realizing there were too few of these in the desert, the Colonel had held his tongue. It would be an honor to serve with Billie. Osceola was able to serve only two missions with Billie then finished his tour and returned to Big Cypress.

That had been so long ago when Chairman Osceola himself had held high ideals. Now, educated in the arena of politics and power, other things had become more important than ideals, especially money and the power that went with it. And now, the leadership potential that Billie had displayed in the desert and mountains of Afghanistan and honed to a fine edge with a college education was a threat to Chairman

Osceola's own leadership. Billie was becoming a thorn in the side of the Chairman who had taken him in, made it possible for his college education, and who had trained him and entrusted him with important matters for the Tribe.

"Damn," Chairman Osceola swore to himself, "Everywhere I go on Big Cypress it's Billie Panther did this and he did that. It sets a bad precedent, as if I have done nothing."

Billie had unintentionally raised himself up in the eyes of the people and was an ever-looming threat. He couldn't afford to let Billie's ideals get in the way of his profits; something had to be done to ensure that Billie could not run against him in the next election. He had not remained Chairman of the Seminole Tribe all these years so some upstart with grand ideals could steal away his power. No, he would have none of that. Years of experience had taught Chairman Osceola how to deal with such threats. He must attack as he would kill a snake, quickly and fiercely, but in the realm of politics, that also meant shrewdly. Many of Chairman Osceola`s followers owed him a debt for past favors, a debt which could always be collected because they needed things that he could provide. By keeping the younger generation down, in the depths of despair and dependent on drugs and other vices, Chairman Osceola ruled the Tribal Council with an iron hand. He had a small army at his command for spying and other purposes, like the discrediting of a young upstart. His followers knew if they opposed him, they would be out of the loop, without supply of their wants, wants that in many instances could not be supplied legally. They would not fail him now. Rumors would begin that would force Billie Panther into obscurity.

Chairman Osceola also had connections that reached far beyond the boundaries of the Reservation. He would play both ends against the middle as it were. Neither party would be fully aware of his role or what his interests were. To them, he would be a mere figurehead, someone who got the ball rolling, but then delegated the authority. All parties concerned would naturally assume he was informed and thus, would make no mention of specific details. Some would assume it was for the good of the Tribe, others would say it was for his own benefit; most of the latter would be correct. Thanks to his own ingenuity and tribal money, he had his own jet, helicopter, numerous automobiles, airboats, and other holdings. He would make sure things stayed the way they were. Thus, he began dialing.

A phone ringing in New York City was answered by a pleasant voice.

"Yes, may I speak with Paul Lorio please?" Chairman Osceola asked.

"May I tell him who is calling sir?" the secretary asked.

"I am Chairman Billy Osceola of the Seminole Tribe of Florida."

There was a slight pause; footsteps and the rustling of papers could be heard.

"Chairman Osceola, it's great to hear from you. How are things going?" Paul asked.

"Good at the moment. I just wanted to check in with you and find out how the negotiations were going for the landfill." Osceola replied.

"Proceeding on schedule," Paul said. "As a matter of fact, we'll be flying down to meet with some of your people soon. Mr. Panther has been easy to work with. I'm glad you had me contact him."

"Excellent," Osceola said. "I was hoping the two of you would get along. What about my trip to Thailand and other items we discussed?"

"The trip will be scheduled once we are operational," Lorio said. "Your other items will be delivered in the place you specified. As discussed, this will be in complete confidence. It would be unwise for anyone to learn of our mutual interests; now, what about your intervention for our behalf?"

"Two things, first I'll influence the council as much as possible to vote for you and second, I'll make sure I keep a thorn in Billie's side. It will be an opposing politician on Big Cypress. I'd rather not tell you who for the moment, but I'm sure you'll figure it out soon enough," Osceola replied. Lorio wasn't about to admit that he already knew who it was.

"Fair enough, I also have my own plans for him" Lorio said. "I guess that will conclude our business on a positive note then. I'll let you know if we need further assistance."

Chairman Osceola pondered the discussion. No matter what happened, good or bad, he would make money off the deal, a prosperous trip to Thailand and receive some very nice perks. No one would ever know of his involvement and if things went awry, Billie Panther would bear the responsibility. It was all in a day's work in politics. He smiled to himself. There was one more call to make. He needed to grease the skids and boost the ego of someone else to ensure loyalty, so that he would always be abreast of current developments. What better way to ensure success than have a distant relative on his side? Dialing a number, he put the receiver down and pressed the speaker button.

"This is Councilman Osceola."

"Solomon, it's great to hear your voice. How have you been?"

"Doing pretty good Chairman," Solomon replied. "What can I do for you?"

"How familiar are you with the landfill negotiations?" Chairman Osceola asked.

"I'm involved in pretty much everything where the Tribe has to make a decision on important matters. But sometimes I don't agree with the way Billie Panther makes his." Solomon replied.

"Well, that's what I wanted to talk to you about," Osceola said. "You know that I have always been able to work better with you than anyone else, counted on you when the chips were down. There's just no one on Big Cypress who understands the problems as well or knows what's really best for the Tribe. I'm not sure if you're aware of it, but Mr. Lorio and his entourage will be visiting Big Cypress in a few days to check out the site, meet with council members, to get a feel for the business environment down here prior to the meeting. I want you to be there for every part of the negotiation process. Keep an eye on Billie and make certain he's looking out for the best interests of our people. If he slips up, you'll be there to help and who knows, perhaps eventually regain your office."

"Don't worry Chairman," Solomon replied. "You can count on me. If Billie does slip up, I'll be there so we can take advantage of his mistake. You can bank on it."

"Good, I'll leave it in your hands," Osceola said. "Just let me know if you need anything. I can't tell you how much this means to the Tribe, Solomon. You'll be well rewarded."

Chairman Osceola smugly pressed the speaker button, clasped his hands behind his head and swiveled in a full circle in his leather chair, a broad smile on his face. "A little flattery will get you everywhere," he thought. He cast his gaze over every inch of his lavish office, decorated with the finest mahogany conference table and desk money could buy and the most elaborate Indian artwork, paintings and artifacts; many were one of a kind. He felt great pride in his accomplishments because he had created this, made it all possible. Sure, he had gotten rich from the Tribe, but it was justified. Without him and his leadership, the Seminole people would still be poling dugout canoes across the sawgrass.

Didn't he deserve all he had taken for himself? The people were happy and prosperous, the goal of any reigning monarch. For many years he had led his people with wisdom. It was necessary to keep some of them down so that he could succeed and for the best interest of the majority. The tribal members he kept down were incapable of functioning in the white man's world anyway; they always would be. But he took good care of them, provided them with their needs, a place to stay, food, the necessary drugs, and their favorite drink, alcohol. They bothered no one and when he needed a favor, they were more than willing to help.

Chairman Osceola had been raised in harsh times. Like many of the Seminole men, he had wrestled alligators for tourists, hunted, fished and done all kinds of odd jobs to survive in a harsh environment that gave no quarter to an uneducated, poor Indian. Tribal members had been persecuted his entire life. He himself as much as any, but despite this, when the call came, he had served his country. As a result, his eyes had been opened. In doing so, he had learned leadership along with politics.

His destiny was in his own hands and he intended to fulfill it. Having achieved the highest and most respected position in the Tribe, Osceola felt he had accomplished all he could as an individual; there was yet one thing more for him to complete, the training of the true Seminole leader and way of the wise elder. He had been working for years with the Medicine Man to learn the magic of the Seminole and of the swamp. Having learned most of the necessary rituals and spiritual ways, he was in the final stages. Yes, on the very pinnacle of complete power. The way of the transparency was the greatest achievement any Seminole could have. Once learned, he would be able to enforce his will and bidding as he chose. He would be like a god. Lately however, the

Medicine Man had seemed slow in teaching him the final phases. He must find out why, but with cunning, else the Medicine Man would not complete the task. Osceola also knew that Billie was working infrequently with the Medicine Man. That had become painfully clear at the last Green Corn Dance Ceremony, a sacred Seminole ceremony, a ceremony that only Seminoles could attend. Osceola had noticed that the Medicine Man seemed to favor Billie. If Billie learned the way of the transparency, it could spell the end of his own reign. He made a mental note to visit with the Medicine Man and resume his training as soon as possible. If he could only complete his transparency training, he would get rid of the Medicine Man and have total control of the Tribe. He would be able to influence any member at will. No one could stand in his way and he would be fabulously wealthy and powerful, his ultimate goal. It was with great resolve that he intended to visit the Medicine Man, soon.

Chickee

CHAPTER 3

The twin engine Beechcraft Bonanza was bucking a nasty westerly wind as it touched down on the small, shell-rock runway adjacent to Big Cypress Tribal Headquarters. Dust billowed behind the plane as it rocketed down the runway. Billie and several others stood waiting as it rolled to a stop. When the propellers ceased turning, Genesis walked up to the airplane and opened the door. Paul's entourage began filing down the short steps, one by one.

"Paul," Billie said, extending his hand, "Nice to see you again."

"Likewise," Paul said. "Let me introduce my associates. You know Mike and Blayde, and this, gesturing with a wave of his hand, is Monique Sandow."

"The pleasure's mine," Billie said, admiring her beauty, almost gasping. Monique was dressed in blue jeans and a provocative white silk blouse.

"Let me also introduce ourselves. "This is Genesis Motlow our constable, Jacob Cypress, Councilman Solomon Osceola, and my son James." Genesis was eyeing Blayde. One could feel their disdain for each other. "I'll turn you over to the capable hands of Solomon," Billie said. "He's in charge of the show today."

"We'd like to begin your visit by showing you around the swamp and then, the prospective landfill site," Solomon said. "First, we'll begin with an airboat tour. Just step into these vehicles and we'll be on our way."

The group drove about 50 miles to Shark Key to meet up with the airboats. As they drove along, Solomon was trying to determine the best way to approach the newcomers. If he could make a good impression, it would help him in his bid for re-election against Billie the next time around. He resented the fact that Billie, who was half his age, had won the last election. Although Solomon was old and graying, most tribal members respected him and the wisdom his age represented. He still carried a great deal of weight around the community. His desire was to make Billie look incompetent if he could. Solomon realized it might prove due to Billie's education. However, his youth still made Billie susceptible to rash and impulsive decisions.

As they arrived at their destination, the party began walking down the docks to a large touring airboat capable of seating the entire party. Billie and Monique boarded last. Monique sat on the outside so she could trail her hand in the water, like a little kid. Billie stood up, turning to face most of the group.

"Genesis will be our swamp guide today," Billie said. "He'll be telling you some history and facts about the unique swamp we call home."

The airboat slowly slipped away from the dock, gradually accelerating until it skimmed along the surface of the water, over the sawgrass. There was a light breeze carrying the scent of rain along with the musty odor of the swamp. The passengers were awed by the vast expanse of the glades; an overpowering flatness that stretched across the visible horizon. They settled into a gentle swaying motion as the airboat sped deeper into the sawgrass and cypress swamp. Alive with plants and animals, spectacular and abundant, elusive, mysterious, and microscopic, the swamp was like a magnet, compelling them to explore it. Sawgrass gave way to open lily-pad ponds, cypress flats, and endless hammocks. The sky looked ominous and brooding to the south. Dark and threatening, thunderstorms were brewing for a typical August afternoon. Now that his passengers were stunned by the river of grass, which outsiders call the Everglades, Genesis began his story.

"Many people believe the glades are filled with quicksand, teeming with alligators and slithering, poisonous snakes, steamy vine-choked jungles and hordes of insects," Genesis said. "While it can be deadly, the glades encompass an extensive region which is so varied that its true essence cannot be captured in any one definition. The Everglades is a low place on a low land. They are barely above sea level, although from the hip deep water surrounding us, most people would tend to disagree. The best way to think of the glades is as a river of grass. It's the largest saw-grass marsh in the world."

"At one time," Genesis continued. "The glades covered all of south Florida. Before 1958, Lake Okeechobee was unbridled, and as the seasons came and went, the lake would swell and shrink depending on how much rain we received. During the rainy season, which lasts from about late May to November, the lake would swell tremendously from summer rains and hurricanes. In 1926 and again in 1928, large storms caused the deaths of over three thousand people. Natural streams were flooded, houses underwater; it was a major catastrophe. In some areas it was told how entire houses, people and animals were washed down the canals, rivers and streams. No one could help them. So, in 1958, construction for a levee named Hoover Dike was completed around the entire circumference of Lake Okeechobee. Now, the lake is approximately seven hundred square miles in area: that's about fifty-three miles in diameter. It's the second largest freshwater lake in the United States. Only Lake Michigan is larger. In case you're wondering, Okeechobee is a Seminole name. It literally means "land of big water."

"I could go on about the history," Genesis said. "But let me tell you more about the glades themselves and why they are such a unique environment. It's necessary that you know this if we want the landfill to coexist with this one-of-a-kind ecosystem. The Seminole name for the Everglades or, river of grass is Pa-hay-okee, which is pronounced pah-HIGH-og-geh, meaning "grassy waters." There are currently about eleven million acres left of the Glades. The majority has been destroyed by the white man and his insatiable appetite for more of everything. The water of the glades flows southwesterly toward the Gulf of Mexico. The basic soil types found in the area are sand, muck, marl, and various mixtures of the three, including limestone formations. Beneath the glades and into Florida Bay, flows the Key Biscayne aquifer. It is truly an underground river. Because of the growing population, there have been numerous sinkholes appearing. You may have heard of them on the news. Sometimes entire houses, cars, and yards are swallowed up. This is happening because the Key Biscayne is being pumped dry. The aquifer buoys up the land above it because the water that flows through it is incompressible. When too much demand is placed on the aquifer to deliver water to the growing population, air pockets are formed between the top of the aquifer and the soil above them. The soil above the pocket collapses and presto, you have a sinkhole that swallows all around it."

"The hammocks you see," Genesis said, pointing. "That's those small islands, are called hammoka, which means "garden place" in Seminole. They are made up of gumbo limbo shrubs, but can also be of live oak, mahogany, cabbage, or other plant species depending on whether you are in the middle of the glades or on the edges of the swamp. The weather in the Caribbean affects us quite a bit, mostly because Florida is surrounded by water on three sides. The strong winds and hurricanes we have carry a variety of wind- borne plant seeds and birds to south Florida. This influences all the flora and fauna."

They were now very deep in the glades as Genesis continued his narration. "We are traveling through what is called by the locals "pine islands," that consists of slash pine, saw palmetto and hardwood hammocks," Genesis said. "A good example is that one to your left. These are cut by narrow glades of sawgrass and grassy marsh and very convenient for airboat travel. This is much the way it looked before Dade County cities such as Miami sprawled over the land. A little ahead, you can see the cypress swamp that consists of bald cypress, cypress flats, and clusters of cypress knees covered with water and alligator flags."

"Notice," Genesis continued, "that the larger bald cypress grows along deep water in slow-moving creeks like the one we're in now. The alligator flags we are moving through used to serve as a marker for our alligator hunts. We knew when we saw them, there were usually alligators around. If you'll look way out to your right, there's a large flat with a mixture of sawgrass and dwarf cypress. This is commonly called a "cypress flat" and generally has much shallower water. The shallow water is no problem for airboats since they can travel over wet grass with only an inch or so of water. The dwarf cypress is the same as the larger ones, but the soil is much poorer, so they don't flourish as well. Also, the sawgrass, as you might suspect, makes foot travel difficult in the glades, but not impossible to the experienced. I'll tell you more about that later."

Genesis continued his narration as the airboat slipped easily through the swamp.

"It's so pristine and primeval," Monique stated.

"Yes," Billie said. "It's easy to be seduced by the flowing water and serenity of the swamp. Enchanting and peaceful, but it can be very dangerous to the inexperienced."

"You love it here," Monique said. "I can see it in your eyes."

"It is home," Billie said. "I couldn't imagine living anywhere else. Nothing can compare to the serenity, beauty, pristineness, or mysteriousness of the Everglades."

"God," Monique said. "It's so flat, so vast."

"To the untrained eye," Billie said. "Look over there. That's a cabbage head. A hammock with cabbage trees instead of gumbo limbo like we passed way back in the sawgrass. And look at that plant up there on that small cypress tree. See the one with the red flower." Monique nodded yes. "The locals call that an air plant, but its real name is common bromeliad."

"Why do they call it an air plant?" Monique asked.

"I guess because it's barely attached to the tree," Billie said. "It seems to have a symbiotic relationship with the tree. If you remove it, there are no roots and you can take the plant home, stuff it in some moist Spanish moss and it will continue to grow. People used to think it only required air to live."

"This place is so intriguing," Monique said. "I can see how one would fall in love with it. Are these hammocks you pointed out where your people live?"

"We're not that far in the dark ages," Billie said laughing. "In the past, before the white man came, we lived on them in our chickee's. Also, when the Indian hater President Andrew Jackson tried to exterminate us, we moved deeper into the swamp. We lived on them then, we showed President Jackson and his soldiers who the best warriors were. Today, some of our people still live in chickee's on small hammocks here and there, but tourists never see them because they are so remote. You'll find most Indians are very private."

"You sound bitter about it," Monique said.

"The Seminoles have fought three wars against the white man," Billie said. "Mostly because of Andrew Jackson himself. People have only recently discovered he wasn't the great president they thought he was. Anyway, we reluctantly signed a non-aggression agreement with the United States Government in 1962. The agreement was that we wouldn't commit any hostile actions against them. It was not a peace treaty because those are no longer issued by the government. We always seem to end up on the short end of the stick when we have any dealings with the white man, especially the government agencies such as the Bureau of Indian Affairs."

Monique didn't know what to say. She was trailing her hand in the water alongside the airboat, looking out across the swamp. Billie was looking at her. She was so beautiful, yet he knew that no matter what happened, she would never stay here, while he would always remain on the reservation. If he didn't help his people, who would? Billie caught a movement out of the corner of his eye. Instantly, he reached over and jerked Monique's arm upward, just in time. The moment her hand cleared the side of the boat, an alligator's jaws snapped shut like a steel trap. A second longer and Monique would have been minus a hand or entire arm. Everyone was startled by what happened, but none more than Monique. She was white as a sheet, trembling uncontrollably.

"Are you okay?" Billie asked.

"Thanks to you," Monique replied as she grabbed him and hugged him tightly. "That scared the hell out of me. I thought Genesis said alligators were mostly docile animals."

"They are," Billie said. "However, that one is a mother guarding her nest." "See," Billie said, pointing. "They are very aggressive when guarding a nest or if they have little ones. Don't ever grab a baby gator. The mother will instantly explode into an ominous display of aggression."

"I'll keep that in mind," Monique said.

"Good thing Billie was along," Paul said. "You'll have to show him your appreciation." Paul was eyeing Monique with a knowing look that Billie couldn't see.

"I do owe you a debt of gratitude," Monique said to Billie. "I'd like to make it up to you somehow."

"Don't worry about it," Billie said. "Just help me get that landfill project so I can provide jobs for my people."

"We'll certainly do what we can," Monique said.

"Give me New York anytime," Blayde said, standing. "Thugs are easier to spot than gators."

"Yeah, I bet," Genesis muttered under his breath.

As Blayde sat back down, he put his hand along the railing of the boat as it slid through the sawgrass; it was sliced like a razor.

"Damn it!" Blayde screamed in pain, holding his hand. "What the hell is this?"

"It's sawgrass," Jacob said. "It has teeth like a saw blade. If you look at the edge closely, you can see them. The old timers call it "jagged grass". You know, because of the teeth."

"Yeah," Genesis said, grinning. "It's sharp like your namesake Blayde. It'll rip the clothes right off your back. That's why foot travel is difficult in the glades. If you're not experienced, a mile in the sawgrass will leave you ripped, bleeding, and naked. Even with experience, you'll be cut, and your clothes sliced to ribbons. Kind of fun, don't you think?"

"Is everything around here lethal?" Mike asked.

"Nah," Jacob said. "The swamp is your friend if you don't fight it. The Medicine Man says if we link our mind with the swamp, we can do anything, even raise the dead. It's part of the mysticism of the Glades. Although some laugh, given the age of the swamp and the alligator, no one can easily dismiss the Medicine Man's wisdom."

"Be that as it may," Mike said. "You can keep your swamp. I prefer the cities and their night life."

The airboat tour completed, the group had traveled back to the main community of Big Cypress and mounted two swamp buggies, amazing vehicles capable of traversing the deep waters and muddy marshes of the Everglades. They had huge tires; as tall as a man and sometimes two feet wide. They were macho-looking vehicles. Definitely not something you would like to see on your bumper through the rear-view mirror. After traveling a short distance, the two swamp buggies arrived at the prospective landfill site.

"You've all seen the site plans," Billie said. "This is the place. Since we'll discuss it at the meeting, our time will be better spent if you study the surrounding area to get a feel for how the installation could affect the environment."

"This might be a good time to separate so we can talk among ourselves," Paul said.

"Agreed," Solomon retorted. "We'll meet you back at headquarters."

"Paul," Billie said. "Just follow us and remember, these vehicles have no brakes, so be careful."

Each group separated; Indians on one swamp buggy and Paul's entourage on the other. They were following a winding road through a slough that passed by hammocks, sand bottom ponds, and sawgrass. They saw several cotton mouth moccasins and once a rattlesnake swam in front of Paul's buggy. "I thought rattlesnakes couldn't swim," Blayde said, surprised. "I suppose everything can swim in a land that is ass deep to a giraffe in water," Mike replied, smiling.

The sloughs were teeming with life. On more than one occasion they saw huge alligators. Just the sight of them made the city people's skin crawl. Like a snake, there was something about them that looked dark, foreboding, evil; they truly were prehistoric. Yes, that was it, prehistoric, representing millions of years of evolution. They seemed to be waiting for someone to fall into the water. Like a vulture waiting for death or a predator for its hapless prey. Small wonder they were called the caretakers of the glades.

"I hope you know what you're doing Billie," Solomon said. "This landfill can be a big environmental risk."

"They've proven safe when installed correctly," Billie said. "I intend on supervising the construction myself. There is no way I'm going to risk damaging our land."

"Don't feed me that garbage," Solomon said. "What about our kids? And what about these guys? Are they on the up and up? I've heard through the grapevine that they are linked with the mafia."

"Yeah, and the swamp is just full of snakes and gators lying in wait to kill you." Billie said. "It is just rumors. Don't worry. I'm not going to purposely do something that would jeopardize ours or our children's future. You know what the installation of this landfill will mean in terms of dollars to the tribe and a chance for employment for residents here on Big Cypress. Remember, this reservation is isolated; it's not in the middle of town like our reservation in Hollywood. You can't just walk to work in Immokalee, Clewiston or Ft. Lauderdale."

"I know that, just remember I'll be watching you closely Billie," Solomon said. "Screw this up and I'll have my old job back."

"You'd like nothing better, would you?" Billie asked.

"Couldn't think of a nicer thing," Solomon grinned.

Genesis was listening intently to the conversation. When Solomon had turned away, sure he had rattled Billie and made his point, Genesis leaned over to Billie.

"Solomon may be right Billie," Genesis whispered. I've done some checking on those guys and they may not be what they've told us."

"Meaning?" Billie queried.

"Well," Genesis said. "When Mike and Blayde were out for the last meeting you had, I pulled them over for speeding. I didn't know who they were and when they mentioned you, I let them off with a warning. However, I ran their names through a friend of mine in the Miami police department. Turns out they both have criminal records. I'm not sure how bad yet, but I think you should be aware of it. I'll check on it further and keep you posted."

"If you're going to, make damn sure you're discreet," Billie said. "I don't want to screw this deal up before it gets started just because someone's heard a few ugly rumors. Our people need those jobs."

"I know," Genesis said. "If I think it's necessary, I'll talk with you again."

Blayde was not fond of what he was seeing. "I don't like this fucking place. It just doesn't feel right. And that Genesis gives me the creeps. This whole thing seems like a mistake. If the swamp is as dangerous as we've seen today, what about those Indians? It's like New York. People who grow up in a rough place are usually rough. Those people are dangerous boss."

"Perhaps but let me do the thinking. What you think doesn't matter," Paul said. "Do what you're told. That's what I pay you for. If the Indians get out of control, take care of them."

"I'm with Blayde on this one boss," Mike said. "Something about this place doesn't feel right."

"Don't wuss out on me now," Paul said, anger creeping into his voice. "This is merely a different environment, but people are people. Deal with it."

"Paul, I don't like it here either," Monique said. "But I do like Billie. The money will be well worth it."

"Holy hell," Paul exclaimed, exasperated. "Quit complaining all of you. Monique, just work your magic on Billie and keep him in the dark. If any of you screw this up, Don Cilatro will make sure we're all dead."

"It'll be done right boss," Mike said.

Paul retrieved a cell phone from his briefcase, not surprised that he got a signal since line-of-sight went forever out here and placed a call to New York.

"Don Cilatro," Paul said. "Yes, Paul Lorio here. The landfill looks like it will proceed as planned. No, don't call me; I'll let you know when we can receive shipment. It will be a while. Even if we get approval, the site still needs to be constructed. Don't worry, if I screw this up, I'll shoot myself. I'll call you when we get approval."

Paul hung up the phone. "The big boss is anxious. He's already getting clients lined up for chemical shipments. This deal will be the sweetest yet; lots of money for all of us."

Just ahead of them, Jacob had stopped his swamp buggy in the middle of a pond. They were watching a flock of roseate spoonbills in breeding plumage. The birds were rhythmically swinging their spatulate bills from side to side. Several of the Indians were laughing. Trying to see what they were watching Mike was not paying attention as he approached the rear of Jacob's swamp buggy. Before he knew it, he was right on their bumper. Too late to swerve and unable to brake, Mike rear-ended them. The collision sent Solomon flying through the air into the pond. He did a somersault in midair and landed on his back side. The splash was so big that Billie and Genesis were soaked with water. The comical nature of Solomon flying through the air gave everyone a good, well needed laugh.

Solomon, looking like a wet rat, stood up on the pond bottom, sputtering as his head emerged from the water. "I fail to see the humor," Solomon said; everyone laughed harder.
"People on the receiving end rarely do," Paul yelled, unable to control his laughter.
"Looks like you're a little wet behind the ears Solomon," Jacob teased.
It was hard for everyone to control their laughter as Solomon crawled back onto the swamp buggy and they headed for headquarters.

Upon return, each member of the group went different ways for one reason or another. Paul, seizing the opportunity, sought to meet with Solomon and sway him for a positive vote. He knew he had a great deal of animosity toward Billie; thus, a careful approach was necessary. With the others now out of site, Paul walked up to Solomon.

"Mr. Osceola," Paul said. "Would you mind if I asked you a few questions."

"Not at all," Solomon replied. "Let's step into this office, we can chat privately."

"What is on your mind Mr. Lorio?" Solomon asked.

"Well," Paul said. "I'm sure you're aware of the aspects of the landfill proposal. You're also aware of each of our goals in this joint venture. Since we're going to be having the meeting to approve or disapprove the resolution, I'd like to know where you stand on the issue. What are your feelings about it?"

"I could be persuaded to jump on the wagon," Solomon said. "It looks like a good idea."

"What would it take to get you on for the ride?" Paul asked.

"What were you thinking of?" Solomon queried back warily.

"Not speaking for Billie, my group could certainly make it worth your while, if you know what I mean," Paul said.

"It may require quite a lot to make it worth my while," Solomon said. "I have a reputation to think of."

"I'm sure we could keep your reputation intact," Paul said. "No one need know about this except the two of us."

"Very well then," Solomon said. "Something worth my while might be in the neighborhood of five figures; off the record of course."

"Alright," Paul said, "Off the record, how about two hundred thousand?"

"I couldn't have come up with a better figure myself," Solomon said. "That'll get you my approving vote and a show of support until the resolution is passed and I'll help you persuade all the others."

"Excellent," "Paul said, shaking Solomon's hand. "I'll have Mike deliver you a care package tomorrow. He'll call you to discuss a time and location."

"It's a pleasure to work with you Mr. Lorio," Solomon said. "Perhaps in the future, we can continue this relationship. Why don't you exit first? I'll follow in a while so no one is the wiser about our little chat."

"Very well," Paul said, shaking hands. "I do appreciate your support. We'll all achieve our goals on this project. It's just a matter of getting it off the ground."

Paul turned and left the room. Solomon sat down in a chair looking out the window. "What a fool he mused to himself." I was going to vote for it anyway, now I'll make two hundred grand in the process. Not only that, but I'll also still give Billie a hard time if anything goes wrong. Things couldn't be better. The only thing that could possibly improve my current situation would be if Billie made a drastic error judging the hydrology of the site and a few people became ill. A greedy politician could always hope. Still, the offer from Lorio worried him a little. Why would someone want to pay him so much for his vote? He knew they needed his vote to get the resolution passed, but was the money they were going to make worth that much to them? Well, he mused, 100 years is a long time, and much money could be accumulated over that time.

Mike could only guess what was in the package on the seat beside him, although he had a good idea. Having called Solomon, he was instructed to drive along the dirt roads on the west end of Big Cypress until he saw a freshly broken tree branch in the road. Upon seeing it, he was to throw the package, a padded manila envelope, out the passenger side window into the grass and keep driving. He had been driving for about forty minutes and had already passed this area once. Suddenly, ahead in the road was a branch, not there before. Mike depressed the control button for the passenger side window, and it powered down. At the same time, glancing furtively about, he picked the package up in his right hand, holding the steering wheel with his knee as he leaned to his right.

Solomon had watched Mike pass by once from the front seat of his jeep. Parked conveniently behind a group of cabbage palms, he was mostly invisible to potential onlookers. After Mike passed by, Solomon cut a frond from the nearest cabbage palm, walked through the cabbage head and surrounding grass, then threw the palm frond into the middle of the road. He casually strolled back to his jeep, took out his binoculars and thoroughly glassed the surrounding area for signs of others. Satisfied all was clear, he settled back into his seat and waited. After a short while, he heard Mike's car speeding down the graveled road. Watching it carefully, Solomon could see the manila package flung out the window as the car passed without slowing.

"So nice to work with professionals," Solomon thought as he carefully looked about before retrieving the package.

He picked up the cabbage frond and threw it into the weeds alongside the gravel road as he walked back to his jeep. His heart was pounding with excitement as he sat down in the front seat, his hands shaking as he opened the envelope. Out fell three bundles of cash, each wrapped neatly with a rubber band. The three bundles consisted of a variety of bill denominations ranging from twenty to one-hundred-dollar bills, both old and new. Solomon took his time, savoring the money and even smelling it; he slowly counted. The total was as agreed. Taking great care, he placed the cash back into the envelope, stuffed it in the glove box and locked it. With a large smile on his face, he cranked the motor and eased his jeep from behind the cabbage palms, heading for home.

Jagged Grass

The day had finally arrived for presentation of the resolution to the council and all tribal members. A previous meeting had been held with various officials who served with the state of Florida, the water compacts with neighboring ranchers, tribal leaders and the South Florida Water Management District. At that meeting, all concerns had been addressed, palms greased, and everyone satisfied that the project would be beneficial, not only to the Seminole, but to the people of south Florida. The residents of Dade and Broward Counties would find it pleasant for the growing trash mounds to be out of sight and out of mind. The white man was more than happy to let the Indians live with the stench and ugliness of their unwanted trash. The Seminoles would make their money and get the jobs, but they'd also inherit more problems than they bargained for. Such was always the case with these types of projects. Neither the managers or people they served would remain happy, but they would learn to suffer the small problems in return for the needed cash dividends and created jobs.

All participants had gathered at Seminole Tribal Headquarters in Hollywood, Florida, on the corner of Sterling and A1-A, in a large meeting room. The council members from each of the Seminole's six reservations were on stage along with Paul Lorio. The room was packed to capacity by tribal members. Christina and Monique were sitting in the front row. Solomon, delegated with the responsibility of starting the meeting, walked to the microphone at center stage.

"As council representative of Big Cypress, I'd like to welcome everyone," Solomon said. "As you know, we'll cast our votes today to decide the future of the proposed landfill project. Based on your vote, we can enter into a joint venture with Mr. Paul Lorio who represents Apex Incorporated and the Seminole Tribe of Florida. At this time, I'd like to turn the meeting over to Billie Panther who has been heading up the project and prospective tribal interests. He'll be able to answer any questions you may have."

"Thank you, Solomon," Billie said. "I've discussed the benefits of the project to many of you already. It will bring needed jobs to Big Cypress and substantial revenues to the Tribe, not only from the waste but also from the methane collected for energy production as the waste decomposes. In the process, it will help improve our standard of living. So, let's begin with all of your questions?"

"What's the risk of this site poisoning our water at Big Cypress," a tribal member asked.

"Minimal," Billie said. "We use the most current technology with clay and plastic liners at the bottom of the fill. This includes state-of-the-art drainage systems. You can see the design in your handout."

"What if the thing springs a leak?" another tribal member asked. "Can you detect it?"

"Not immediately," Paul said, stepping up beside Billie. "However, we will have monitoring wells installed for that specific purpose. Also, the site is elevated above the original land surface by several yards like the old Indian mounds Billie showed us near Chokoloskee. Any leakage should be soil adsorbed by the clay liner. No contaminants will reach the groundwater or surrounding surface waters."

"What Paul is stating is correct," Billie said. "Any risk to the environment would be minimal at best. You would have to intentionally dump hazardous waste to have the kind of bad effects you're suspicious of."

"If you can assure us it's safe," another tribal member said, "we're behind you."

Many others muttered their approval. The tribal members present were looking around at each other shaking their heads, trying to form a consensus.

"Do we have your word on safety Billie?" Solomon asked.

"You do, Solomon," Billie affirmed.

"This is all fine, but how do we know that Lorio isn't going to screw us like every other white man we've dealt with?" asked another tribal member?

"You have both my word and a written agreement," Paul said. "You still own the land, and we are joint partners. If I back out, you own it all, which leaves the tribe in a win-win situation. Also, considering the money we can make, I'm not going anywhere."

The room grew quiet as members pondered what Paul had said.

"Are there any more questions?" Solomon asked. There was a long pause. "Alright then, I'll give you a couple of minutes to decide and then we'll vote."

For the next few minutes, the room buzzed with conversation as individuals and groups of tribal members voiced their opinions to each other. Billie, Solomon, and Paul roved the room to help dispel fear and answer questions that were not previously voiced. There was some occasional bickering over a difference of opinion. It was like a primary caucus atmosphere. Gradually, the room fell silent; everyone had made up their mind. This would be a public vote, so one had to make sure they were on the majority side.

"It looks like we've come to a consensus," Solomon said. "Let's cast our votes. All in favor?"

The majority of tribal members raised their hands. The vote among the council members on the stage was unanimous.

"All against?" Solomon asked.

Only three tribal members raised their hands.

"Mr. President," Solomon said. "We have a majority in favor of the resolution. The proposal is carried; the resolution is passed."

There were shouts of joy as the silence held during the voting became a crescendo of approval. Both Paul and Billie sighed in relief. Many were exclaiming that finally Big Cypress could join the rest of society by having available jobs for workers. Paul and Jacob were shaking hands on the stage, beaming at each other. It had been a long, difficult battle for both of them. Monique stepped onto the stage to congratulate Paul and Billie. Christina also made her way through the crowd to Billie.

"Congratulations Billie," Christina said. "You've worked on this for a long time. I hope you're happy. Can we talk now?"

"Thanks," Billie said. "I'd love to talk. There's something I need to tell you."

At that moment, Paul and Monique walked over.

"Billie, you didn't tell us you had such a lovely admirer," Monique said.

"Paul and Monique, this is my good friend Christina Jumper," Billie replied.

"It's such a pleasure to meet you," Monique said. "What kind of work do you do?"

"I teach school, third grade," Christina said.

"Sounds fascinating," Monique said with a small smile.

"A noble profession," Paul said. "I'd like to know more about it sometime, perhaps over lunch."

"Some other time," Christina responded. "I'm late for an appointment. Nice meeting both of you. Would you call me, Billie?"

"I'll give you a call tomorrow," Billie said as Christina turned and made her way through the crowd.

CHAPTER 4

Construction of the landfill site had been going on for months. Trucks, bull dozers, and other heavy equipment were moving at a swift pace. Billie had supervised the entire construction phase with the assistance of Paul, Mike and the construction foreman. He was certain the landfill would operate without problems and that any type of contamination would be avoided.

An earthen mound had been formed. It was massive and took up the space of several city blocks. Once the mound had been formed, clay and geotextile liners had been put in place, along with a high-tech drainage and a ventilation system to increase microbial activity. Tiny microbes and bacteria would get the air and energy they needed to degrade harmful contaminants. Eventually, the contaminants would become the food supply of the organisms and would be eaten up before they would have a chance to reach the groundwater. The ventilation system would also pipe the methane produced by the bacteria as they decomposed the garbage to an onsite facility that would convert the methane to electricity for the community on Big Cypress. Billie, other council members and the tribe in general were excited about the new source of energy, an added dividend worth the expense of the system.

The crews were performing the last phases of construction on the site. After this day, pending final inspection, the site would be ready for operation. Billie met Paul by the office on his way out.

"Well," Billie said. "That does it. The site is complete. Now all we need to do is watch the money roll in. As a matter of fact, Jacob and several other council members have been soliciting business from waste management companies in Dade and Broward Counties. They have already managed to sign several clients to long term contracts."

"That's great," Paul said. "I have several associates who will begin helping you on that next week. Between us, we'll have more business than we can handle."

"Everyone is excited about this Paul," Billie said. "It's the first time they have really believed we could accomplish our goals. That's great for tribal moral. I want to thank you for all you've done and before I forget, take this." Billie hands him a key.

"What's this for?" Paul asked.

"It's the gate key," Billie replied. "Now that we're through, I won't need it. Since you have the hundred-year lease, the land is in your custody. As long as you abide by the agreement, you have complete control over who comes and goes on the site."

"Nothing should change," Paul said. "All employees will be free to come and go as they please during work hours. You also have the same privilege. The only thing we may have a problem with is that non-employees will need to check in at the office when they enter the site. That's mostly for liability and insurance reasons. You know how people like to sue these days."

"Don't I though," Billie said. "I'll likely call before I come out, if not, then I'll check in as you wish. I'll pass the information on to the rest of the council members and the Seminole PD. However, it's likely you'll be getting calls from them quite often so they can bring a few hot shots out on tours of the new site."

"No problem," Paul said. "The site will be made available to them. It's really nice to work with people of your caliber, Billie. It's not often a deal goes as smoothly or as profitably."

"Thank you," Billie said. "The council feels the same way. And, just in case (writing a number on a piece of paper), should you get some unruly members out who have had a little too much to drink or cause you a hindrance, this is the number for Seminole PD. Give them a call if you need to. Anyway, I have to run. Let me know if there is anything I can do for you."

"Roger that," Paul said as Billie climbed into his truck and drove away.

Mike and Blayde had been watching from inside the office. A trailer set up as a temporary until construction could begin on a permanent structure. They walked out to meet Paul.

"What was that all about?" Mike asked.

"Nothing," Paul said. "Billie just returned the gate key. We have total control of the site now, so let's get the last job finished. Where are the blueprints?"

Blayde handed Paul a set of rolled blueprints that he spread across the hood of a nearby pick-up truck.

"Add these disposal pipes," Paul said, pointing and tracing them on the blueprint with his finger. "Have them penetrate to about mid-depth. When we bring our chemicals in, we'll use these for dumping. Don't let anyone see you install them. I want the tanks and pipes installed tonight. The bentonite and geotextile liners have to be in place first, so make certain that you don't puncture either liner. We'll be able to use this site for years."

"Okay," Mike said. "The tanks we purchased are a little larger than those we used in Seattle. They will have small puncture holes just like before."

"Excellent," Paul said, "The more volume, the better. Blayde, if anyone sees you tonight, ace their ass, but make it look like an accident."

"My pleasure boss," Blayde said.

It was 1:00 a.m. The crew was hard at work and had almost finished installing the last tank. They were just beginning to bury it when the sound of a car penetrated the still night air. The crew could see headlights snaking toward the site far down the highway. As the car drew alongside the front gate, it slowed.

"Damn," Mike said. "Kill the lights. We can't let anyone see us. I hope Blayde is awake out there."

Blayde, who had been posted as a lookout near the main gate, was smoking a cigarette. The mosquitoes were awful; you could reach out and literally grab a handful. Blayde had insect repellant burning on the dash console; it didn't help much. He wanted to roll down the windows, but the mosquitoes were just too thick and hungry. Sweat was dripping from every pore as he sat in the hot, humid cab of his truck. His clothes drenched; anger built with each droplet of sweat. He was cursing Lorio for being in such a forsaken hell hole. His anger was about to erupt into a physical demonstration when he noticed a car approaching. The car slowed as it passed. Blayde could tell the female driver didn't see him but was watching the site. The instant the car passed, Blayde noticed the lights at the site switch off. "Damn," Blayde thought. "That's my cue, time to take care of business."

Blayde cranked the engine to his truck and squealed out after the car. "Wrong place at the wrong time, bitch," Blayde muttered to himself. Blayde had the pedal to the metal and was gaining on the car quickly.

Mary Jane saw the lights at the landfill site as she passed and wondered why the crew was working so late, making a mental note to talk to Genesis. It was pleasant to think of him. They had been dating for quite a while now. Marriage was a certainty, a welcome relief to the loneliness she felt when Genesis wasn't with her. Wrapped in deep thought, she was returning home from a long day in Hollywood working with mentally challenged children, some of whom would be in her next class. She loved what she did, but it took so much energy. Sometimes Mary Jane felt like a car battery, which when cranked continually, slowly ran down. She was looking forward to getting home and taking a hot bath. Then, maybe she'd call Genesis, just to wake him up and tease him. Who knows, maybe he would come over. The thought excited her. Mary Jane was so wrapped in thought that she didn't notice the headlights following her until they were right on her bumper.

"Why don't you just go around," she thought. "There's no one else on the highway."

Suddenly, the truck rammed her. Terror struck Mary Jane in the heart like a dagger. She panicked. The truck rammed her again. In a futile attempt to escape, Mary Jane sped up, pressing the gas pedal to the floor. Still, the truck was on her bumper. It hit her again. She was frantic; so afraid the scream in her throat couldn't escape. Realizing she couldn't get away; she slowed the car. At that moment, the truck rammed her and the bumpers of the two vehicles locked together. Mary Jane panicked even more, trying to get free. The car was difficult to steer; she pushed the pedal all the way down. As the car leaped forward, the bumpers of the two vehicles unlocked. Mary Jane's car catapulted ahead, lost traction and began to fish tail. "I wish Genesis were here."

It was the last thought Mary Jane had as her car, going eighty miles an hour, left the highway, flew through the air like a flying squirrel, and landed upside down in the roadside canal knocking her unconscious.

Blayde cut his lights and pulled off the shoulder of the road, exited his truck and walked around to the passenger side to observe his destructive handiwork. As he stood watching for signs of life to emerge from the wreck, he pulled a pack of cigarettes from his shirt, lit one and took a long, slow drag. He blew smoke into the still night air, watching it as it encircled the stars in the jewel-studded sky. Patient as a leopard watching its prey, Blayde stood. No cares, no worries, just a job. Satisfied that the driver was dead, he strolled back around the pick-up, stood up on the driver-side running board and looked into the black water of the canal. There were only a few bubbles visible in the moonlight. "Good riddance, bitch," Blayde said as he flicked his cigarette into the canal. He stepped down into the cab and drove away.

The early morning mist had just burned off and Freeman could barely discern the green of the trees as dawn approached. A deputy for Seminole PD, he was making the final leg of his patrol. It had been a long night. Seventy-two thousand acres, almost 113 square miles, was difficult to patrol. In a time when drug dealers would land on a deserted road to exchange their contraband for money, it was impossible to be everywhere at once, so only the most isolated roads were patrolled.

Several times that evening, Freeman has shown his spotlight at low flying planes to keep them off his roads. He had stopped the cars the pilots were supposed to rendezvous with and had run them off the reservation. The license plate of each one had been radioed to headquarters. Today, the department would run the plates to determine who they belonged to, then sheriffs in the surrounding counties would be notified. Each car had been thoroughly searched, but nothing had been found. It could only mean they stashed their money so they could reclaim it later. Freeman made a mental note to go back after he was relieved from his shift and make a search of the surrounding area where the cars had been stopped. Maybe he'd get lucky; his kids would have their college tuition far in advance.

Freeman was having a hard time staying awake until he saw the broken glass, scarred pavement and rubber marks on the road. It was as if he had been shot. Sleep fled from his mind as the excitement of a potential investigation entered. In an instant his heart was pounding; adrenaline began flowing like the Mississippi River. A few caffeine tablets couldn't have made him more alert. The police cruiser he was driving came to a screeching stop as he unconsciously depressed the brake pedal. He literally jumped from the car almost before it stopped and began inspecting the highway. He tried to imagine which direction the car was headed as he attempted to recreate the scene. Had there been a terrible accident or had someone simply been rear ended. Freeman looked up and down the road and decided where the initial impact had taken place. Walking to that point, he began to study the tell-tale signs on the pavement. Like tracking a wild boar, he knew he would satisfy his curiosity.

The first items he noticed were small, broken pieces of red taillight lenses followed by swerving tire marks on the pavement and a few yards farther, yellow glass spread out in a fan shape. Next, were large pock marks in the asphalt of different shapes and sizes. These abruptly ended at the edge of the road where there were only a few skid marks on the grass adjacent to the painted line on the pavement, which continued like an endless ribbon to the horizon. It had to be a rollover Freeman was thinking. "I wonder when it happened." He'd have to call Genesis and ... "Wait a minute," Freeman thought. "What's that?" Not seeing a car directly, he had been looking across the nearby pasture and then along the canal when he noticed an oddly shaped shadow on the water. He scrambled down the steep bank like an armadillo on the run.

The car was sitting on its roof, its four tires barely submerged below the surface of the water. Immediately, not knowing when the wreck had occurred, Freeman removed his shoes, wallet, and gun belt. He dove headfirst into the tepid, coffee-colored water and swam to the car. He swam around the car and then, beneath the surface, nothing was visible. The water was too murky to see more than a couple of feet. He tried to feel around inside the car, extending his arms as far as possible to detect the presence of a body. None could be found. Out of breath, Freeman, swam to the surface and then tried several more times. The result was the same.

Freeman swam to water's edge, climbed the steep embankment and reached into his cruiser for the radio. "Dispatch," Freeman said. "This is car one."
"Dispatch, go ahead," a pleasant female voice responded.

"Have you had any reports of an accident last night or yesterday on Snake Road?" Freeman asked.

"Negative," the dispatcher replied.

"I was afraid of that," Freeman stated as he let out a heavy sigh. "You better tell Genesis we have a submerged wreck about five miles south of the community. I'll need divers, a tow truck and you better send an ambulance. Tell them to prepare for the worst."

A crowd was gathering when Genesis arrived, after all, the Res as those who lived there, didn't have much excitement to speak of. He had to worm his way through the onlookers to the accident scene. The car had barely emerged from the water as he walked up. A diver had hooked the winch from the tow truck to the undercarriage of the vehicle and then, began the tedious task of reeling in the wreck, like hauling in a lifeless whale. Two divers were pulling Mary Jane's body out of the water. Genesis had to turn away as the paramedics placed her cold, discolored corpse onto a stretcher and covered her with a sheet.

Freeman had seen Genesis pull up and watched him as he made his way through the crowd. He could only imagine how Genesis must feel. Just a few days before, Mary Jane and Genesis had decided to take the big step. It was all Genesis had talked about. He was looking forward to being a husband and someday soon, a father. Genesis showed no emotion; his facial expression was unreadable. Perhaps the white man was right, Indians showed very little emotion at any time. Once, a female reporter for the Miami Herald had stated that to look upon the face of an Indian was to look upon a blank canvas because they never smiled, laughed, or showed any emotion. If she could only know of the situation that confronted Genesis at this moment and photograph the expression on his face, Freeman was sure she would say, "See, I told you so."

Freeman strolled over to where Genesis was standing next to the tow truck.

"It was Mary Jane," Freeman said, "Looks like she lost control. Right now, there's no sign of alcohol or foul play. I'm sorry Genesis. I know how close you were." Genesis made no indication he had heard Freeman as his piercing eyes inspected every detail of the accident scene. Finally, he spoke. "Have an autopsy done right away," Genesis said. "I want to know the time of death. This couldn't have been an accident. Mary Jane's driven this road a thousand times. Go ahead and take the car to the impound lot. We'll look at it later."

"Do you want me to inform her parents?" Freeman asked.

"No," Genesis replied with a sigh as he gazed steadfastly toward the landfill site across the pastures. "I'll do it."

Freeman saw a small tear roll down Genesis's cheek.

Genesis pulled his police cruiser to a stop along the old dirt road. Almost unable to think and still in complete shock, he could not remember anything as difficult as what he had just done. Mary Jane's parents still lived in a chickee so they could provide her, as an only child, all they had to offer. Her dad had wrestled alligators, worked as a hunting and fishing guide, and gigged frogs for local restaurants in Miami to help put her through college. Mary Jane's mother had worked her fingers literally to the bone making Indian beadwork necklaces, earrings, ceremonial jackets and dresses, and key chains, as well as woven baskets. The hardships Genesis had suffered in Afghanistan had not prepared him for what he had just done. At least there, he had himself to rely on. Now, he couldn't even do that. All his soul cried out to have let Freeman tell the parents of Mary Jane's death, but that would not be the proper way.

They had been as amiable as they always were, but as the awful news Genesis had to tell was comprehended, he could see their hearts wrenched from within, the unimaginable agony that shown on their faces. The parents had broken down in tears; Genesis had cried with them. If only he could hide under a rock, in a cave, or for that matter, the depths of hell, he would feel much better. Anything rather than tell them of the death of their only treasure in life and his own agony from the loss. He felt like his insides had been wrenched out; the stress was intolerable; he felt so alone. The word itself seemed to have a tragic meaning. Genesis could never remember feeling alone. He had always been linked to the land around him, never needing another. But, after meeting Mary Jane, the wall he had built between himself and rest of the world had crumbled as he learned to love and trust her and cherish the memorable moments that were now only a memory.

He put his hands over his eyes and sobbed bitterly, not for her parents, but for himself because at that moment, his life was empty. The two of them were no more. Nothing he could do could repair the injury to the heart of the anguished parents or to him. His only consolation would be to discover what had happened, what had caused the accident. In his heart, he knew it had something to do with the new landfill project. Something seemed wrong about it. Perhaps it was the people who had to be accepted as part of the project. Could it be because of his dislike for Blayde? But Genesis was a professional. He wouldn't let personal feelings clutter his judgment. No matter what happened, he was certain the reason for the accident would be forthcoming.

It was late afternoon when Genesis pulled into the police impound lot on Big Cypress. Afternoon thundershowers surrounded the area, lurking like demonic, blue-gray demons on the horizon. Freeman was already at the lot inspecting the car. Genesis sat in his car for a moment watching him. "A good deputy," Genesis thought. "We'll get to the bottom of this."

"Found anything?" Genesis asked as he approached the car.

"Nothing that would indicate another vehicle or any kind of mechanical damage," Freeman said. "The coroner gave a rough estimate of about 12:00 p.m. as the time of death. Do you think she could have dozed off?"

"I suppose it's possible," Genesis said. "Keep looking. If you find anything suspicious, I want to know immediately. I'll be in Billie's office."

"Don't worry," Freeman said. "If I find anything, you'll be the first to know."

Genesis and Billie had been friends for a long time. After Genesis had been sent home from Afghanistan, he had stayed in the military until he was able to take an early retirement. During the years after Afghanistan, he had been stationed as an instructor at Ft. Bragg, North Carolina for the LRRP unit which he had served with during the war. It was during this time that Billie began serving with the unit. They had hit it off right away and when Genesis found out Billie was from Big Cypress, he was thrilled. Billie was only in for three years. He did a very short stint in Afghanistan as an eighteen-year-old kid and the three years had passed quickly. It saddened Genesis to see Billie leave; they had become such good friends. Billie went off to Yale, where he had worked hard for seven years. Genesis and Billie kept up their relationship through letters and phone calls. As luck would have it, Genesis retired the same time Billie graduated and they found themselves back at Big Cypress trying to help the Seminole Tribe into the new age of high tech. Chairman Osceola had helped them in various efforts and they had both become successful men. But, because of their remote location, they often felt they might as well be on the moon. Their technology lagged far behind the real world. Nothing that should work did and things that should be easy weren't.

Genesis was thinking about the good times he and Billie had shared for the last fifteen years. Though about eighteen years Billie's senior, they were more like brothers. As Genesis walked into the office, Billie stood up from behind his desk.

"Sorry to hear about Mary Jane," Billie said as he shook his hand and gave in a long hug. "Did you talk to the family?"

"Yeah," Genesis said. "They took it real hard. It was heart wrenching to have to tell them."

"I'll visit with them later and try to help console them, but what about you?" Billie asked. "How are you coping?"

"I'll deal with it," Genesis said.

"I know how you deal with things," Billie said. "Remember, it's me you're talking to. If there is anything I can do, just say the word. I know how close you were. God, I'm sorry Genesis."

"Thanks for the offer," Genesis said. "I'll get through it somehow."

"Do you have any idea how it happened?" Billie asked.

"No, not yet," Genesis said. "I have a gut feeling, but I'm reluctant to say."

"Spit it out," Billie said. "We've been friends too long. Let's hear it."

"I think it was deliberate," Genesis said. "I think one of those goons of Lorio's did it."

"I understand how you must feel," Billie said. "But don't jump to any conclusions. Take a day or so off and we'll talk again. Once your head is clear, maybe you'll be able to concentrate better."

"No need," Genesis replied. "I want to check around and see what I can find out about those guys. If I find anything, I hope you'll listen."

"Of course, I will," Billie responded. "We've been friends for a long time. Even my dreams won't come between that. If you find something, I'll be all ears. Just promise you won't do anything rash without absolute proof."

"Don't worry," Genesis said as he arose to leave. "I won't go off half-cocked without a good reason."

Billie stood watching him as he walked out. He felt for the man. Memories from his own past came flooding in and his eyes began to mist over. From his own sad experience, he knew what his friend was feeling. Genesis was never one to show emotion or affection. Mary Jane had become his whole life. They were always together, and Genesis never ceased talking about her. Now, Genesis was alone again. Pushing his late forties, Genesis would likely become a loner. Billie was worried that he might do something rash, but at the same time, he had never known Genesis to be anything except the consummate professional. And that's what bothered him. If Genesis suspected someone at the landfill site was responsible for the accident, there was cause for concern.

Billie tried to think of every incident and conversation that had led to approval of the resolution that permitted construction of the site. While he wasn't extremely fond of all the participants involved in the operation, there was nothing that cast suspicion on Lorio or his associates. Billie had to put it out of his mind. Right now, he had a celebration party to attend. He hoped to be able to talk to Christina and let her know how he felt about her. Not only had he promised his mom, but he had also promised himself. While he was at the party, he'd check out Paul and his men and try to get a feel for them and whether or not Genesis was justified in his accusations.

James Tindall

CHAPTER 5

The banquet hall was alive as Billie walked into the grand entrance. Everyone who had been involved in the project was in attendance. He would need to be careful tonight because politics would be foremost on many of the other council members' agenda. They would try to jockey for position and use every advantage to obtain more votes for upcoming tribal elections. Billie's goal was to avoid them if possible. The only thought on his mind right now was to find Christina and have a quiet table so they could talk.

Billie wound his way between banquet tables and across the dance floor. A band was on stage tuning instruments, adjusting microphones and speakers and going through last minute preparations before their performance. Not far from the stage, Paul and several others were deep in conversation.

Almost at the same instant, Paul looked up and caught Billie's eye. He motioned for Billie to join them.

"Well, Billie," Paul said as he walked up. "We made it. In another week, the landfill will be receiving its first shipment of waste. You'll have your jobs, and we'll all make a ton of money. By the way, I heard about the auto accident, sorry. Please don't hesitate to call us if we can help in any way. We would like to send flowers and condolences if you can tell us where".

"I appreciate your offer," Billie responded. "It appears that the car simply ran off the road late at night. Anyway, let's not talk about the tragedies in life. I'm glad the landfill operation has gone so smoothly. That is a miracle around here."

"I understand," Paul said. "Every large group is a bureaucracy. Sometimes, delays can't be helped, but sometimes they also are not accidental."

"To a long and prosperous relationship," Paul added as he hoisted a glass of champagne.

At that moment, Monique, sexily dressed, joined them. Paul glanced knowingly at her and nodded his head. Monique understood clearly. It was time for her to begin working her feminine charm on Billie. As she appraised Billie, she thought that this would be the nicest job she had ever had. The money would be easy, and Billie would be another trophy on her wall. Monique was sure he wouldn't suspect a thing. It was simply a matter of being casual, moving in at the right time and alienating Christina. Most women she met were jealous of her beauty, the cattiness always surfaced. Christina would likely be no different, especially if she thought Monique was making a move on Billie. Tonight would be an excellent opportunity to begin. The band had begun playing softly in the background.

"To all of us," Billie said as he toasted the group.

"Billie," Monique said. "Come dance with me."

"I really shouldn't," Billie replied.

"Oh, come on," Monique pleaded. "Paul ..."

"Go ahead Billie," Paul implored. "It'll be fun. Besides, she may not forgive you if you don't."

"Well, if you insist," Billie said as he grabbed Monique by the arm and walked her to the dance floor.

Christina was making her way through the crowd, trying to reach Billie. She arrived too late to attract his attention. She watched in disappointment as Billie began dancing with Monique. Her disappointment turned to jealously and then boiling anger, yet knowing it was most likely an innocent part of entertaining the new partners. "How dare him," Christina thought. She briefly thought about cutting in but opted to stand idly by and watch unaware that Monique was plying her cunning trade.

"Well," Paul said, sidling next to her, "Our noble and beautiful schoolteacher. How about a dance?"

"I don't think so," Christina replied.

"Come on," Paul said. "You're going to hurt my feelings if you reject me. You know, not many women would turn me down." As Paul was talking, Christina looked across the dance floor at Billie. Monique was holding him tight and kissing him on the lips.

"What did you do that for?" Billie asked.

"No special reason," Monique said. "You merely saved my life from an alligator and have shown me such a good time, I couldn't resist. Besides, you're so cute and sexy. Why don't you come over to my place tonight?"

"I don't think that would be wise," Billie said.

"Perhaps not," Monique replied. "But it would be fun and very hot."

"Don't tempt me," Billie said. "I might not have enough self-control to stay away."

"That's what I'm counting on," Monique retorted, grabbing Billie's buttock and gently thrusting her hips into his as they began a bump and grind dance. She was very good and very sexy. Billie was having a difficult time keeping everything in perspective. He found himself lusting after her.

Christina couldn't believe what she was seeing. Monique and Billie were so close it looked like they were painted together. Christina's eyes flashed in hot anger as she watched. If looks could kill, Billie and Monique would be black toast. Christina immediately decided to take advantage of Paul's offer.

"I mustn't hurt your feelings," Christina snapped. "I can't let you go back to New York thinking us inhospitable."

As Christina grabbed Paul by the hand, Paul could see that his plan was working perfectly. Monique was doing an outstanding job. Not only had she succeeded in wrapping Billie around her finger already, but she had also made Christina very jealous, a perfect opportunity for Paul to make moves on her. In addition to his work Billie would have so many personal problems he'd never be around the landfill site.

Christina and Paul were quite the dancers. Both moved gracefully and rhythmically to the music. Before long, a crowd had gathered around them as they danced. They were like Ginger Rogers and Fred Astaire. It seemed there was nothing they couldn't do.

Billie also noticed. He couldn't help but think he had driven her to dance with Paul. If he had only waited a few more seconds, it would be him dancing with Christina. He desperately wanted to talk to her; to tell her how he felt about her. Billie decided that he would grab her at the first opportunity. As the music ended, everyone on the dance floor around Paul and Christina applauded their skill and finesse.

"Wow," Paul exclaimed. "You were great. Where did you learn to dance?"

"In college," Christina said. "Florida State University has some wonderful dance classes. I took every one of them."

"It shows," Paul said. "How would you like to go to lunch tomorrow?"

"Here's my number," Christina said as she handed him a business card. "Call me early tomorrow morning and tell me where." She turned and disappeared into the crowd. Paul couldn't help admiring her honesty and openness. He supposed most people would think she was rude because she was brutally honest like a small child. Christina Jumper was anything, but a child Paul thought to himself. This was one beautiful woman. As Paul watched her go, he thought how nice it would be to have her by his side in New York. He could and would hide his profession from her. "Just think", he thought to himself, "I'd have two of the nicest looking women in town." The thought intrigued him as he silently wondered how he could accomplish it.

Billie had separated from Monique and was able to catch up to Christina as she made her way through the crowd to the door.

"Christina," Billie said as he approached from behind. "It's nice to see you. If you have a minute, I'd like to talk."

"Do you mean nice to see me or her," Christina snapped, nodding in the direction of Monique. "It was hard not to notice your professional behavior. I thought we had something going and then I see you with her, kissing and grinding."

"That was nothing," Billie said. "She was just..."

"I know what it was," Christina exclaimed. "I'm not blind or dumb.

"I can explain," Billie said.

"There's nothing to explain," Christina said. "If you'll excuse me, I have an early day tomorrow."

"I thought we were going to talk," Billie said. "I've been planning on it all week. Can we talk tomorrow?"

"I have a date tomorrow," Christina said. "Look Billie, I know it hurt when your wife was killed, but you have to quit blaming yourself. I've been waiting for you to make a decision for a long time. I won't wait forever. Now, it appears that I must weigh all my options."

"What the hell is that supposed to mean?" Billie asked. "You're going to start dating others before we can talk?"

"I'm not getting any younger, Billie," Christina said. "And you've shown no romantic interest for a while."

"Please," Billie pleaded. "Be patient for a little longer."

"I'm fresh out of patience," Christina said.

"But..." Billie added.

"Good night Billie," Christina said as she quickly walked away.

Billie couldn't believe what had just happened. Was it his entire fault? He had been trying to talk to Christina all week, had promised his mother and himself he would and now, when he was desperate to spill his feelings to her, she had turned him off, as easily as flicking a light switch. Had it been because of the innocent kiss from Monique? He realized how it must look, but Christina should know of his feelings for her. After all, Billie had not dated anyone besides her since his wife had been killed. As long as he lived, Billie didn't think he would ever understand women. Watching Christina walked away, anger and resentment welled up inside him. His eyes trailed after her, watching her from the entryway as she drove off. He did love her, but she seemed too impatient, everything always having to be her way whenever she decided or, no way. He would need to reevaluate their relationship.

Paul and Monique had been watching Billie and Christina as they talked.

"From the expression on her face, I'd say you did a great job tonight," Paul said as he intently analyzed the two.

"I almost had Billie talked into coming over to my place," Monique said. "Christina's jealously will simply make things easier. A few more days and he'll be eating out of the palm of my hand. Christina is such a fool. Her sniveling, impatient, condescending attitude will only drive Billie away."

"What do you think is going through Billie's mind now?" Paul asked.

"Right now, he's asking himself if she really loves him, or if it's something he did," Monique said. "He's thinking she should know that he loves her. But he's also angry as hell that she won't take a moment to reason things out with him, hear his side of the story. Isn't it wonderful what an innocent kiss will do?"

"You knew," Paul asked.

"Of course," Monique said. "I watched her walk in. I knew she would react this way. Almost any woman would. And, like most women, she wants to point the finger of blame first before she knows the facts. Once the anger begins it subsides only slowly and, if something happens to reinitiate it well, that'll be good for us. I just wonder why so many women are so blind?"

"What do you mean?" Paul asked.

"Everyone except Christina can see that Billie is in love with her," Monique replied.

"How wonderful for us," Paul said. "Our job will be that much easier."

"And Billie will be a very nice perk," Monique added.

About a week later, Genesis and Freeman were meticulously inspecting the wreck again. Like a team of forensic scientists, nothing escaped their gaze.

"What about these dents?" Genesis asked, pointing to the rear bumper.

"They are consistent with a rollover type accident," Freeman said. "I would be suspicious of them myself, but there's no paint or scrape marks that would indicate a collision from another vehicle."

"Damn it!" Genesis exclaimed. "Nothing about this accident makes any sense. I want you to keep an eye on our new friends at the landfill site. But don't be obvious."

"You're much too nice, Genesis," Freeman said. "Assholes are more like it. Don't worry, they won't know they're being watched."

Genesis climbed into his cruiser and drove down the street. He had a meeting with Jacob at the diner. They had planned to discuss a few details about the case over a cup of coffee. Genesis couldn't understand how Mary Jane could have just left his life so suddenly. They had plans to be married in a couple of months and now she was gone. Surely the Great Spirit wouldn't be so callous after all Genesis had been through. It had to be those thugs. It just had to be. There simply wasn't another plausible explanation.

As Genesis parked his car, he noticed that Jacob had already arrived. He strolled into the diner and stopped just inside the door. His piercing eyes quickly scanned the room and spotted Jacob at a corner table.

"Just like him", Genesis thought. "No wonder the white man thinks we're anti-social." Jacob was always at the farthest location from a speaker or a door. He always said it was because he didn't trust people, never liked to turn his back to anyone. Genesis walked to Jacob's table and sat down.

"How are you holding up?" Jacob asked.

"I'll survive," Genesis said. "It just won't be the same without Mary Jane. We had grown so close."

"I know," Jacob said. "Billie feels for you too. We both know the pain you're going through."

"I appreciate your concern," Genesis said. "But I'll be alright. I just need some time to think about everything. Anyway, that's not what I want to talk to you about. I want to discuss my suspicions with you."

"What suspicions?" Jacob asked. "You're talking about the accident, aren't you?"

"Yes," Genesis said. "It couldn't have been an accident."

"I understand your suspicions Genesis," Jacob said. "However, unless you can get proof, your suspicions are as useless as tits on a boar hog. It'll also jeopardize our new opportunities with the landfill. We've waited for an opportunity like this for a long time. But you already know this."

"I'll get proof then," Genesis said. "Those thugs had to be responsible. I won't rest until I find out what happened."

"Just be cautious, we don't need any trouble at this juncture, and you know we'll back you up if you find it wasn't an accident," Jacob said.

"Well, speak of the devils; there are your favorite people now."

Genesis turned in his seat to see Mike and Blayde at the counter. "Bastards," Genesis muttered under his breath. "They have to be up to no good." Genesis and Jacob watched the two as they stood in front of the counter deciding what to select from the menu hanging on the wall behind the cashier. It was fairly obvious to Genesis that Blayde was in a foul mood. Genesis rose from his seat and closed the distance between them.

"What the hell's a punji?" Blayde asked. "Why don't you heathens speak English?"

"For future information, it's a soda pop. And, another thing, we live in our own nation and teach our own culture," the cashier replied. "Since you're going to be our guest for a while, it wouldn't hurt you to learn a little about us. Maybe then, someone might actually like you."

"Why you Indian slut," Blayde hissed, cocking his fist. As his hand started forward it was jerked to an instant halt as Blayde was spun around. His back smashed into the counter. Genesis's severe looking face was barely an inch from his own as he released his vise-like grip.

"Got a problem?" Genesis hissed at Blayde.

"Yes," the cashier stated. "He does."

Blayde was feeling bold and cocky. "Why don't you take her place asshole, or are you afraid to take off your badge?" Blayde asked.

"I wouldn't be so smug," Genesis said. "It would be easy enough to arrest you for what you just did."

"You mean easy for you," Blayde said. "That way, you won't have to face me man to man."

"Don't let your bulldog mouth overload your puppy-dog ass," Genesis said as he removed the badge from his shirt and put it into his pocket.

Jacob stepped between the two would-be combatants. "You don't want a piece of this ex-LRRP," Jacob said. "Best if you leave things be before he jacks your jaw, son."

Mike had stayed out of things because he knew how Blayde's temper could be. Things had happened too fast; the situation had quickly gotten out of control. Mike had to act quickly if he was going to avoid a confrontation. Mr. Lorio would be extremely displeased if they caused trouble with Seminole PD. It was important to keep a low profile and Mike had always been level-headed and cautious. He stepped forward, next to Jacob to prevent Blayde and Genesis from punching each other.

"You were in Afghanistan?" Mike asked.

"Yeah," Genesis said. "2008 to 2010."

"You have my respect, sir," Mike said. "I had several relatives there. We all owe you a great debt for your service."

"It's refreshing to know someone is actually on our side," Genesis said. "Afghanistan veterans have always felt alienated."

"You shouldn't," Mike said. "There are many who support your service, anyway my apologies again for my young friend. He still hasn't learned any manners."

"I'd be happy to teach him some," Genesis said curtly.

"You could try," Blayde said. Genesis took a step forward.

"Let's go Blayde," Mike said as he grabbed Blayde by the arm and half pulled, half dragged him from the diner. Genesis, Jacob and the cashier watched them leave. Three sets of eyes drilling into their backs.

When Blayde and Mike were in the parking lot, out of hearing range, Mike could hardly contain his anger.

"What the hell's an LRRP?" Blayde asked.

Mike exploded in fury.

"You stupid son-of-a-bitch," he yelled. "Don't you know anything? It's someone with nerves of steel that has faced armed men, wild animals, hunger, thirst, extreme fatigue, and booby traps in close quarters combat, deep behind enemy lines. I was told about Genesis. That man used to crawl around in the dark in Afghanistan with a knife and .45 pistol, hunting the enemy. His nickname by the enemy was 'the ghost.' Didn't you listen to my briefing to Mr. Lorio? He and his group were a bullet sponge for the insurgents in Afghanistan. Getting shot at and stabbed is a picnic to him. Hell, those guys did things that would make most wise guys puke. Wise up, he was a former hand-to-hand knife and empty hands instructor at Ft. Bragg and apparently the best the U.S. Army ever had. Jesus Christ, you really fucked up this time Blayde."

"Finally, someone who might be a challenge," Blayde said.

"Look, dumb shit," Mike said. "You stay away from that man. We don't need or want trouble with the law. Focus on cooperation instead of alienation or you will find yourself wearing a set of concrete shoes."

Paul was looking forward to lunch with Christina until he got an irritating phone call.

"Okay, I'll be out soon. Sorry, I thought it would be great to have lunch today," Paul said. "However, something's come up at the site and I have to get back. I've asked Monique to join us. When she arrives, I'll leave you and her to get acquainted."

"That's too bad," Christina said. "I was looking forward to some interesting conversation."

"Tell you what," Paul said. "Billie told me there's a swamp race coming up soon. Perhaps we can be partners. That will give us a chance to talk."

"I'll hold you to that," Christina said.

Christina looked up to see Monique entering the restaurant. "I can't believe I have to have lunch with her," Christina thought. After the performance she put on the other night, kissing Billie in front of the whole tribe, it was difficult for Christina to feel anything but animosity toward her. Since Monique had arrived, she had been with Billie at every opportunity. Why? Sure, she had to get the project done so the landfill would be operational, and everyone would be happy. But there was something about her that bothered Christina. She seemed to bring out the worst in her. As Christina thought about how she had cut Billie off at the party, she realized she should probably apologize, but it was Billie who had kissed another woman. Christina strained a smile as Monique sat down.

"Later then," Paul said as he rose to leave. "Take good care of her, Monique."

"I will Paul," Monique said.

"It's so nice to finally have a chance to talk to you," Monique said. "Billie's told me so much about you."

"Like he would know," Christina said sarcastically. "We spend so much time together."

"I think he's a real gentleman," Monique said. "What's he like?"

"You see more of him than I do," Christina snapped, instantly regretting it. "Why don't you tell me."

"Look Christina," Monique said, feigning innocence. "He's only shown me around. There's nothing between us."

"Could have fooled me," Christina said.

"Christina," Monique said. "Oh, I see, you're referring to my kiss the other night. It was only a thank you for him saving my arm or life or both from the jaws of an alligator. I'm not here to try to steal him from you. I'm here to help Mr. Lorio."

"I'm sorry," Christina said with a sigh. "It's just that things haven't been going well lately."

"Understandable," Monique said. "I can see how teaching could get on your nerves. So, tell me about yourself. Where do you teach?"

"I actually teach at Big Cypress and in Hollywood," Christina replied. "I really enjoy the children. They're so innocent and alive."

"How did you meet Billie?" Monique asked.

"I was offered the position here and met him at a school function through his son," Christina said.

"Well, I'd say he will make quite a catch to the woman lucky enough to land him," Monique said.

"That's probably the one thing we can both agree on," Christina said.

"By the way, "I was going to ask Billie about your people, their culture and history. Could you tell me more about them?" Monique asked.

"That's a big question," Christina replied. "There's so much to tell. Sure you're ready for a history lesson?"

"I'd love one," Monique said.

"Okay, I'll teach you the simple basics about the Seminole Tribe, just like I do for my students," Christina said.

"During the early 1800's," Christina began. "The Creek Indians in Alabama and Georgia began to push southward into Florida to escape the increasing pressure of white settlers in the north. These Hichiti-speaking Indians were followed by another group of Creeks, the Muskogee's in about 1814, after the Creek war with the U.S. forces led by Andrew Jackson. In 1821, Spain ceded Florida to the United States. By this time, our hunting parties were pushing deeper south to find game. They would be gone weeks at a time and brought back valuable information about southern Florida.

Concurrently, the skirmishes between the Seminoles and the white settlers became more frequent. Mostly, they were angry at us for providing shelter and food to runaway slaves. The white settler's raids on the Seminole became harsher and they finally forced us into a reservation in central Florida. Like always, they promised us much, but what we got in return was starvation and misery. Our people were dying. Angry, our leaders retaliated by raiding the white settlers who demanded our immediate removal by the government. So, in

1830, Andrew Jackson, the Indian-hating president, began his policy of Indian removal. Essentially, every Indian east of the Mississippi was to be moved west to the "Great American Desert," thought to be useless. After all, if the whites didn't like it, it must be a good place for Indians.

Jackson began to move us out by force along the "Trail of Tears" to Oklahoma. Almost five thousand began the journey, but few finished it. The soldiers and the hardships of trail life took its toll. Some of our Seminole bands, led by the famous war chief Osceola resisted. His name alone was frightening, meaning "fierce warrior" or "fierce one." Our success was legendary. He killed an entire battalion led by Major Dade in central Florida near the current town of Bushnell. They have named a park for him where the battle took place, Dade Park. The army pursued this band of Seminoles and so began a series of three wars with the whites. The final war was during 1855 to 1858. Gradually, the war petered out. Andrew Jackson's legacy was a poor one. His private war had cost the U.S. twenty million dollars and 1,500 soldiers their lives. The soldiers went home with their tails between their legs. The mighty Seminole remained.

The truth is none of it had to happen. If the white men in power were not so greedy, we could have lived in peace. Once the soldiers left, we were forgotten. Our people lived in villages on the hammocks you saw on the tour. In chickee's, the huts supported by cypress poles and open to the breezes. They raised crops like corn, squash, and oranges, also sugarcane and beans. We hunted and traded animal skins for money, which we used to buy what we needed most to survive.

In 1928, a road called the Tamiami Trail, which linked Tampa and Miami, ended our secluded way of life. Another blow was dealt when the whites, in their never-ending thirst for more land, began draining the Glades. We were forced from our traditional campsites and eventually resettled in permanent settlements in various locations in Brighton, Hollywood, Immokalee, and Big Cypress. Our cousins, the Miccosukee live along the Tamiami Trail. Our main industry now is tourism. We have adapted to everything the whites have done. Some are good to us, most are not. The ones who are not still look upon us as heathen savages, worthless bums, and welfare recipients of free government money. If they would simply realize that we don't get free money and that our people are hardworking individuals like themselves, we would all get along much better."

"You sound proud of your heritage," Monique said.

"Why shouldn't I be?" Christina asked. "Our people's life was the land. The ancient Seminole used to sail and pole dugout canoes, laboriously burned and chopped from cypress trunks, across the Everglades and Florida Bay. They lived off the land and asked nothing except to be left alone. We never signed a peace treaty with the U.S. Finally, after much pestering and insistence from the U.S. Government, we signed a non-aggression agreement in 1962, mostly because of disputes about our reservation territories. Once it was all settled, we have lived in relative peace as an independent people, a sovereign nation within a nation. Now, there are those who would take our land back."

"Why?" Monique asked.

"Because it's a valuable resource," Christina said, "Especially in terms of water rights, what we call blue gold, and agricultural productivity."

"Surely the government won't steal your land," Monique said. "They couldn't get away with it today."

"It's not likely," Christina said. "But that hasn't stopped many from trying. In lieu of that, they constantly try to regulate how we pursue commerce that will help our people. This has been done mainly in the areas of bingo hall operations, casinos, and tobacco sales."

"Interesting," Monique responded.

"Tell me," Monique said. "I notice that Billie's son has a different last name than he does. Was he married twice?"

"No," Christina replied. "The Seminole Tribe is a matriarchal society. All children take their mother's last name, not the father's. We are separated into eight clans: bear, bird, deer, otter, panther, snake, wind, and toad. The toad clan is sometimes called big town. Some clans have become extinct when the last female of the clan passed away. An example of one of these is the alligator clan. Each child is a member of the mother's clan."

"Well," Monique said. "I don't think I'd want to be a toad, not enough handsome princes around." They both laughed.

"What's this wagon I've heard some of you mention that Billie is on?" Monique asked. "Is he an alcoholic?"

"Don't you know?" Christina asked. "He wears it like a badge of courage. He hasn't had any alcohol and has been performing cleansing rituals for two years. He was coming home one night with his wife. A man was stranded in the middle of the road. He couldn't see him."

"And?" Monique asked.

"Billie hit the man," Christina continued. "He lost control of his car. The man and Billie's wife died. He blames himself. Although he had a couple of drinks a few hours earlier, there was barely any trace of alcohol in his blood. It wasn't his fault, but he still blames himself."

"Such guilt would be understandable. The loss of two lives is probably hard to take." Monique said. "Don't you think you need to give him a little more time?"

"Where do you get off?" Christina asked angrily. "He's had quite enough of my time, and so have you. You seem to have plenty of it, why don't you give him some more? Good day!"

Christina arose so fast, the chair she had been sitting in crashed loudly to the floor. Everyone in the restaurant stared as she hurried out the door. Monique was smiling. "I will spend more time with him," she whispered to herself. "All I can. You're such a fool to let your petty jealously of me come between you."

As Christina climbed into her car and sat down, she slumped forward and began pounding the steering wheel with her fists. Tears trailing down her cheeks, she couldn't believe how she had acted. Her goal was to keep Billie away from Monique. Now, she had given her approval to spend as much time with him as she wanted; all because she couldn't control her anger and most of all, her jealously. Perhaps she had been too curt with Billie, unwilling to listen. "Damn," she thought, "He's wanted to talk, and I've refused. Billie must feel awful. I need to talk to someone who can give me some advice. Billie's mother would be the perfect person."

Freeman had pulled onto a small side road, obscured by shrubs and palmetto to watch the landfill site. He had been there for hours and had seen nothing suspicious. From his observations of the past few days, he was sure Genesis had him on a wild goose chase. This meant that Mary Jane's accident had been just that. He really felt for Genesis but thought that his emotions were clouding his professional judgment. However, none of that mattered now. Freeman had gotten lucky. When he had gone back after his shift the day Mary Jane died, he had found drug money stashed neatly behind a cabbage palm. Counting it had revealed a whopping seven hundred thousand dollars. Something that many people dream of had actually happened to him; he could hardly contain his glee. Already, he had opened accounts and trust funds; his children would have their educations paid for, he'd purchase the farm that had always been his dream and in one week, he would no longer be on the tribal police force.

Unknown to Freeman, he was being watching from behind a small grove of trees. Blayde had noticed the police cruiser as it passed on the main highway. He knew they would be coming. It was bound to happen sooner or later. "Well, the sooner the better," Blayde thought. He had been itching for some action and seriously doubted whether or not any of the local Indians would be worthy of his talent, except perhaps Genesis. After all, he had grown up on the roughest streets in the Bronx. He was considered one of the best knife fighters in New York. Late one night, after he had mugged two separate men and cut them to pieces, leaving them dying on the street, his buddies had nicknamed him "the blade." The name had stuck, so he used it with a slightly different spelling. Perhaps today he would be able to test this deputy who was sticking his nose in places it didn't belong.

Paul was sitting at his desk in the landfill office working over budget figures for his new enterprise when the phone rang. It was his new client Karla Phenning, a ruthless woman who cared for nothing except money. Paul admired her for that. He always knew where he stood with her.

"We're ready on this end," Paul said. "You can make your first delivery next Thursday. What do you have?"
"We need to dump some benzene, TCE's (tri-chloro ethane), PCB's and other miscellaneous solvents," Karla said. "The PCB's mixed in are only in trace amounts. There's about seven hundred gallons."

"The underground storage tanks we've rigged will hold that much," Paul said. "But that's more than we anticipated for your first shipment, especially with the amount your other associates are bringing in. We will need to charge you extra because your shipment combined with theirs will incur great risk for us due to discharge time."

"How much?" Karla asked.

"Our cut will be one and a half million," Paul said.

"Why that's highway robbery," Karla exclaimed.

"Considering the cost of legal disposal, it's a bargain," Paul said. "And as I said, this much material requires substantial risk on our part."

"If I'm going to spend that much money, I need to know the site is secure," Karla stated. "I don't want things to get nasty."

"Rest assured," Paul said. "We have things well in hand. A state-of-the-art security system and the facility is completely fenced. We've signed a hundred-year lease and have carte blanche on the property as long as we don't get caught."

"If someone catches you, kill them," Karla said. "There can be no links back to me. I don't care what you do or how you do it. We can't afford any screw ups."

"There won't be any," Paul said. "Trust me."

"Very well," Karla said. "I'll prepare the first shipment for next Thursday. It will arrive in the early a.m. hours. Be ready on your end. And Paul, next time you're in New York stop by for a drink at my place."

"I'll just have to do that," Paul replied. "Call me Wednesday to confirm your shipment. Take care now."

It's beginning to pay off already," Paul muttered to himself as he hung up. Glancing through the office window he was surprised to see Billie Panther entering the main gate. Paul rose from his desk and strolled out the door to greet him.

"I hope this is just a social visit," Paul thought to himself. Billie skidded his four-wheel drive to a stop directly in front of Paul and thrust his arm out the window to shake hands.

"Looks like things are going well," Billie said as he motioned to all the activity going on at the site.

"Couldn't be better," Paul said. "The shipping schedule will be in full swing in a few more days. As soon as we get the scheduling process smoothed out, we'll be bringing in several hundred loads per day. This will mean twenty new jobs for tribal members, plus the fifteen we have on staff now. How does that sound?"

"I'm very pleased," Billie replied. "So is the Council. They still worry about possible contamination, but given the progress we've made so far, their fears are diminishing."

"Yeah," Paul said. "Now that they see the money aspect of our hard labor, they're all for us." They both laughed.

"Ain't that the truth," Billie stated. "Money makes all the difference."

"So, tell me," Paul said, "how do you feel about it?"

"Like I've reached the end of a long struggle," Billie replied. "I've worked hard to get something like this out here. Now that I have it, we'll move on to other things."

"What are you thinking about?" Paul asked.

"We've been cattle ranchers for a long time," Billie said. "Probably expand more into ranching and agriculture, maybe a rice or fish farm. I'm also thinking about a safari business for tourists. You know, take them site-seeing in the heart of the glades. I can see it now, "Billie Panther's Safari and Outfitters."

"Given your success so far, I'd say you'll do just fine," Paul said.

"Well, I really just wanted to drop by and say hello," Billie said. "Before I go, I'd like to invite you to the race we're having."

"Is that the "Jagged Grass Challenge" you've been advertising?" Paul asked.

"Yes," Billie added, "A race through the swamp. It's a way for us to stay close to the land and it's a lot of fun."

"Sounds interesting," Paul said. "What's involved?"

"The race has three legs," Billie replied. "The first is a swamp buggy race, followed by poling in authentic dugout canoes through a slough, and then an airboat leg to complete the race. The first leg is fifteen miles through the cypress swamp and flats. The dugout portion is about three miles through snake- and alligator-infested stagnant marsh and cypress heads and the airboat phase comprises the last twelve miles."

"That sounds really fun to me," Paul said skeptically.

"You'll do fine," Billie said as he laughed. "Besides, since you're new, you'll be assigned to an experienced partner."

"With you?" Paul asked.

"No," Billie said. "The race is coed. You'll be partnered with a woman. Any choices?"

"Well, the only woman I know out here besides Monique is Christina," Paul replied. "Could I have her as my partner?"

"An excellent choice," Billie stated emphatically. "She's a formidable opponent."

"Will Monique be your partner then?" Paul asked.

"Yes," Billie said. "The other racers don't want to be saddled with a beginner. It won't matter though, I'll win anyway." Billie was beaming.

"We'll see about that," Paul said. "I never lose. It's bad for my image."

"Prepare to have your image tarnished," Billie grinned.

"Shall we make a wager?" Paul asked.

"Tell you what," Billie said. "I'll bet my finest quarter horse against five thousand dollars."

"Deal," Paul retorted. "If I win, you also have to take care of it for me."

"Done," Billie said.

"On a more serious note, Billie," Paul said. "It's time now, like we discussed before, that the site will be closed to all except employees and clients."

"You're authorized to do what you need to do according to the lease terms," Billie said. "Just let me know if you have any problems."

"I appreciate your cooperation," Paul said.

"Anytime," Billie said. "Look, I have to run, see you at the race."

Paul stood watching Billie as he pulled away. "This is almost too easy," Paul thought. Now that site security is taken care of, nothing will stop our chemical shipments. They'll be arriving at night when no one's around; funny how darkness always brings out the worst sorts he mused. Oh sure, the trucks will be spotted once in a while, but it would be easy to make an excuse for them. The trucks had the wrong delivery address, they were just bringing supplies or fuel; almost any excuse would work. Not even the tribal police would be able to stop them as long as there was no direct evidence of illegal activity. Things were definitely looking up.

James Tindall

CHAPTER 6

"Curse Paul," Monique thought as she sat in the hot diner, sweat dripping from her brow, fanning herself with a menu. Time with Billie was going well. Monique could tell he was attracted to her, but he was still elusive. No doubt because of his feelings for Christina. He'd get over her soon enough. A few more days with him and Monique was confident Billie would do just about anything she wanted. She would have to make certain the timing was perfect. If she could only get Christina to blow up at Billie, make him really angry, then he would be ready for the kill. She'd close in and Billie would never know what hit him. She guessed it was worth a little sweat for the money she would make, and the fringe benefits that Billie provided. At the moment life couldn't be better, except for a little air conditioning. Monique was wiping the sweat from her forehead as Paul walked into the diner.

He ambled to the table and sat down, already in mid-sentence as he whispered to her.

"How are things going with you and Billie?"

"Better than I had hoped," Monique said. "I've basically been given carte blanche by Christina to spend as much time with him as I want."

"Excellent!" Paul exclaimed. "I want you to make sure he stays occupied so that he's out of my hair. He's busy anyway, but with you as an extra diversion, I won't have to worry about him. Our first shipment is arriving next week."

"Everything's under control," Monique said. "I'll work my magic; you just work yours. You don't need to worry about a thing."

"Good," Paul said. "I've just found out something that should make your job easier. We've been invited to this "Jagged Grass Challenge" in a few days. You'll be paired with Billie and I'll be with Christina. It will be good opportunities for both of us to, shall we say, grow closer."

"I see you've hit it off with Christina," Monique said. "Be careful. She's not as easy as you think. She'll be using you to get to Billie. I'm not sure what her game is, but I know she's in love with him."

"We all use each other Monique," Paul said. "I'll let her think she's using me to get to Billie, but I'll be using her, and you'll be using Billie. Just like an orchestra. Don't you love being the conductor?"

"Yes, I do," Monique said. "But what I really like are the personal rewards."

The alligator wrestler was putting on quite a show as Billie, Timmy, Genesis, and Jacob watched the prize they had captured on Big Cypress.

"Goliath has drawn quite a crowd," Timmy said as he looked around.

"Thanks to us," Jacob said. "Next time, they can have all the fun."

Suddenly, the twelve-foot, half-ton pre-historic lizard launched itself at the wrestler, who easily stepped aside as its cavernous jaws snapped shut.

"On second thought, we didn't have it so bad after all."

"Yeah," Genesis said. "I'll tell the wrestler you want to trade places with him."

"Not on your life," Jacob said curtly. "You'll never see me stick my hand in a gator's mouth. Hell, that man must have a death wish."

"You remember the guy who had his arm broken in fifty-seven places last year on the Miccosukee Reservation?" Genesis asked. "That damn gator twisted his arm like play putty. He's still recuperating; told me he wouldn't be doing any more alligator wrestling but would consider women's mud wrestling."

"That must make us dumb asses then," Billie said as he strolled up. "We caught the damn thing."

"Hey Billie, isn't that Christina over there by the snake pit?" Timmy asked, pointing.

"Yeah," Billie replied. "Excuse me will you, I need to talk to her."

As Billie walked away, Timmy goosed Genesis in the ribs. "Look at that," Timmy said. "I don't know about you, but I'd have a difficult time wanting to talk to a beautiful woman who jumped on my ass every time I tried to discuss something with her."

"Haven't you heard?" Genesis asked. "It's called love."

"Honestly though, Timmy is right," Jacob said. "She's about as friendly as a snapping turtle cornered in an airboat. If she treated me the way she treats Billie, she'd have gotten her walking papers a long time ago."

"There are always two sides to a story," Genesis said. "You may not think so, but that woman would do anything for Billie. I just don't think she's always aware of it. She just tends to let her emotions talk first. Besides, if you were competing against someone who could be a Playboy Centerfold, you'd be a bit snappy too. The key is good communication, but it ain't there yet."

"I suppose you're right," Jacob said as the three of them watched Billie make his way through the crowd.

"Hell, I know I'm right," Genesis said. "You ever heard the joke about the man who found the genie in a bottle?"

"No," Jacob said. "But I have the feeling you'll tell us anyway."

"One day," Genesis began, "a guy was walking down the beach. He stepped on this bottle and looked all around. Seeing no one, he stooped down to pick it up. Finding the bottle all corked up, he opened it. Out pops this genie and says he'll give him one wish for freeing him from the bottle he had been trapped in for so long. Well, the man said, I'd like to go to Hawaii, but I can't fly or take a ship because they make me sick. Would you build me a road to Hawaii so I could drive? The genie thought about it for a moment and then said. No, I couldn't do that. Do you realize how much material it would take to build such a road, how long the pilings would need to be? No, you'll have to make another wish. The man thought a minute and then said okay, this will be easier. I'd like to be able to understand women, why they're different from men, their thought processes, and more about their feelings. You know, I'd like to find out what really makes them tick so I can get along better with them. The genie thought it over for a minute then asked, "Do you want a two lane or a four-lane road to Hawaii?" Jacob and the others burst out laughing. When they had stopped, Genesis cut in. "Now you understand what Billie's up against. It's not as funny when you think of it that way." They all cast their gaze back toward Billie with a renewed understanding, glad they weren't in his position.

Billie was trying to think about what he would say as he wriggled through the throng of people surrounding the wrestling pit. It seemed that each time he had tried to talk to Christina recently that he had put his foot in his mouth. Christina noticed Billie as he approached. She kept her eyes focused on the snake pit, watching the warrior perform. She was trying to get the conversation with Monique at the restaurant out of her mind. She still couldn't believe what she had said. Although she was sure Billie wouldn't know, it still gnawed at her gut thinking that she had given Monique an even better opportunity to be around Billie. Concentrate on something else; that's what she had to do as she watched the warrior in the pit, surrounded by lethal serpents. She just couldn't seem to rid herself of the underlying anger.

The pit was filled with coral snakes, copperheads, eastern diamond-back rattlers and cotton mouth moccasins. Some of the rattlesnakes were over six feet long and as large in diameter as a man's leg. The snake pit Indian was moving about with seemingly little concern for his own safety as the serpents struck at him.

"A snake can't really see you because of poor eyesight," he panted, addressing the crowd, excited from his own adrenaline flow. "This rattlesnake senses my body heat through pits under its eyes. Watch it strike as I walk toward it." The Indian stepped straight toward the poisonous viper as it struck like lightening. Just as the snake struck, the Indian moved his leg to the right as it was in mid step. The strike missed as the man tossed the serpent back with his control stick. "See," he said, as he walked toward the snake and it struck again. "It detected my body heat, but when I moved my leg just as it struck, it missed. I'd like to caution you not to do this at home or in the woods. I do it every day and if you're not careful, you'll get bit. If you get bit around the neck or head area by such a large snake that hasn't eaten in a week or so, you'll receive a full dose of venom and likely will not survive."

"Quite a show," Billie said as he joined Christina.

"Why don't you jump down and join him," Christina retorted smartly. "It might inspire you, hurry your life along." No sooner had the words left her lips than Christina wished she could have them back. She winced at herself for saying them and secretly wondered how Billie could put up with such coldness. "I must get my emotions under control," she thought. She looked at Billie in the instant the words exuded from her mouth; he seemed indifferent to the comment. Inside, he was far from indifferent and tried to imagine why she always seemed to drip venom and how long he would need to tolerate it.

"I know you're sore," Billie said. "Can we talk?"

"Do we have anything to talk about?" Christina asked.

"I certainly hope so," Billie said. "I talked to my mom and she suggested I talk to you and let you know how I feel; I wanted to do that. I probably should have told you long ago."

Christina watched Billie from the corner of her eye as they walked to a nearby table and sat down in the shade.

"Just how do you feel about us Billie?" Christina asked. "You're always so charming and then I see you in the arms of another woman, kissing. What am I supposed to think?"

"She kissed me," Billie retorted. "She said it was because I saved her from being bitten by the alligator on the tour. I didn't initiate anything. The kiss just came out of the blue."

"Don't be so naive," Christina said. "Monique wants you. Given the way I feel now, she can have you."

"What have I done to you?" Billie asked, raising his voice. "I've spent all my free time with you, which has been very limited. I've not dated another woman for two years. I thought we had a mutual relationship going, but lately, you've treated me like the proverbial dog. Every time I've tried to talk to you, you get all pissed off and we never get to finish our conversation. What do you want?"

"Yes, you have spent time with me," Christina replied, ignoring his question. "But you've always been preoccupied with her."

"Her who," Billie responded. "Who the hell are you talking about?"

"Your dead wife," Christina screamed. Several onlookers glanced in their direction, almost expecting a full-blown fist fight.

"You won't forget her."

"How can you expect me to?" Billie said, raising his voice. "I'm reminded of her every day. Every time I send James off to school and every night when I put him to bed, I see her reflected in his face. Not to mention the wonderful times we shared. We were together for a long time. It's not easy to forget something that was part of my life for so long, something that fit like a well-worn glove."

"That's exactly what I mean," Christina said. "I'm not saying you have to forget her completely, but you need to move on. I can't play runner up to a dead woman. I understand you'll have her memory; it will never go away. I don't want you to lose that, but you have to release her, not her memories, her. She's gone Billie."

"That's easy for you to say," Billie said as he slumped forward like he had received a blow in the stomach. "You didn't kill her."

"Neither did you." Christina said softly. "It was an accident. Even if you hadn't had a couple of drinks and she hadn't been in the car, the man would still be changing a tire on that dark lonely highway. They would both still be just as dead, whether it was you driving or someone else."

"I've tried to come to grips with that," Billie said. "But I have trouble not feeling responsible, feeling the awful guilt associated with the consequences of what happened. And until you have to live through the same thing and wear the same shoes, who are you to judge?"

"Until you come to grips with it, we don't have a future Billie," Christina said. "And I'm not judging you."

"That's not fair," Billie pleaded. "I thought we had something."

"I'll tell you what's not fair," Christina said. "Me having to wait on you for the next week, month, years, or whenever the hell you decide to live in the here and now. Until you do that, we have nothing."

"And I thought of all people, you'd understand," Billie said. "You know I have feelings for you and am trying to work out my problem so we can have a future."

"You have a damn funny way of showing them," Christina said, exasperated.

"Are you that willing to just forget everything?" Billie asked.

"Let me explain myself Billie," Christina said. "You know I lost my own mother. I haven't forgotten her, and I do think about her often. I'll always have the good memories we shared and when I think of her, I can see her face. I can feel her near, and as long as I feel that she'll never be dead. It's part of the immortality in all of us. We all live on, even after we're gone."

"I understand that," Billie said. "But your mother died naturally.

"Shut up and let me finish," Christina said. "I've gone on, despite the loss. Mother would have had it no other way. Billie don't forget your wife or the good times you shared. I can live with those memories and I'll never try to make you give them up or be jealous of them. However, I need all your heart, not part of it."

"I'll think about that," Billie responded. "I'll go see the Medicine Man."

"You do that, but hurry up," Christina said. "It's me or else. I won't share your heart with another, and I won't keep waiting. Look, I've got to run. Call me later." Christina squeezed Billie's hand as she rose and walked away.

As Christina hurried off, tears filled her eyes. "Damn it," she thought bitterly, "I'll never learn to listen well. It was bad enough at the party, now I've given him an ultimatum. What a stupid thing to do. It's obvious he's trying to work things out and now I've stepped on him, again. He won't keep climbing the ladder forever. Next time, I'll let him talk and not say anything. He was trying to open up and I slammed the door. I really need to get control of my own emotions before I lecture others."

As Billie watched Christina leave, he didn't know what to say or what to think. He could only put his hands on his hips and look dumbly at his feet, hanging his head like a tired dog. Maybe Christina wasn't right for him. Was she trying to tell him that politely, trying to let him figure it out for himself so she wouldn't offend him? He began to get angry. No matter how he tried to talk to her, it didn't work and losing a parent, while difficult, was not the same thing as losing someone you spent night and day with for years, someone so close that you could tell what they were thinking. The tenseness inside Billie began to grow, ready to burst at any moment. He felt mentally and physically sick and began to resent Christina for what she had said and how she was acting. It would be different if he was seeing other women, such as Monique, but he was faithful. Maybe that didn't count for much anymore. Hell fire; damn it to hell! Why did relationships with women need to be so difficult? He had always seemed so sure of his relationship with Christina, but now began to wonder. Maybe the Medicine Man could help. Hopefully, he had more wisdom in such matters than young men.

Timmy, Genesis, and Jacob, though occupied by the alligator wrestling, couldn't help noticing the conversation between Christina and Billie. Even from where they were, it was evident things weren't going well for their comrade. Three sets of eyes followed Christina as she walked away. They quickly returned to Billie.

"Look at that," Timmy remarked. "He looks like a whipped dog. I told you she was no good for him. I tell you; she'd be damn lucky to ever see me again. How can you treat someone like that?"

"I don't know what's going on," Genesis said as he watched Billie stomp the ground with one foot. "But I've never seen Billie look like that. She may have kicked him one too many times."

"Well," Jacob drawled. "They'll work things out, if the other woman doesn't get Billie first."

"Yeah, she's after him like white on rice," Timmy said. "The way she looks, how could you blame Billie if he fell for her?"

"I hope they can work things out," Genesis said. "This white girl might look good, but she's not for Billie. I hope he can see that. Still, when someone shuts the door continually and the other has it open, the choice for the path of least resistance is often a mindless one."

The makeshift parking lot on Big Cypress was filling quickly. The day of the "Jagged Grass Challenge" was at hand. All Seminoles were wearing traditional, colorful, patchwork clothing. Many of the male members of the tribe had really gotten into the spirit of things and were marked with war paint. Some carried spears, others bows and arrows, and still others antique and modern type firearms, including muskets, 30/30 lever-action rifles and black powder pistols and powder horns. Genesis was temporarily assisting several deputies, making certain parking was convenient for all the guests arriving to watch the race. It was important for the tribe and essential that good hospitality was shown to all. There were reporters from most of the larger newspapers including the Miami Herald.

"What a day," Genesis thought as he waved in a car. "Better make sure everyone is on their best behavior. Ninety-five-degree weather and high humidity were not conducive to bringing the best out of people." Genesis was waving in a young white couple who stopped briefly to get directions. The mother was holding a young baby on her lap.

"Will the race begin on time?" the young woman asked.

"Yes," Genesis replied. "If you'll just park right down there on your left, you should have no trouble getting a good seat in the stands?"

"Do you think there will be some refreshments suitable for our baby?" the woman asked.

"Certainly," Genesis replied. "Oh! What a cute baby." Genesis touched and tugged the infant's fingers. The baby, looking at Genesis's severe, dark features, began to cry.

"It's okay," Genesis managed to blurt out. "I'm a good Indian." The parents laughed.

"It's alright," the father said. "He's just afraid of strangers."

Genesis smiled as the car pulled away. The deputies seemed to have everything under control, so Genesis walked to a newly constructed chickee that served as race headquarters.

Everything about the race was as authentic as possible. Chickee's were set up to house the refreshment stands, ticket sales, race headquarters, and first-aid station. Genesis checked to make sure everything was being done properly. The reporters weren't likely to write a favorable article if they became displeased with a lack of adequate services or a race delay.

R ace contestants were busy making last minute inspections of their vehicles. Paul and Monique, walking around the massive vehicles, were awestruck by the size of the tires, as tall as a man and more than two feet wide—a miracle of engineering. Paul grabbed Monique by the arm and walked her to the rear of one of the large, metal behemoths.

"Remember what we discussed," Paul said. "Use every opportunity to win Billie over. I'll do the same with Christina. This will be our best chance to achieve our goals concerning them."

"Don't sweat it," Monique said. "Everything's under control."

Paul walked over to Billie who was inspecting his swamp buggy. It was next to Christina's as Monique walked between the two buggies so she could overhear the conversation.

"Are you ready to get your butt kicked today?" Paul asked.

"I think it's the other way around," Billie said, smiling. "Christina is a worthy opponent, but you're outgunned and out classed."

Christina, who was sitting atop her vehicle, was silently killing Monique with her looks when she overheard Billie's remark.

"Quit blowing hot air Billie," Christina yelled. "I'll be looking back at you at the finish line."

"Just ante up," Paul said. "You're going to lose this and more."

"Don't count your chickens before they hatch," Billie said. "Just put your money where your mouth is."

The race announcer had climbed his tower and there was a crackling sound as the microphone sputtered to life.

"Ladies and gentlemen, may I have your attention," the race announcer said.

"You all know the race rules. It's a combined thirty-mile competition; fifteen miles on the swamp buggies, three miles in the dugouts across the slough, and twelve miles in the airboats. The first to cross the finish line wins. However, this year we have a new rule. If you fall out of the dugout in the slough, you'll be penalized three minutes on your time. This means, even if you cross the finish line first, you could wind up second or third place or maybe not place at all."

"Can you knock an opponent out of their dugout?" Timmy asked, yelling above the noise of the crowd.

"As a matter of fact, you can," the race announcer said. "You will be allowed to bump and run in each event with the exception of the swamp buggies."

"What are we waiting for then?" asked a competitor. "Let's have some demolition canoeing." The audience roared, some of them yelling taunts at various contestants.

"Several more points though," the announcer interrupted. "Be careful out there. We don't want the gators to carry any of you off, although I'm sure most of you would be too bitter to suit their epicurean palette. The water's deep this year, so I hope you brought your scuba gear. Stay in the designated routes for the swamp buggy portion of the race so we can protect the environment. It's time to begin the festivities. Proceed with your vehicles to the starting line."

The swamp buggies roared to life, the noise from the engines deafening. As a group, they headed for the edge of a small flag pond just in front of the stands. Each buggy was positioned on an imaginary line between sets of surveyor's flags as racing assistants lined them up.

"Racers ready," the announcer yelled, looking left and right. The announcer raised a small flag made of Seminole patchwork. About to drop the flag, there was an interruption in the line as two swamp buggies had rubbed axles with each other. It took several minutes to separate them; the crowd looked on with great curiosity. The problem finally resolved; the announcer quickly dropped the flag. The buggies were off in a frenzy of churning tires, slinging mud, and roaring engines. The first rows of spectators were drenched in swamp ooze as the buggies, obscured from their view, disappeared behind a high-flying wall of mud. The rest of the audience roared in laughter at the sight.

Billie had his seat belt fastened tightly as they spun off.

"How long will this last?" Monique yelled over the roar of the motor.

"It'll take about half a day depending on how deep the water is to cover the entire route," Billie yelled back.

"What's this?" Monique asked, picking up a diving mask that was resting on the seat.

"The water can be very deep sometimes," Billie replied. "Our heads may actually go under the surface for several seconds."

"You've got to be kidding me," Monique exclaimed! "How can the engine run under water?"

"We have a push board to keep water away from the engine fan and that's a snorkel attached to the carburetor so it can breathe underwater," Billie said, pointing.

"It's just a rubber tube," Monique said.

"Yeah, not as fancy as the commercial ones, but it'll do the job," Billie quipped. "It's permanently glued to the lip atop the carburetor and is tied down about every six inches. If the engine doesn't stall, we'll be able to traverse any water up to about nine feet for a short period."

A swamp buggy pulled up on their left side trying to cut Billie off before they reached a narrow road leading into the cypress swamp. Whoever got there first had a good chance of maintaining the lead for the first leg. Billie sped up. The other driver tried to maneuver; too late, he hit a cypress knee and knocked his right front tire off at the axle. The swamp buggy toppled onto its front bumper to an immediate stop, spilling its occupants into the swamp.

"Sorry," Billie yelled back.

"I talked to Christina the other day Billie," Monique said. "She seemed angry at you and me."

"Furious is more like it," Billie said as he grimaced while downshifting and grinding gears.

"What did she say?"

"She told me more about your culture and also about your accident," Monique replied.

"How thoughtful of her," Billie remarked sarcastically.

"It's okay Billie," Monique said. "I understand. It really wasn't your fault."

"Yeah," Billie said. "Everyone else was so guilty, they're dead."

"I'm sorry," Monique said. "I didn't mean it like that. I'd like to talk when the race is over." She slid next to him in the seat.

Mud was flying off Christina's tires like black oil. Both she and Paul were black, covered from head to toe. Unable to pass, Christina was right on Billie's bumper. Sparks flew from her eyes when she saw Monique slide next to Billie and then glance over her shoulder with a sly smile. Christina sped up and was about to ram Billie's bumper. Remembering she could be disqualified, she backed off.

"Pass him, or I'll owe him money," Paul said.

"How much?" Christina asked.

"Five grand," Paul stated.

"If we win, Christina said, "I want half."

"Done," Paul said. "Just win at any cost."

"We'll have to be a little daring then," Christina said as she gunned her engine.

Christina tried to pass as the cypress swamp opened up but was cut off by another buggy that was a little faster on the throttle. She zipped around it as they wrongly anticipated her passing on the opposite side, then cut back in front of them.

"Eat mud," Christina yelled to the driver.

"Looks like I've found quite the jockey," Paul said. "You're very intriguing you know."

"I'll take that as a compliment," Christina said.

"I've been meaning to ask you," Paul whispered throatily as he leaned near. "Since we weren't able to have lunch, how would you like to have dinner with me tonight? The sky's the limit."

"How could I refuse," Christina said. "I hope you have a thick wallet; it's going to cost you."

"Somehow, that doesn't surprise me," Paul said, laughing.

"It really won't cost you," Christina said pointing to Billie's buggy. "It'll cost him. We're going to take all his money today."

"A woman after my own heart," Paul grinned.

With the adrenaline flowing through their veins from the race, sound reasoning seemed to escape them all.

Christina managed to pull her swamp buggy alongside Billie, but still couldn't pass. She and Monique exchanged looks—if they could only kill. Christina started to take advantage of an opening, but Billie closed the distance and forced Christina into a large clump of sawgrass. Momentarily stalled, she got quickly back into the race.

"That was deliberate you toad," Christina yelled at Billie.

"I'm not going to roll over and die for you," Billie yelled back.

"Yeah, don't I wish," Christina mused.

"Come on," Paul said. "Pass this swamp rat."

Monique was grasping Billie's thigh tightly. During the excitement he hadn't noticed. He was about to reach down and remove her hand but decided it might be better not to offend her. Somehow it seemed pleasant and was the only affection he'd had for some time.

"She's pretty good isn't she," Monique said.

"Yes," Billie responded. "But I've got a few tricks up my sleeve."

"Look," Monique exclaimed. "It looks like open water."

"Hold your breath, we're going under," Billie said.

Monique visibly sucked in her breath as the swamp buggy plunged into the open water. Both the buggy and their heads disappeared briefly beneath the surface. The only visible part that protruded above the water was the snorkel. They began to reappear a few seconds later.

"Eee haa," Billie managed to gasp as his head resurfaced, "Slick as scum on a swamp."

"This is definitely a bad hair day," Monique said.

Billie looked at her and burst into laughter. Monique's makeup was running in dark rivers down her face.

"Umm, Princess Running Face," Billie said.

"That's not fair," Monique moaned. "I looked so good today. I was hoping you would notice."

"Oh, I noticed," Billie responded. "It's hard not to, especially now. You look like you're in a wet t-shirt contest."

The white t-shirt Monique was wearing was clinging to her wet body, the nipples on her breasts clearly visible through the fabric.

"Maybe I should take my shirt off so I can get dry," Monique mused. "What do you think?"

"My carnal side would love it," Billie replied. "But I don't think Christina or Paul would appreciate it."

"Well then, I'll just have to do it in private," Monique said. "How would you like to dry me off?"

"Don't tempt me," Billie said, smiling shrewdly. "I might not use a towel."

"Christina's swamp buggy, with several others close behind, followed Billie and Monique into the open water. Seeing the open water too late, one buggy tried to steer right, lost momentum and stalled, disappearing in the coffee-colored water. The driving team floated to the surface and barely managed to get out of the way as another swamp buggy plowed into the water behind them, meeting the same fate. The open water was quickly becoming a swamp buggy graveyard.

Finally, out of the deepest water, the buggies found the going easier. Mud flew as Billie, Christina, and several other buggies jockeyed for the lead. One pulled out of the pack and tried to pass on the left and just as suddenly hit a submerged stump, ripping the oil pan open and throwing the driving team forward off the buggy into the mud and water. The riders of the remaining buggies were having a great laugh at their misfortune. Behind them, a monitoring vehicle quickly contained the minor oil spill and began cleaning up the mess.

Jagged Grass

Freeman was sitting alone in his police cruiser adjacent to the landfill site. The palmetto and small scrub oak obscured his vehicle from view. He was contemplating how he would enjoy his newfound freedom from his lucky treasure find. "Well, he mused, "I should at least give them their money's worth during my last week." With that in mind, Freeman exited his vehicle and began making his way through the chest high palmetto and undergrowth closer to the landfill. He had noticed several vehicles that seemed to be abandoned in a small grove of oaks. Having talked with Genesis several times over the last few days, he was convinced that Mary Jane's wreck had not been an accident. But there had to be a link somewhere. He would really like to pull the pieces together for Genesis, whom had been a good friend, confidant, and teacher to him for many years.

As Freeman approached the hammock, he could see two trucks that were semi camouflaged to prevent detection. Looking around carefully, he saw no sign of activity and carefully slipped across an open, grassy meadow. At first glance, the trucks appeared to be normal, but almost immediately Freeman noticed that the front bumper of one was padded with a heavy, black rubber. Closer inspection revealed a section of rubber that had been torn with minute particles of paint within the damaged area. The small specks were the same color as Mary Jane's car. "So, this is why it looked like an accident."

Freeman's gun was suddenly jerked from its holster. He immediately turned to face his unseen assailant.

"You shouldn't stick your nose in other people's business," Blayde whispered raspily. "It's unhealthy. Let's go. Blayde motioned with the gun and marched Freeman through the woods to a large cypress head. As he walked, Freeman knew the only chance he had was to get the gun away from Blayde. If he could just knock it away, he was sure the hand-to-hand combat skills Genesis had taught him would win the day.

In the middle of the cypress head was a large gator hole. When they reached it, Blayde stopped.

"End of the trail, Injun'," Blayde said. "I heard how good you people are with knives. So, tell you what I'll do, I'll give you a sporting chance."

"That's more than I need," Freeman said curtly. "You know you won't get away with this. Genesis is on to you."

"Oh, but I will," Blayde chided. "I killed the female bitch in the car and now you're going to become gator bait. See." On the far side of the hole, a large alligator was sunning itself. "As for your friend Genesis, he'll meet the same fate or worse. You see, we're prepared for every contingency."

"So, you're a tough son-of-a-bitch," Freeman said. "Are you going to play motor mouth all day, or are you going to show me what you got?"

Blayde tossed Freeman's revolver into the gator hole. He reached behind his belt and pulled two identical daggers forward. Sunlight glinted off the cold steel of the eight-inch blades. He tossed one to Freeman.

"Let's tango dickweed," Blayde said.

"Alright you scrotum licking scum ball," Freeman said. "Let's see if you can learn the swamp-man hustle."

Blayde lunged at Freeman who side stepped and cut Blayde deeply across the right shoulder. Blayde drew back in surprise. He had underestimated his foe. Blayde regained his balance and the fight raged back and forth. Freeman was making a quick darting slice when his foot hung in the undergrowth and Blayde slashed him across the chest, stomach, leg, and back. Freeman managed to get a slice in on Blayde's left arm in the melee. By now, they were panting and struggling to maintain alertness, each bleeding like a stuck pig.

"You're good," Blayde said. "But, not good enough."

"Swamp-man hustle isn't done yet," Freeman panted. Losing blood quickly, he was on the verge of passing out. Realizing he must get the fight over with fast or die, Freeman lunged at Blayde once more and sliced him across the chest. Just when it looked like Freeman would end the fight, gaining an advantage over Blayde, he lost his footing and balance in the mud. In the briefest instant, Blayde stabbed him in the chest. Freeman collapsed onto one knee.

"Out hustled you huh swamp man," Blayde teased.

"White bastard," Freeman said, unable to move or protect himself. As quickly as it had begun, the fight was over. Blayde stepped forward and sliced Freeman across the throat. As life ebbed from his body, Freeman's last thoughts were of his children. With a shudder, he fell backward into the gator hole. Blayde watched him for a while as he rested, then grinned with glee as the resident gator pulled the body beneath the water.

Blayde was wondering who had taught Freeman how to work a blade as he picked up the other knife and stumbled back to the landfill office. He realized that had the fight been on level ground, he would be in Freeman's place. "Just goes to show you," he thought, "the most skilled don't always win; a good thing in this case." He dragged himself into the office looking like a blood-soaked rag. Mike, sitting behind the desk, jumped up in surprise at the sight of him.

"What the hell happened to you?" Mike asked.

"I had a party called the swamp-man hustle," Blayde replied. "Think you could stitch me up?"

"Let's go into the bathroom."

Growing up in the Bronx, Mike and Blayde were as adept as surgeons at sewing human flesh. While Mike cleaned him and sewed his wounds shut, Blayde relayed his story, wincing from the pain of each suture.

"Shit!" Blayde exclaimed. "Watch it will you."

"Quit whining and hold still," Mike said. "It's your own fault you're in this mess. You better hope to God Lorio doesn't cut your dick off for this."

"Let me worry about that," Blayde said. "He would have done the same thing given the circumstances. Maybe I won't tell him."

Blayde put on fresh clothes and walked out the office door. His cuts were beginning to throb, making him irritable and angry. One of his crew, Danny, was standing nearby.

"Danny," Blayde said. "Do you see that police truck parked over there in the shrubs?"

"Barely," Danny said.

"I want you to take it to the Tribal Police Office," Blayde said. "Leave it in the parking lot behind the building. Wipe it clean. I don't want any prints on it. And make damn sure no one sees you."

"We'll take care of it boss," Danny said.

Danny swallowed hard as he walked off to carry out his assignment. He motioned to another fellow to help him out. He wondered who Blayde had killed and hoped it didn't bring the police out. Already on probation for armed robbery, any offense would send him back to the joint. He'd die before going back.

"John," Danny said. "Get in your truck and follow me. I'm going to take that truck over there to the police station. Stay right behind me and be as inconspicuous as possible."

"Okay," John said, "Whatever you say."

When Danny reached Freeman's cruiser, he put on a pair of gloves and found a rag and bottle of water in the vehicle. He wet the rag and wiped the vehicle from roof to running boards, beginning with the inside. Every glass, handle, knob, and smooth surface was wiped clean, including the outside of the vehicle. Sure that there were no prints remaining, he climbed in. Luckily, the keys were in the ignition; he cranked the engine, eased the vehicle into drive and headed down the dirt road to the highway. Once there, he cautiously looked in both directions. When he was certain no other vehicles were in sight, he pulled onto the paved roadway and maintained the posted speed limit into Big Cypress community.

Upon reaching the area of the police station, he slowed down, intently observing every building and car. He hadn't passed any vehicles on the way in and no one was outside. Everyone must be at the race that had been the topic of discussion the last few days. Those not at the race were inside, staying out of the hot, humid weather and taking advantage of the air conditioning. Danny parked the cruiser in a corner of the parking lot so it wouldn't draw attention. It was beneath a large oak tree. He cut the motor and looked carefully about. Not a soul in sight. John pulled up alongside the parking lot and Danny ambled over like he had all the time in the world. "Let's get out of here," Danny said. John eased away. No one had seen them; they were certain of that.

James Tindall

CHAPTER 7

Billie pulled his swamp buggy to a stop as he and Monique hit the ground running. Several other buggies, including Christina's, were right behind them. They had reached the edge of the cypress swamp and had to run across a narrow strip of marsh for about a hundred yards to reach the dugout canoes that were waiting for them. The running was tough going. They had to pump their knees up and down like crossing small hurdles in the thigh-deep water. By the time Billie and Monique reached the canoes, they were gasping for breath.

"Climb into that one," Billie said, pointing. "Just sit down and hold onto the edge with your hands, face forward. Let me do the poling."

Monique took her position while Billie held the canoe stable. He hopped in lightly, picked up his ten-foot pole and they were off on the next leg of the race. As they pushed into the deep-water slough, other dugouts, not far behind, disappeared from view. Billie pushed the dugout forward in smooth, paced strokes. Deeper into the swamp, passing groups of yellow pond lilies, hyacinths, and bald cypress cloaked in tapestries of Spanish moss.

Christina quickly lost sight of Billie and Monique. Imagining the worst, jealousy was getting the best of her.

"Who's that?" Paul asked, startled. He was pointing at a Seminole warrior a scant five feet distance, well camouflaged with his surroundings, wearing traditional warrior dress consisting of a wide red head band, colorful cotton shirt with striking yellow colors and light leather pants with moccasins. He was standing very erect atop a large cypress trunk surrounded by Boston ferns, holding a steel tipped spear in his right hand as if it were a part of his body. Wearing three diagonal stripes of war paint across his cheeks, his eyes were piercing as daggers, no sign of an expression on his countenance.

"He's a sentinel," Christina said. "They watch us during this phase of the race. If we fall out of our dugout, they report it to race officials."

"Nothing left to chance and no cheating I suppose," Paul said.

"That's right," Christina said, grinning. "You know how slick we Injun's can be."

"Personally," Paul said. "I've never met anyone like you before. You make me feel alive. I'd like to get to know you better. What can I do to impress you?"

"Just be yourself," Christina said. "Having a nice dinner is a good start. You never know what will happen, so let's just take things as they go."

"I have to return to New York soon," Paul said. "It would be very nice if you could accompany me. I'll pay for everything."

"That's a generous offer Paul," Christina commented, not wanting to offend him. "I'll think about it."

As Christina poled the dugout, she watched Paul closely. He seemed well mannered and was particularly good looking. Suave and sophisticated, he was also relaxed and appeared to get about everything he wanted in life. At least she hadn't seen anyone refuse him. And, one thing was certain, he was very wealthy. He had expensive tastes in clothes and every time she had seen him, he was wearing a different watch. Today, it was a diamond studded Rolex. She would think about his offer alright, very seriously. Who knows what might happen? If they got along, he had everything any woman would ever want. But thoughts of Billie began to cloud her mind. She must not let herself get distracted.

Billie was soaked as he poled the dugout along, dripping with sweat, like a horse that had just run a race. Only, he wasn't in lather. The shade of the cypress was a welcome respite from the blazing sun this hot August day. As Billie studied Monique, he couldn't help but be turned on by her beauty. Wearing form fitting blue jeans and a snug t-shirt commemorating the race that she had purchased that morning, there was no way to hide her female endowments. She had the looks of a Playboy centerfold and model all rolled into a tidy package. She was also athletic and graceful. "Who could refuse a woman such as this," Billie wondered as he silently asked himself if he could ever afford to be alone with her.

"What is that flower up there?" Monique asked, snapping Billie out of his thoughts.

"It's a leafless ghost orchid," Billie said. "While plentiful, they're rarely seen."

"The green leaves it has are so pretty," Monique said.

"Those leaves belong to a fern," Billie said. "This particular orchid is usually found close to the fern. Botanists believe they may have a symbiotic relationship, but they don't really know."

"Anyway," Monique said. "It's very elegant."

"Much like yourself," Billie responded.

"That's the sweetest thing anyone's ever said to me," Monique said.

"I find that hard to believe," Billie said. "You are a very beautiful woman."

"Come over to my place tonight," Monique said sexily. "I'll show you just how lovely."

"I better not," Billie said. "You might have trouble getting rid of me."

Billie was poling the dugout through open water along the edge of some bald cypress amidst alligator flags. He was thinking he had to keep his distance from Monique. If he went to her apartment, there's no telling what would happen, and he wasn't sure he was strong enough to resist the temptation she presented. Abruptly, Billie noticed Monique shaking. She was peering into the alligator flags.

"There's a a alligator," Monique stuttered, frightened. "It's coming this way."

"Don't worry," Billie said. "It won't ..." Billie was cut short as Monique tried to stand in the dugout, before she realized what was happening, they were both submerged in the swamp. Monique thrashed about wildly, panicking as she remembered what had happened on the airboat when Billie had yanked her hand up just in time. Now here he was again, holding her in his strong arms. Monique was clinging to him tightly as he managed to calm her down. She kissed him passionately. Billie responded in kind. He could feel himself becoming aroused. Monique was also aware of it and felt she was finally getting to him as they managed climb back into the boat and continue, unaware that a sentinel was watching them.

"I was about to say it would not bother us because it wasn't nesting," Billie remarked.

"I'm sorry," Monique said. "I didn't mean to dump us."

"Don't worry about it," Billie said. "At least we got cooled off. By the way, were you serious about tonight?"

"What do you think?" Monique asked.

Genesis was on his radio trying to contact Freeman who was supposed to help them work the crowd so no one got too rowdy.

"Has Freeman checked in?" Genesis asked.

"No," said the dispatcher. "He hasn't shown up yet."

"When was the last time he contacted you?" Genesis asked again.

"The last time was about 10:00 a.m.," replied the dispatcher.

"Alright, have him call me as soon as you hear from him," Genesis said as he switched off his radio.

Genesis couldn't understand why Freeman hadn't checked in. It wasn't like him. He had always been prompt. As a matter of fact, Genesis couldn't recall a single time of tardiness or irresponsibility. He wished all his deputies were as conscientious as Freeman. It was only a matter of time before he showed up. Genesis was certain of that. Until then, the crowd would have to be worked by himself and one other deputy.

Christina was wrapped in thought as she poled the dugout along. Wondering how she could get back with Billie. She definitely needed to soften her tone, be a little more patient, at least until she heard him out. That much she owed him. When Paul spoke, it startled her.

"How did you learn to be so self-reliant?" Paul asked.

"I grew up with three brothers," Christina said. "A real tomboy."

"I'm not trying to butter you up," Paul said. "But it's refreshing to meet a woman with your good sense and abilities."

"Oh, I don't know," Christina said. "There are plenty of women like me. I'm not unique."

"You're dead wrong," Paul said. "Women like you are very scarce these days."

"I'm flattered," Christina said.

"You should be," Paul responded.

"Look," Christina said, pointing. "We're almost to the airboats. There's Billie."

Her abrupt change in topics didn't go unnoticed.

"Catch him at all costs," Paul said. "I never lose and don't want to make a habit of it now."

"Don't worry," Christina said. "For five grand, I'll catch anyone."

Billie and Monique were just coming out of the slough. Christina's dugout and several others were not far behind. As they reached the edge of the marsh marking the finish line for the dugout leg of the race, Billie and Monique jumped from the canoe. Monique fell flat on her face in waist deep water. Billie grabbed her arm, jerked her onto her feet and began racing to the airboats about one hundred yards away.

"Hurry, everyone is on our tail," Billie yelled.

"Don't wait on me," Monique cried. "I'll keep up."

It took all of Monique's strength to keep up with Billie. He was like a wild animal she thought as they made their way to the airboats. They hopped onto the nearest one. Billie climbed into the driver's seat and cranked the airplane engine. It sputtered as it tried to run one second and die the next.

"Hurry," Monique screamed. "They're closing on us."

"I'm working as hard as I can," Billie said.

The airboat suddenly roared to life and they were off like a shot. Billie and Monique looked back over their shoulders to see about five more airboats roar out after them. Billie's boat was beginning to put considerable distance between them when the engine sputtered and died.

"Damn," Billie screamed. "It's got to be the filter. Tell me how close they are."

Billie jumped down under the protective cage that surrounded the prop and hurriedly detached the fuel filter, drained it, blew it out with his mouth and reattached it.

"Looks like it had water in it," Billie said.

"They're about a quarter mile away," Monique said. "There's five of them."

Billie jumped back into the driver's seat and cranked the engine. It fired up and Billie gunned the boat forward, giving it full throttle. By the time the boat picked up speed, the other boats had surrounded him. The race was now a six-way tie. Christina had pulled her boat directly alongside Billie's.

"Looks like you're going to owe me," Paul yelled.

"The race isn't over yet sucker," Billie screamed back.

"We'll see who the sucker is in a few minutes," Paul said.

Billie veered his boat and rammed Christina's boat in the side. Paul was sent sailing through the air into the water and sawgrass.

"Sucker," Billie yelled back, laughing.

Christina had to slow her boat and turn it around to pick Paul up. She was now too far behind to catch Billie. The lead changed back and forth. Another boat tried to ram Billie who pushed back and forced the other boat into a hammock, dry docking it. The driver shook his fist at them, yelling unheard obscenities. The remaining three boats, scrambling to beat Billie, ran into each other, stalling. Billie finally pulled ahead and crossed the finish line. The race official lowered the flag as Billie roared through. Spectators were yelling their approval.

"Congratulations Billie," the official yelled. "Pull up over there where the other airboats and buggies are parked."

There were picnic tables and lots of people on hand to celebrate the race. As Billie pulled his boat up to the edge of the hammock a throng of spectators surrounded him, slapping him on the back, giving him the thumbs up. Two minutes later, Christina and Paul arrived, followed close behind by another boat. The remaining contestants straggled in one by one. Paul made his way over to where Billie was standing.

"What the hell was that?" Paul asked. "I almost drowned."

"Just a race," Billie replied calmly. "Didn't Christina warn you we could play tag?"

"No!" Paul roared. "You should have done that."

"I don't have to do a damn thing," Billie replied. "I wasn't your partner."

A raucous party had erupted in the background drowning out the sounds of Paul and Billie's conversation. The race official wandered over to the contestants and crowd. He had a walkie talkie pressed to his ear as he approached Billie and Paul.

"I hate to interrupt your fun Billie," the official said. "One of the sentinels just informed me that your partner fell out of the dugout in the slough. Is that true?"

"Yeah," Billie replied softly.

"Then, I'm afraid that Christina and her partner have won," the official said. "Despite your time advantage, she beat your penalty time by about thirty seconds. You are actually in third place."

"So," Paul said sarcastically. "Even your cheating couldn't help you. Like I said, I never lose."

"I didn't cheat," Billie stammered. "You just got lucky."

"Just have my registered quarter horse waiting," Paul said. "Do you like to ride Christina?"

"Depends on what kind of mount I have," Christina mused as she tried to play Billie's emotions. "The harder, the better."

"I'll have it ready," Billie said as he angrily eyed Christina. "Next time, you will lose. Let's go Monique."

As Billie turned to leave, Monique looked directly at Paul, who smiling, gave her a wink that only the two of them could see. Monique exchanged looks with Christina and smiled slyly. "Too bad you're such a fool," Monique thought. "Billie's all mine tonight. Keep treating him like a dog and perhaps I'll even take him back to New York with me." Monique turned, rushed to catch up with Billie and put her arm through his. Looking back over her shoulder, she could see that Christina was red with anger.

Genesis had returned from the race to find Freeman's 4x4 cruiser in the parking lot. Walking inside the headquarters building, he crossed the lobby to the dispatcher's desk. The dispatcher was a pleasant elderly woman with soft eyes and a pleasing smile.

"Where's Freeman," Genesis asked.

"I don't know," the dispatcher replied. I noticed his vehicle in the parking lot but haven't seen him."

"When did you notice his vehicle?" Genesis asked.

"About five hours ago," the dispatcher replied. "It's funny, one minute the parking space was empty and the next, there was Freeman's vehicle. I thought he would be around after a few minutes. When I didn't see him, I tried to contact him on the radio. He didn't answer. Do you think something is wrong?"

"I hope not," Genesis said as he hurried out the door.

Genesis jumped into his cruiser and began searching the entire community for Freeman. The first place he looked was his house. As he pulled into the driveway, he noticed Freeman's personal truck. About time, Genesis thought. Why hadn't Freeman shown up today? As he walked to the door, he was mulling over possible reasons in his mind. Nothing made sense. It was out of character for Freeman to have been absent without at least calling. Genesis softly rapped on the door. Freeman's wife, Frieda, answered.

"May I speak to Freeman?" Genesis asked.

"He's not here," Frieda replied. "I thought he was still at work. Is something wrong?"

"No," Genesis said. "There was just something I wanted to discuss with him and thought I'd drop by on the way home. He's likely at the office. If you see him, tell him to give me a call when he gets a chance."

"Okay," Frieda said. "I'll tell him."

The last thing Genesis wanted to do was alarm Frieda unnecessarily. Freeman's likely just out goofing off. He had been acting very happy and a little strange the last few days. Almost like he had no worries in the world. The next stop Genesis made was the elementary school, then the tribal gym, followed by Freeman's favorite fishing hole. He had searched every place he could think of for about two hours and was getting very frustrated and angry. As he passed the community store and diner, Genesis saw a familiar truck and pulled into the parking lot. Pausing just inside the doorway, he scrutinized the patrons. At a small table in the corner sat Jacob Cypress, a cup of coffee in one hand, a cigarette in the other. Genesis strolled over, slid out a chair and sat down.

"Those things will kill you," Genesis said.

"Something's bound to," Jacob responded. "On the tube the other day, scientists were reporting that sugar can cause cancer. Of course, that was with mice. Turns out a person would have to eat five-hundred pounds at a time to get the same results. The key is moderation. So, what can I do for you?"

"Something strange is going on," Genesis said.

"What do you mean?" Jacob asked.

"Freeman was supposed to go out to the landfill site and snoop around," Genesis said. "I just wanted him to keep an eye on things for a while and then meet to help us with security at the race this morning."

"So, what's the problem," Jacob asked.

"He hasn't come back yet," Genesis replied. "I have looked everywhere for him. His cruiser appeared this afternoon, rather mysteriously, in the police parking lot. His personal truck is at home and his wife hasn't seen him."

"That is odd," Jacob said. "It's not like Freeman to take off without notifying someone. Maybe something is troubling him. Did you check his favorite fishing hole?

"Yes," Genesis said. "No luck there either. And this morning when I spoke with him, he acted like he didn't have a care in the world. As a matter of fact, I don't think I've ever seen him happier. If you must know, I think those thugs at the landfill site have killed him. I've had this awful nagging feeling for the last couple of hours. Something is definitely wrong."

"I tend to agree," Jacob said. "But accusing the landfill operators is a serious matter. You shouldn't say things like that without something to back them up."

"Listen," Genesis said. "Talk to Billie about it for me. In the meantime, I'll get proof."

To satisfy his own curiosity about Genesis's suspicions, Jacob drove to police headquarters and took a look at Freeman's cruiser. It looked strangely clean for having driven around the shell-rock roads on the reservation. He walked into the building and began looking for Joe, the resident fingerprint expert and found him sitting at his desk filling out a crime report.

"Jacob," Joe said, standing up and extending his hand. "How the hell are you? What brings you out this way?"

"I have something I need you to do for me," Jacob said.

"Just name it," Joe said. "I can't begin to count the favors you've done for me."

"How long would it take you to dust a car for prints?" Jacob asked.

"Only a few minutes for a basic inspection," Joe said. "Why?"

"Get your equipment and come outside with me," Jacob said. "I'll fill you in."

A few minutes later the two men emerged from the office and walked to Freeman's cruiser. Joe took out his kit and began to dust for prints. He began with the driver's door.

"Hmmmm," Joe said. He followed the door with the hood, the tailgate, the passenger door and the top of the bed. "Hmmmm," he added again. Next, he crawled inside and dusted the steering wheel, dash, inside door panels and rearview mirror. He kept repeating himself over and over.

"What do you mean by, "Hmmmm?" Jacob asked as Joe climbed out of the cruiser.

"It's very strange," Joe said.

"What?" Jacob asked, exasperated.

"All I can tell you is a that a ghost must have been driving this car," Joe said. "It's like something you'd find after a major crime. I didn't find a single print; there should have been hundreds. This vehicle has been wiped clean. I'm certain of it.

I'll check further if you want, but I doubt the results will change."

"Go ahead," Jacob said. "If you find anything, let me know immediately. I'll be at Billie's office."

Billie was rummaging through his office drawers searching for a pencil when Jacob tapped at the door. Glancing up, Billie motioned him in.

"We've got a problem," Jacob said.

"I've had one all day," Billie replied. "I lost my horse in a bet."

"To whom?" Jacob asked.

"Paul Lorio," Billie said.

"I'm disappointed in you Billie," Jacob said. "You know the Medicine Man won't approve. What has he told us so many times? Bet with the white man, drink his whiskey, Indian get screwed."

"Yeah, yeah," Billie murmured. "I'm so pissed. Damn it all to hell. So, what's your problem?"

"Freeman is missing, can't be found," Jacob said. "His police cruiser is at headquarters and his personal truck is at home. Genesis suspects foul play. Just to be sure he wasn't a little emotional about Mary Jane's accident, I had Freeman's cruiser dusted for prints. We didn't find one print. The vehicle has been wiped clean."

"Have you checked with his wife and his friends?" Billie asked. Jacob nodded affirmative. "This sounds serious. What's Genesis doing about it?"

"He's looking into it," Jacob replied. "He wants to find proof of his allegations before accusing anyone. He thinks the thugs at the landfill site did Freeman in."

"Why in the hell would they do something like that?" Billie asked. "Especially with so much at stake."

"Maybe Freeman saw something he shouldn't have," Jacob said. "I don't have a clue."

"The way I feel now," Billie said. "I'd like to believe they did. It would be a great opportunity for me to get my horse back. But we can't blame them without proof. Look into it and for God's sake, be discreet; don't do anything rash."

"I'll keep you posted," Jacob said as he hurried out the door.

Billie couldn't believe that Paul or any of his gang would kill Freeman. It just didn't make sense. If they were brought under suspicion, the hundred-year lease would revert to tribal control and they would lose everything. The tribe would own the landfill outright. But, if they did kill Freeman, why? What could they possibly gain? Billie couldn't stop thinking about it as he closed his office door, hurried home, took a shower and was on the road to Hollywood. He had a nice dinner planned with Monique.

As he drove down Alligator Alley, Billie was grateful for the darkness. The glare of the sun was gone and driving at night was easy on his eyes. He loved the feel of the cool, humid night air as it streamed over the windshield of his Corvette convertible and tore through his hair. Billie forced the thoughts of Freeman out of his mind as he focused on Monique. He was excited at the prospect of dinner with her. For the past few days, he had been torn because of his feelings for Christina, but she hadn't even tried to listen to him. It was almost as if she were dropping hints to tell him indirectly it was over. People just didn't have guts anymore. It would be nice to have dinner with Monique, just so he could see for himself if he still felt as much love for Christina as he thought he did.

There was no doubt that Monique heightened his male lust. She was a gorgeous woman. Billie couldn't help thinking about the kiss she had given him earlier when she fell out of the dugout canoe. He almost laughed aloud thinking about the incident, how terrified she had been of the alligator, but the kiss was truly magnificent. It was not simply a peck on the cheek. It was a deep, tongue probing, thrusting, passionate kiss. Almost as if it were the only one she expected to get from him. However, she had alluded to the possibility of playing a little bedroom buddy tonight, a frolic in the hay as it were. Billie would have to be careful. He dared not think about it or it may become a reality and at this point, he no intent of being unfaithful to Christina. That issue would have to resolved before he considered another woman. He had always felt that Christina was the one for him, but now he was unsure.

He finally arrived at Monique's rented apartment. Rapping softly on the door, she answered, ready to go. She closed and locked the door behind her. Turning, Monique slipped her arm around his as they walked to the car.

"What a car," Monique exclaimed. "Is it yours?"

"Yes," Billie said. "One of my personal rewards to myself. I really enjoy driving and a Corvette convertible makes it more fun than you can imagine."

"I don't know about that," Monique said. "I can imagine a lot."

Billie opened the door for her. As she sat in the low seat, Billie couldn't help noticing long, sexy, muscular legs protruding from beneath her skirt. Heading out of the parking lot, he turned south on A1-A, toward Miami.

"Where are we going?" Monique asked.

"To a nice seafood restaurant near the beach," Billie said. "I hope you like it."

"I've been dying for some fresh seafood," Monique said as she pecked Billie on the cheek. She leaned her head against his chest as she placed her left hand in his lap. It made Billie feel guilty and exhilarated at the same time. Her touch and perfume were intoxicating.

"I hope you didn't get too frightened today," Billie said. "Although, your reaction was not unlike that of most people unfamiliar with gators."

"It terrified me," Monique said. "After the incident on the tour, I was certain it was going to tear me to pieces. Your being there made all the difference." She squeezed his arm tightly. "I always feel safe when I'm with you, kind of invincible."

"Thanks for the compliment," Billie said. "It's not often I make people feel that way. Seems like most of them are a little unsure of me."

"That's because they don't know how sweet you are," Monique said. "You know, most women, including me, would think a man like you would be quite the catch."

"Would they now?" Billie mused. "And what makes you say that?"

"Because you're strong, good looking, friendly, kind, intelligent, and educated," Monique replied. "An awesome combination. If you become rich too, you'll have to beat women off like flies."

"I am rich," Billie replied. "I have my health, a good son, and a very large endowment from a stranger I helped one day."

"Guess I better be really nice to you then," Monique said. "This calls for some pampering."

"Don't pamper me too much," Billie said. "It wouldn't be good for my health, if you know what I mean."

"Like this?" Monique queried as she ran her hand seductively along Billie's thigh and groin, arousing him.

"Alright," Billie whispered hoarsely. "You better stop before we wreck. Oops, saved by the restaurant. We're here." Billie pulled the car into a parking space and they entered the restaurant arm in arm.

Monique loved the ambiance. It was a mixture of Caribbean and European. The lobster was delicious. Her mind was on Billie. Despite her goal to seduce him and keep him out of Paul's way, she really liked him. He was kind and considerate, a real gentleman. Unlike Paul who used everyone to get what he wanted; Billie was like a shining emerald. Everything he touched seemed to sparkle and everyone liked him. Just thinking about him turned her on. "Wow", she thought, "how long had it been since she felt that way about someone?"

"I'm really sorry I kept you from winning the race today," Monique said. "It's too bad really, Paul will be gloating about it for weeks. I'd like to make it up to you."

"I never should have bet with him," Billie said. "Besides, it wasn't your fault and just being here with you is great, all the reward I want."

"Oh, I can think of something better," Monique said.

"Something big I hope," Billie said.

"Oh, trust me," Monique said. "It is."

Looking at her, Billie couldn't figure out the excited look in her eyes. It must be the wine she had. Perhaps she was getting a little tipsy. A good reason why Billie no longer drank.

Paul had taken Christina to a local night spot to celebrate their victory. Both were on the dance floor kicking up their heels. Having had several glasses of wine, Christina was not her usual self. Her inhibitions had disappeared as she did the bump and grind with Paul. She was certainly attractive. Paul had the passing notion that she would easily be the winning contestant for a Princess Pocahontas contest. The light-yellow blouse Christina wore highlighted her dark skin and jet-black hair. Paul was captivated by her.

The hour was growing late when Christina finally decided she had enough dancing. She stumbled to their table and took a seat.

"I think I've had too much to drink," Christina said. "I'm really out of it, do you think you could take me home?"

"Sure," Paul replied. "I guess we have had a pretty full day.

As they drove to Christina's apartment, Paul was thinking about how great the day had really been. Winning the race against Billie further enforced his own high opinion of himself. He could do anything, anytime, and much better than others. Paul's conceit was only limited by his arrogance, which outwardly appeared as a high degree of self-confidence. He was a true narcissist. Perhaps that was why women responded to him so well. They were like putty in his hands. He seemed to be able to mold them at will, at least until they found out what he was really like. With Christina, he intended to never let her find out. Now that the landfill had been approved and constructed and he controlled the site for the next one hundred years, Billie would no longer be an obstacle. He had made up his mind that he would pursue Christina at every opportunity.

Paul had to help Christina out of the car and up the walkway to her apartment. She fumbled in her purse for several seconds before she was able to find her keys. It was difficult for her to find the keyhole, so Paul assisted. He leaned her against the outside wall as he unlocked and swung the door open, then reached in to find the light switch.

"I've had a splendid day today," Paul said. "You're a wonderful woman."

"Flattery will get you everywhere," Christina murmured as she leaned forward and kissed him. Paul responded fervently.

"Why don't you come in for a night cap," Christina said as she grabbed his hand and led him into the apartment closing the door behind them.

"Let me change into my bath robe," Christina said. "I'll feel more at home that way."

"Be my guest," Paul said as she left the room.

Within a minute or two she had returned wearing an ankle length silk robe. Though it fit loosely, it did a poor job of hiding Christina's sexy body. She sat down on the sofa next to Paul and faced him, crossing her legs.

"So," Christina said. "Tell me more about yourself. I don't even know what your likes and dislikes are."

"Not much to tell really," Paul said. "I grew up in the Bronx in New York. My dad was a plumber. We barely made ends meet. At a young age I figured that being an entrepreneur was one of the best ways to make money in life."

"How so?" Christina asked.

"When I was about thirteen, my father bought me a car," Paul continued. "The engine was bad and though I wasn't of legal age to drive, my father said I could repair the engine over a period of time. I did some checking and found out how much it would cost, but I also found out a car that was sold in pieces was more valuable than an entire car. Some friends and I decided to go into business getting old cars and then chopping them up and selling them for parts. My father couldn't believe it, when on my sixteenth birthday, I got him to sign the papers so I could buy a brand-new Pontiac Trans Am with cash."

"Your father must have been very proud," Christina said. "Do you get along well with him?"

"We got along well," Paul said. "But he was killed about seven years ago in a liquor store hold up. He was getting a six pack when a couple of hoods came into the joint to rob it. They killed the cashier and several patrons."

"Gee," Christina blurted. "I'm sorry to hear that. I know how you must feel. My own mother passed away from cancer. It was a slow, very painful death. Watching her waste away in the hospital was hard to bear."

"A terrible way to go," Paul said softly. "You know, we're not so different after all. We come from different backgrounds but have the same attitude about things. Makes me wish I could have met you many years ago."

"You're so nice," Christina said as she leaned forward, put her arms around Paul's neck and kissed him passionately, thrusting her tongue deep into his mouth. Paul stretched her out on the sofa and began kissing her body in every conceivable place. Christina was writhing in excitement. It was strange the effect alcohol had on people.

"Let's go into the bedroom," Christina whispered.

Paul picked her up and carried her across the floor laying her gently on the bed. He lay down beside her and began fondling her breasts, kissing her softly. Christina was moaning, but suddenly began thinking that something was wrong, someone else was involved. Then, it came to her, Billie. It was difficult to try to clear her mind.

"I'll be right back," Paul said. "Don't go anywhere."

He walked into the bathroom and took out his wallet, searching for some protection. He couldn't find any. "Damn," he thought, "it must be in the car." Paul slipped out of the apartment, leaving the door ajar and searched his glove box. Finding what he was looking for, he returned to the bed. Undressing himself, he again lay down next to Christina and began where he left off. Abruptly he noticed she was not responding. She had fallen asleep.

Frustrated, Paul decided it would be best to wait until she had her full wits about her. He dressed and left her a note thanking her for the wonderful day and hoping they could continue where they had left off at a later date. He put the note on her nightstand and gently covered her with a light sheet. Christina looked like an angel as she lay so peaceful upon the bed. Paul was determined to make her his angel. Besides, she would think he was even more of a gentleman for not taking advantage of the situation and that could earn him a few kudos. Christina would be coming back for more not realizing that he would become her puppet master.

As Billie arrived at Monique's apartment, he couldn't remember the last time he had felt this good. Monique had been great, building him up instead of tearing him down. He couldn't help thinking how different she was from Christina. She was a great conversationalist and a good listener. He had been physically turned on all evening. The smell of her hair as she leaned her head against his chest, her perfume, and her personality. Even though she was so good looking, she was quite a capable woman. Definitely not of the bimbo type mold. Monique was resting as Billie pulled into the driveway.

"We're here," Billie said softly.

"Won't you come in?" Monique asked, sitting up.

"I really shouldn't," Billie said. "Tomorrow will be a busy day for me."

"Please," Monique pleaded. "I'll fix you an orange juice or something. There's a much better way to end our evening."

"Alright," Billie said. "But, just for a little while."

As they entered the apartment, Monique walked into the kitchen, opened the refrigerator and pulled out a carton of orange juice.

"Make yourself at home while I pour us some juice," Monique yelled from the kitchen. "As a matter of fact, why don't you put on some music."

She walked to the cabinet and retrieved two large glasses. In a narrow cabinet above the stove, Monique found a prescription she often used. It was a small bottle of Valium. She rapidly crushed two of the tablets and put them into the bottom of Billie's glass and poured the juice over them. "Billie will never know what hit him," Monique thought, as she stirred the contents of the glass well.

Billie was looking around the apartment when Monique walked in and gave him his glass.

"Quite a place you have here," Billie said.

"Yeah, not bad for a rental," Monique said. "Go ahead, put on some music. I need to slip into something a little more comfortable. I'd also like to take a shower to relax. Do you mind waiting while I do that?"

"No," Billie said. "I suppose I could stick around that long."

Billie could hear the water running in the shower. Although it would probably be best if he left, he couldn't draw himself away. Having already gulped his orange juice down, Billie took a seat in front of the stereo and sorted through various compact discs. He selected a romantic classic and slipped the CD into the player. As he listened to the soft music, the Valium began to take effect. Once the reactions began, they progressed rapidly.

The drug began to depress his central nervous system as the therapeutic effects were beginning a full press. His muscles were so relaxed, he didn't want to move, couldn't move. Billie had never felt so good. He felt not only relaxed, but happy, not a care in the world. It was as though he was slipping into oblivion as he lay back onto the floor staring at the ceiling. Monique was suddenly standing above him, looking down at his face. She looked like she had just stepped out of a Victoria Secret catalog wearing a light lavender lacy bra and panties to match.

"Wow!" Billie whispered. "You're stunning."

"It's all for you," Monique said as she lowered herself down on top of him, straddling his lap and bending forward, pressing her body against his.

"We shouldn't, Christina ...," Billie managed to whisper.

"It's payback time handsome," Monique said. "We only worry about ourselves tonight. It's just you and me."

Billie tried to fight it, but having been robbed of his will power, succumbed to Monique's advances. She pressed herself hard against him, kissing his neck and nibbling his ear lobes before planting a sensual kiss on his mouth as she unbuttoned his shirt and erotically massaged his chest. She moved up on him as she removed her bra and stuffed the nipple of one of her large breasts into his mouth, rubbing his crotch with her free hand. Billie no longer had any resistance as he returned more than she gave. Monique unloosed Billie's belt unbuttoned his slacks and removed them, along with the rest of his clothes. She stood over him, performing an alluring dance to the beat of the music as she very slowly removed her panties.

Watching her, Billie could feel himself become aroused. HE could not remember the last time as Monique sat down on him and thrust his large manhood deep inside her. She was writhing like a snake as she pumped up and down. Billie gave her a little assistance, placing both his hands on her buttocks, he gently raised and lowered her. Both were in ecstasy as they made love most of the night, falling asleep just before dawn.

Billie awoke the next morning with the sun streaming through the window. For an instant he couldn't remember where he was, then it dawned on him. Next to him lay Monique in all her sexual splendor. As he looked at her, he felt guilty for what had happened. How could he have done this? For the life of him, he couldn't remember what had happened last night. But, at the same time, given how his life had been going, he was elated and felt more alive than he had for a long time. Actually, after thinking about how Christina talked to him each time they had met lately and the tone of her voice, the feelings of guilt slowly subsided. But who knows what tomorrow will bring? The unexpected always seemed to pop up. No time for such thoughts now.

Billie jumped up and hurriedly showered. Lucky he was an Indian, his beard growth was so slow, no one would notice he hadn't shaved this morning. As he exited the shower, Monique arose and joined him.

"You missed some spots," Monique said as she licked them off with her tongue. "I think you should come back to bed."

"I can't," Billie said. "Today's a full day. I've got six meetings and if I don't get my butt out of here, I'm going to be late. The first one is with Solomon. Being late would really satisfy him."

"How about tonight?" Monique asked. "Can we get together again?"

"Assuming I get finished in time, I don't see why not," Billie said. "I'll give you a call one way or the other."

"I'll be looking forward to it," Monique said as she continued to arouse him.

"Knock it off," Billie said. "I'll never get out of here."

"That's what I'm counting on," Monique replied smiling. "Hard to let go of a good thing, if you know what I mean."

"Oh, I think I have an idea," Billie said as he reached out and pulling her close, squeezed and licked her naked breasts. Her nipples immediately began to swell as she wiggled in delight. As much as he hated to leave, Billie sat down and began to pull on his shoes. Monique threw her naked body atop him and pinned him to the bed.

"Come on now," Billie said. "I can't be late."

"You can't go until you give me a kiss," Monique whispered.

Billie put his arms around her as they stood up, holding her off the floor as he kissed her as hard as he could. She pressed forcefully enough against him to feel his hard body and throbbing manhood.

"See," Monique pleaded. "You know you want to."

"Yes, I do," Billie responded. "But want and need are two different things. Let me go and we'll continue this later."

"Alright," Monique said. "You better call me today."

"Don't worry," Billie said. "I'll call you so much you'd wish phones didn't exist."

Golden rays of sunshine filtered through Christina's window the next morning, rousing her from a peaceful sleep. She had a headache from the night before. As she lay upon the bed, she stared at the ceiling until she was fully awake. Suddenly, what had happened the previous evening dawned on her as she jolted upright, looking about. Paul had gone. Noticing his small note, she picked it up and quickly read the few lines he had scribbled. At first, she was pleased at the sentiments and attention, then reality settled.

For the last few weeks, she had been giving Billie a hard time for neglecting her, but at the same time, he had remained faithful to her for several years as they dated. She knew he had not seen another woman during that time and now look at her. Christina had betrayed his trust, and not only his trust, but her own self confidence and esteem. At seemingly the first opportunity, she had fallen for another man. Mentally tormented, she didn't even know if she had slept with Paul last night. Everything was such a blur. Whether she did or not, there was no excuse for her. How would she tell Billie? Could she? How would he react? She wouldn't blame him if he walked away completely given her attitude and treatment of him these last few weeks. What a dolt she was. It was almost as if she wanted to drive him into the arms of another. And now look at the predicament she was in. At that moment, Christina felt so alone. A great pang of guilt washed over her as she bowed her head and cried softly, tears of disappointment trickling down her cheeks.

CHAPTER 8

Paul, Blayde and Mike were having a heated discussion about what Blayde had done to Freeman. Paul was furious. Blayde's impetuousness had jeopardized the entire operation. If the Tribe found out, it would be the only excuse they needed to close the operation and Paul's illegal enterprise would vanish like a puff of smoke. This bothered Paul exceedingly. With the money he would make on it, both personally and for the mob, Paul would be next in line for Don Cilatro's job. Getting on in years now, Cilatro was sure to pick a successor soon and Paul was doing everything he could to make sure that he was the chosen one.

"You stupid asshole," Paul yelled. "Do you realize what you've done? If they find out, we'll lose millions, we'll be in prison."

"What was I supposed to do, let him connect the truck to the accident?" Blayde asked. "Don't worry, no one will find him. The gator ate him, so there will be no evidence. Even the blood trail has been washed away by afternoon storms."

"Blayde's right boss," Mike chimed in. "I checked. There's no sign or him or a struggle; nothing to connect any of us to him."

"Pray to God no one finds him, or you'll be gator bait," Paul glared. "Both of you get out. I have some calls to make. Check one more time to make certain there's no evidence and don't fuck up again."

Mike and Blayde exited the office and walked across the site to their truck.

"I've never seen him so pissed off," Mike said. "We better walk a fine line, so we don't offend him. I've never heard him swear before; that's completely out of character."

"You can walk whatever kind of line you like," Blayde said. "I'll still do what I please."

"One day your hard-headed attitude will kill you," Mike replied. "I hope I'm not around to see it."

Paul watched the two through his office window. Maybe Blayde had done the right thing, but there was nothing for the deputy to see. The rubber on the bumper could have easily been burned and replaced. Although Blayde was proficient at doing his dirty work, he was so unpredictable. When he returned to New York, perhaps he would find a replacement to bring down who was more levelheaded. Now that things were going well, Blayde and Mike could both use a break.

Paul pulled out his cell phone and dialed. "Good morning Monique," Paul said. I trust all went well last night."

"Couldn't have been better," Monique replied. "We had a most enjoyable time. As a matter of fact, he didn't leave until early this morning."

"Perfect," Paul said flatly. "Just keep on him."

"Oh, I'll ride him every chance I get. He's supposed to call me this afternoon," Monique said. "But he may get tied up."

"Look," Paul said. "I don't care what it takes. Marry him if you have to; just keep him out of my hair."

"Actually," Monique responded. "I've been thinking of just that. He's a nice guy and a girl like me could do a whole lot worse. But don't stress about it, I'll find a way to control him."

"Good," Paul said. "I'll expect a report every day."

As Paul hung up the phone, a large smile spread across his face. He began to hum. If Monique did marry Billie, it would be a great advantage to his cause, but he was certain she was just trying to goad him. Billie was so naive he would even help them fight his own people as long as he maintained employment and kept bringing money to the tribe. Monique would also be on his side, especially for a share of the kickbacks and if she got in the way, well, there was always the possibility of blackmailing her with her past. At the same time, Paul's feelings for her caused jealously and resentment toward Billie.

Paul dialed another number. "Hello gorgeous," Paul said. "We've had a minor snag on this end, but nothing we can't handle."

"You sure you've handled it adequately?" Evelyn said.

"Yes, I'm sure," Paul replied. "You can begin shipment when you wish just notify us beforehand, so timing is exact."

"I'll send it down when I'm ready," Evelyn said. "Once it's on the way, I'll give you a jingle."

"Look," Paul exploded. "If you want your damn crap disposed of you do it my way or it's no deal. The people down here aren't stupid."

"Alright, alright," Evelyn said. "Don't get so testy. We'll be ready in a few days. I'll call you to confirm shipment scheduling."

"Good," Paul said. "I look forward to a prosperous relationship."

As Paul hung up, he was irritated. He would have to pay Evelyn a visit once back in New York. She liked to play with him; he was going to play back. It was not often a person could make millions off a lovely lady and be friends with benefits at the same time. Paul knew he could manipulate her and since he had total control regarding shipments, he was certain a good story could be made up of the difficulty of disposal. A rise in the price would be justified and he would be able to skim a little more money for himself.

It was midnight; the swamp was its typical hot and humid climate; not a breath of air was stirring. Genesis was sweating like a pig as he sat in the dark watching the landfill site. He had ridden a horse into the adjacent woods at dusk and patiently waited for signs of after-hours activity. Every now and then he would look through his night vision goggles, each time to be disappointed. It had been dead all night. The only activity was the buzzing of mosquitoes as they landed on Genesis for a drink of blood. Thanks to the wonders of modern technology, the insect repellant he was wearing kept them mostly at bay. The mosquitoes never sat on his skin for long. Each time he noticed one, he played games with it. Once they landed, he would try to trap them with his index finger against his skin and then roll them between his thumb and index finger into a ball, slowly counting how many he killed. "If anybody ever saw me do this," Genesis thought, "they would think I was sick, crazy, or both. Just like Afghanistan in some respects. A man would do anything to break the boredom of waiting."

As the night wore on, he was conscious of the crickets and frogs singing. Their chorus was deafening. He could hear the horse snort occasionally as it endlessly swished its tail back and forth to keep the mosquitoes away, the chomp of teeth as grass was pulled from the soil, and the creak of the saddle. In the distance, owls had begun hooting. It made him long to go hunting, but he had forsaken it several years before. Somehow, it always seemed to be in his blood and that's what got to him. Since Afghanistan, Genesis couldn't stand to see the spilling of blood. It was therefore incredulous to some why he had chosen to become a police officer. For Genesis, it was a simple matter. He had retired from the military and it was the only job he was qualified to perform; one which Billie had helped him obtain. Besides, there had never been a murder on the reservation, so Genesis wasn't too concerned.

Tired of sitting, he stood to stretch his legs as he took a large swig of water from a bottle he had stashed in his knapsack. Fumbling around in the dark, he was able to pull out a cellophane package, which he unwrapped. The contents were Indian hoe cake and venison. After a few bites and another swig of water, Genesis felt more alert. Except for the crescendo of crickets and frogs in their nighttime chorus, the swamp was quiet. Almost any sound could be heard for miles by the trained ear. They simply floated across the water of the swamp in the still night air. Suddenly, Genesis heard a faint hum, growing louder until the sound was unmistakable; one which he had heard many times on his rounds through Big Cypress. It was the sound of the friction of rubber against pebbled asphalt; the sound of a very heavy truck traveling along Snake Road. Only this time, it was more than one, it was several. Genesis trained his night vision goggles on the gates of the landfill. Four large trucks pulled up, blinked their lights three times and then turned them off.

"Hmmmm," Genesis murmured to himself. "This looks damn fishy. Those aren't garbage trucks, so what are they and why are they here?" He walked over to his rucksack and retrieved a camera with a telephoto lens, set it up on a small tripod, and zoomed in on the site. Genesis glanced at his watch — 0130 hours. The fact that four large trucks of the wrong type arrived so early indicated something illegal at best and sent up a red flag. It was too late or early for any respectable citizen to be up and about. A chill shot up Genesis's spine. As he watched, thoughts of Mary Jane's crash raced through his mind. Perhaps these guys were in cahoots with the drug dealers that frequented the back roads of the reservation; they used the same time schedule to unload their goods on Big Cypress, yet these trucks were too large to likely fit the scenario.

The shadowy outlines of a person were scarcely visible, walking across the landfill to the gate. A faint metallic clinking could be heard as the shadowy figure pulled a large chain from around the gate and swung it open. The trucks pulled inside; the gate was immediately closed and locked behind them. Genesis depressed the shutter button to store the scene digitally. As the trucks pulled up near the office, Paul, Mike and Blayde walked out the door to greet them. Genesis snapped another picture. The trucks appeared heavily loaded as the camera continued to shoot one shot after another. Abruptly, the trucks pulled around the office and across the site a short distance. Although there was some light on the ground, Genesis was too far distant to see what was happening. Unaware the trucks were dumping toxic waste; Genesis took several more pictures. As quickly as the trucks had come, they were leaving. The gate was unlocked, and they were racing out, their flight being recorded on Genesis's camera. However, Genesis could tell they were now empty as he pondered scenarios that might explain what they had unloaded. Perhaps he was too paranoid, and it was just diesel fuel for the site's heavy equipment.

Genesis listened until the sound of the tires humming on the pavement faded completely. What he didn't hear was the last truck, which because of its slight swaying back and forth had stopped near one of the feeder canals on Big Cypress. Some of the chemical hadn't been dumped, causing a slight swerving back and forth due to the unbalanced load. The driver jumped from his rig, opened his vent pipes and pumped several hundred gallons of toxic waste into the water off the bridge. Satisfied the tank was finally empty he was again on his way to catch the others.

Several cars left shortly afterwards; sounds of buzzing mosquitoes, the crescendo of crickets, and hooting of owls were all that remained. He wondered if Mary Jane had seen something like that and been killed for it. But what could it be? So what, if someone saw a few trucks on the site. Maybe they were greedy and wanted to take a few more loads of trash, keep the extra money for themselves. It didn't make any sense. Genesis needed to talk to Billie or Jacob about it. Maybe they had a better idea. In the meantime, he would develop his film and run the pictures by a friend in the Miami police department. The only thing Genesis was sure of was that the trucks had dumped something, the pictures would prove that.

Genesis was late, but it couldn't be helped. He knew Billie and Jacob would understand as he rushed from the parking lot into the building and down the hall to Billie's office.

"About time," Jacob exclaimed as Genesis ran into the room, panting from lack of breath.

"Sorry," Genesis said. "I had to drop my camera off to develop some high-resolution prints from the digital images I took. You'll like what you see when I get them back."

"If it's about the landfill site, I think you're off base," Billie said.

"No, I'm not," Genesis responded. "The images will prove it. I tell you Billie, something is going on out there. Last night, several large trucks arrived and dumped something, then left. They weren't garbage trucks either."

"Maybe they were just delivering some sort of supplies," Billie said.

"At 1:30 in the morning!" Genesis blurted. "I don't think so."

"Hmmmm," Billie mused as he stared at one of the paintings on the wall, deep in thought, his mind racing.

"I think Genesis may be onto something," Jacob said. "It's been several days, and Freeman is still missing. It's not like him. He was happy at home and at work. I smell a possum."

"Agreed," Genesis said. "Something is wrong. I downloaded the images I took last night to a friend in Miami PD. He should have some information for me tomorrow or the day after."

"Okay," Billie said. "Do what you think is best. But remember, there's delicate politics involved here. Let's make certain we have something before accusing anyone."

As Jacob and Genesis were making their way out, Solomon rapped on the door.

"Come in Solomon," Billie said.

"Am I interrupting?" Solomon asked.

"No," Billie replied. "We were just wrapping up."

"Now that we're alone," Solomon said, "I'll get right to the point."

"You always do," Billie said. "I wouldn't expect anything less."

"You think the council seat gives you carte blanche to do anything you want?" Solomon asked.

"I'm not following you," Billie stated."

"Come on," Solomon glared. "You know exactly what I mean. You're dating this white girl, flaunting her in front of the whole tribe."

"For your information, I'm not dating her," Billie said. "I am trying to be a hospitable host and business partner."

"Don't give me that bull shit," Solomon argued. "Everyone knows what you're up to. It's bad enough you're a half breed. Do you want to turn our blood to water?"

"Yeah, I'm a breed," Billie said. "You never let me forget, but you also know how I feel about our people and our heritage. Doing the right thing is what matters, not whom I choose to date or marry. I'll do anything for our people. You know that."

"You'll do anything alright," Solomon said, "Like getting us into bed with a bunch of scum and vermin. I've heard the rumors. Just stop dating the white woman. She's bad medicine. What about you and Christina? Isn't she good enough for you?"

"What about us?" Billie asked.

"Everyone expects you to marry," Solomon said. "I mean the way you've been carrying on and all. Hell, as much as I don't like your attitude, I expected the same. Don't you love her?"

"Yes, everyone knows I do," Billie said.

"Well, tell her," Solomon said. "She needs to know too."

"I think I've made my intentions clear to her," Billie said.

"Uh huh, about as clear as swamp water," Solomon said. "Look Billie, a woman has to be told, they want to hear it in words from the lips. Talk to her before she falls for this white man. She likes you and has said as much when I talk with her at the school."

"I suppose you're right," Billie said. "Tell me, how do you know all this?"

"I'm an old man son," Solomon replied as he turned to leave. "But I have many eyes."

"Many spies are more like it," Billie muttered under his breath. Then he marveled at how understanding Solomon could be. He had a heart after all. Who knows, they could become good friends given the right conditions.

As much as Solomon disliked Billie, he had a soft spot for him and Christina. Actually, he didn't hate Billie at all, just thought he was in his way and out of his league. If Billie would just live up to his potential, he should be chief, Tribal President, rather than a councilman and if he ever runs, I'll support him, Solomon thought as he walked down the hall.

Chairman Osceola pulled his airboat up onto the shore of the hammock. As he walked along the path, he contemplated what he should say to the Medicine Man. How could he cajole him into finishing his instruction and mentoring for the transparency? Two Seminole warriors blocked his path as he approached the small clearing where the Medicine Man, who had heard the airboat pull up, waited stoically to greet him.

"Greetings Medicine Man," Osceola said.

"Greetings Chairman; what brings you out so far, that you have come to see me?"

"I was sitting in my office a few days ago and marveled at the concepts and ideas you had taught me. It made me eager to find out when I could complete my training so that I can better serve our people." Osceola said.

"Thought have I also given to this matter Chairman," the Medicine Man answered. "I think that it may not be wise to continue your training right now, perhaps at a later date."

"Why?" Osceola asked, his voice rising, a hint of anger creeping in. "Is it something I have done?"

"Something you have not done my brother," said the Medicine Man. "You see the office you hold has a great responsibility to the people. Over the years you have done much for the Tribe in the ways of the world, but you have neglected the spirituality of our people the mighty Seminole. While it is true you have provided jobs and money for many, there is a considerable number who lack the necessities of life, and without the necessities of life, the mind and body face the stress and tasks of daily survival. In such a state it is difficult to be humble to the Great Spirit, to be spiritual."

"I can and will work on that," said Osceola. "I give you my word it shall be done."

"Considering what has not been done my brother, your word carries little weight with me," replied the Medicine Man. "It is not only this, but your failure to establish a place for the individual Seminole to give thanks to the higher powers of the Great Spirit. You have known about this for some time and yet, you have done nothing. We talked of this before."

"I realize that," Osceola said, "But, it will cost so much money to establish what you ask. I am working on it, but I need more time."

"What is money compared to the souls of our people?" the Medicine Man asked sharply. "Can you put a price on something that is priceless, something which neither you nor I can comprehend? Can you determine the price of a soul? And what is time but a man-made concept? The mighty Seminole has been here for eons and will remain for eons more, champions of the swamp. You have had too much time already and yet you have done nothing for these things of which I speak."

"Don't you think you're being unfair?" Osceola asked.

"No!" the Medicine Man replied. "It is you who have not been fair. I have asked little of you and have given you much, but you care more for the ways of the white man and the world, the power and greed, than for the well-being of those you should truly serve. Because you have not reciprocated, it leads me to doubt the sincerity and wholesomeness of your spirit."

"You do not know who you are dealing with old man," President Osceola hissed vehemently.

"Ah, the true spirit of the Chairman shows through," the Medicine Man said, frowning. "I cannot teach the final stages of the transparency to such a soul. That is why I have already chosen another. One day, your place to lead will pass and his will come."

"No matter what you do I'll win," Osceola said. "I'll finish the final stages myself. You will not be able to stop me."

"Probably not," the Medicine Man said. "But be forewarned, there is danger in that which you will attempt, more in the destruction of your soul than the death of your body. It would not be wise for you to continue alone."

"I'll show you which of us is wiser old man," Osceola said as he stomped past the guardian warriors."

It was evident the warriors were furious at the Chairman for showing such disrespect to the elder. They eyed him angrily and turned to follow as he passed. The Medicine Man waved them back as he sat without blinking, staring through the Chairman as he strode away.

Billie had been riding his airboat hard for over an hour as he slid it to a stop on the edge of a cabbage hammock deep in the sawgrass of the Florida Everglades. He couldn't help noticing the expensive airboat next to his. There was only one like it in the entire area. Decked out with chrome plated controls and cowling, an eight bladed metal prop on a warp-

Jagged Grass

drive engine, and a jet-black paint job overlain with murals depicting ancient Seminole rituals along each side. It was the epitome of ostentatiousness. To say it was showy and flashy was an understatement. What would Chairman Osceola be doing out here? Billie was sure he was about to find out as he noticed the Chairman striding down the path toward him.

"Chairman," Billie began, "What brings you out this way?"

"That's none of your concern Panther," Osceola retorted. "Are you the one?"

"The one what," Billie asked, unsure about what the Chairman was referring to?

"If you have to ask, then you are not," Osceola said. "Just take care to mind your own business. This is between me and the Medicine Man."

"Very well," Panther said. "It's none of my concern anyway."

Billie watched the Chairman for a moment as he continued down the path. He began to think about what the President had said, but it was none of his business. Other things were more important now.

It had been a long time since he had come to visit the elder. He was so old, Billie didn't think anyone knew his name, at least Billie didn't. To the tribal members, he was simply the Medicine Man. What he spoke carried a lot of weight. No one would argue with his wisdom, gained from years of experience. Yet, as Billie walked up the worn animal trail to the middle of the head, he couldn't help feeling a true kinship with this man. There was no enmity or animosity here, only words of wisdom born of true logic. Whatever the Medicine Man said to him would be of value and would serve as a great help in Billie's struggle to come to grips with his feelings and goals. It had always been so.

Because so few people really knew him and rarely visited, the life of the Medicine Man was the talk of the tribe during

171

community gatherings. He was held in mystical awe by the people, and he always knew who you were and what you were doing. It was uncanny Billie had to admit to himself. The Medicine Man was so remote from the main community of Big Cypress yet seemed to know everything. That was the true beauty of his spirit. He would not condemn, only lecture and disseminate wisdom. As Billie entered the small clearing where the Medicine Man had his chickee, several warriors were gathered before him. They seemed to float like mist from the air, quiet, but deadly. Each was armed with traditional bows and arrows, spears, the ever-present knife, wearing moccasins, and also carrying 30/30 lever action rifles — a favorite among many of his brothers.

Billie was not allowed to pass until the Medicine Man nodded his approval. The warriors were like his private army. Billie knew every tribal member by sight, except these. Although they were listed on tribal rolls, no one knew anything about them. They had all been personally trained by the Medicine Man in the ancient ways of the Seminole and were as fierce a looking group as Billie had ever encountered. They would rival any Navy Seal or Special Forces squad in both guerilla tactics and war operations. History had proven the Seminole was the fiercest of all Indian warriors. The Medicine Man believed that and trained them so well their reputation would continue its own legacy. As quickly as they had appeared, the warriors were gone. It always spooked Billie how they did that.

Very traditional, the Medicine Man required Billie to change into historical Seminole clothing. He slipped into the Medicine Man's chickee and put-on leather pants and leggings made of deer skin, a beaded head band and moccasins. When he emerged, the Medicine Man put three stripes of war paint on each cheek: yellow, red and black,

Tribal colors. The Medicine Man led Billie a short distance through the hammock to a small clearing from which all vegetation had been scraped. In the middle of the clearing was a group of stones that had been heated red hot by the warriors. Near the stones was a gourd full of water; a conk seashell would be used for a dipper. The Medicine Man sat down cross legged on one side of the rocks, Billie on the other.

Billie sensed something was troubling the elder.

"Is something wrong?" Billie asked.

"Nothing I can speak of to another," the Medicine Man said. "It is a private matter. However, I can tell you that some among us lack the respect due elders and have a total disregard for the process by which we do things."

"Ah you refer to the Chairman and his pretentious ways," Billie said.

Without answering the question directly, the Medicine Man scrutinized Billie.

"Do you know of the transparency?" the Medicine Man asked.

"You mean the ability of one to leave the body and perform tasks while in the spirit?" Billie queried. "I mean, I've heard of it, but thought it only a legend."

"Pick up the stone in front of you my brother," the Medicine Man directed. "Can you feel it, see it, is it real?"

"Yes," Billie said. "I can do all those things with it, even taste it."

"Good, so it is with the transparency."

"I never realized...." Billie said, his voice trailing off.

"Panther," began the Medicine Man. "You have the true heart of a Seminole. There are things I know about you that you do not, grand things. This you must believe with all your heart. It is you I have chosen to teach the transparency to. It must be passed on and you are the vessel that should receive it."

"What is it that you require of me?" Billie asked.

"Ah, you ask with an unending loyalty; the sign of the one who should be taught. You must be honest, loyal, benevolent, courageous, and generous to a fault," the Medicine Man said. "But that is only the beginning. You must have charity and good will toward all men, even the whites for in the eyes of the Great Spirit we are all one. Above all, you must cherish the value of the gift of life and of the transparency for the good it can accomplish among our people, among all people. However, the path is exceedingly difficult. To begin it, you must pass the test of life; you must be able to become one with the swamp. Will you learn this?"

"I will do what is required for I know that you will direct me to do nothing that the Great Spirit would not allow us to accomplish."

"Excellent my brother," the Medicine Man said. "Your journey will be long and difficult, yet very fruitful."

The Medicine Man, lapsing into silence, stared intently at Billie. He was old and noble in appearance. His face had high cheek bones, separated with a sharp nose, which gave him hawk-like features. The hair on his head was white as snow and hung just below his shoulders yet full and thick. Without speaking, he picked up the seashell dipper and began pouring water onto the hot rocks. Thick clouds of steam rose, which were accompanied by the harsh sizzling of water on the rocks, partially obscuring Billie from his view.

"You have come far Panther," the Medicine Man said. "The course you have chosen will soon put you in your test of life, to prove your worthiness to lead our people."

"Didn't the army put me in a test of life?" Billie asked. "Afghanistan was no picnic."

"That test was only meant as a struggle for survival," The Medicine Man responded as he added a small portion of water to the rocks. "The true test of life must test survival, obedience, and wisdom. That test is survival in the new world of technology, among greedy men, corrupt government officials, obedience to the Great Spirit and to our way of life, and wisdom from years of learning."

"How do I gain the wisdom of the elders?" Billie asked. "They know all, and I lack the years."

"The way of the wise elder is to watch, listen, and then speak," the Medicine Man said. "Do this and age matters little."

"I try, but it is difficult," Billie said.

"Ah!" the Medicine Man responded. "You speak of Christina. If you wish to win her, speak to her from your heart."

"I'm not so sure anymore," Billie said. "Every time I'm around her she tries to tear me down rather than build me up. But how do you know of this?"

"I know all my brother," the Medicine Man said. "The elder's body is old, but our eyes sharp and the body remains agile."

"I do not know what to do," Billie said. "Christina has not been very friendly to me lately. Nothing I have tried to do has made any difference."

"I would not be friendly either knowing you are playing pig-in-the-blanket, sharing affections with another woman," the Medicine Man said.

"I am not doing that," Billie said. "Monique is just friendly to me."

"The black widow is also friendly before she kills her mate." the Medicine Man said. "Most who want something are friendly until that which they desire is received. But I will leave you to work this out on your own. We have more important things to discuss."

The Medicine Man poured more water onto the hot rocks. The steam completely obscured Billie from his penetrating gaze. Billie was grateful because the Medicine Man's stare was unnerving.

"Your problem," the Medicine Man continued, "is that you wish to see the end from the beginning."

"Well, at least a few steps ahead," Billie responded.

"Ah, you must first learn to walk to the edge of the light and then proceed a few steps into the darkness," the Medicine Man said. "The light will gradually reappear and show the way before you. Trust the Great Spirit. All will work out as designed."

"What if I fail?" Billie asked.

"Failure is not an option!" the Medicine Man snapped.

"Can I count on you?" Billie asked. "Will you be there to help if I stumble in my test?"

"We see all," the Medicine Man said. "We will be there when you think not. Do not fear my brother. If you are worthy to lead this people, you will pass your test of life. Remember that the test comes day by day, not in a single grand act. It is the little things that need attention; all others will take care of themselves. Remember my advice."

When the steam cleared before Billie's eyes, the Medicine Man was gone. Three warriors appeared to further train Billie in hand-to-hand fighting skills. As he was led away, Billie's thoughts kept dwelling on the Medicine Man; he had kept talking about a test. Maybe he knew something Billie didn't or perhaps it was just his experience with life. Billie made a note to ponder his statements. After several hours of intense training, he changed to go back to the civilized world. For the Medicine Man, everything seemed so simple, but in the real world, there were so many compromises to be made. Could you really exist as he did and still maintain such lofty views? What would happen if the white man encroached upon his hammock? Billie was certain there would be war again.

Billie had fulfilled his promise to Christina. After talking to the Medicine Man, his airboat sped across the swamp to his mother's place at Shark Key. As Billie approached, he could see that the previous damage he caused had been repaired. Pulling the airboat up to the dock, he saw his mother sitting at her worktable inside her chickee. Mabel was in the process of completing a beaded necklace when Billie reached her. He bent over and kissed her on the cheek.

"Has Christina talked to you mom?" Billie asked.

"Yes, she talked to me a few days ago," Mabel said. "From what she said, I gathered you didn't take my advice."

"I tried, but I don't know how," Billie said.

"Good grief," Mabel blurted out. "You can wrestle an alligator, but you can't speak to a woman? Talk to her just like you talk to me or Jacob. She's waiting for you to make the first move."

"I've tried to talk to her," Billie said. "But she always cuts me short. There never seems to be the right time."

"The right time," Mabel chimed. "Right times are for buses and trains, not women. When you see her, tell her. That will be the right time."

"Alright, I'll try again," Billie said. "She's bound to listen to me sooner or later."

"I'd make it sooner if I were you," Mabel retorted.

"To change the subject, there's something else I've wanted to ask you for a long time," Billie said.

"And what might that be?" Mabel asked.

"I would like to know about my father," Billie said. "You told me you would tell me about him soon and it's been a while."

"I'm not going to tell you until you clear up your other problems," Mabel said.

"That's not fair," Billie said, raising his voice. "I'm sorry mom; I didn't mean to say it like that."

"It's okay," Mabel said. "But, to hear what I will tell you requires that you have an open mind, uncluttered by thoughts of women or tribal management. Today is not the time."

"Won't you tell me something?" Billie pleaded.

"Okay, I'll tell you a small portion of the story," Mabel said.

"Your father came here to work for the government many years ago," Mabel began. "He was originally assigned in the Bureau of Indian Affairs office. I met him while he was on his first fact finding trip in the old diner on Big Cypress. I can still remember how handsome he looked with his dark skin and hair, wearing his short sleeve white shirt. I was attracted to him right away, even though I knew he was married. He had an easy, polite way about himself, a quick smile and relaxing manner. Everyone liked him, especially me."

"I decided right then and there, Mabel continued, "that I would have this man. So, I set might sights on him and never let up. Every time he was on Big Cypress, I would arrange to be near him. There was always some excuse that would allow me to do so. In time, he fell in love with me too. We began seeing each other in secret. We were so discreet, no one ever knew. Our affair lasted for several years. He wanted to divorce his wife and marry me, but I wouldn't let him. If I hadn't forced the relationship, we would have only been casual acquaintances. I couldn't let him ruin his career and betray his wife for something I had forced him to do."

"You said he had dark hair and skin, was he white?" Billie asked, not daring to breathe as he waited for the answer.

"Hardly," Mabel replied. "He was Seminole from Oklahoma. I had to make up a story so that no one would suspect he was the father. You are full blooded Seminole Billie, but you must not reveal what I have told you to anyone, at least for now. Just remember it was my fault and I wouldn't let him stay. However, you should know that he does stay in touch with me and you have actually met him before. He also paid your way through college, funneled through Chairman Osceola. Even the Chairman doesn't know his identity. The money I make here is okay, but it has never been enough to send you to Yale."

"I never realized," Billie stammered excitedly. "All this time I envisioned my father as a no-good bum who wouldn't take responsibility for his actions. When...?"

"You'll get to meet him when I think you can fully understand," Mabel said, interrupting. "That time is later. You think about what I have told you. Ponder it in your heart and treasure the knowledge; tell no one of this or it could be our undoing. Also, you should know that he asks about you often. I've sent him pictures. He attended your graduation at high school and college. You didn't know he was there, but I met with him."

"Is that why you were so happy at my graduation?" Billie asked.

"Partly," Mabel said, "But, also because I was happy for you and what you had achieved. I never meant for things to turn out this way Billie, but it's my fault, not his. If you need to blame someone for not having a father, blame me. He was willing, but I couldn't let him destroy his whole life for me. We still love each other, and you are his only child. Just be patient and one day you shall meet."

"I'll never blame you mother," Billie said softly. "What you have told me means more to me than you can imagine. It will be my secret and treasure. I can't tell you how happy it makes me feel."

"Good," Mabel said. "You take care of your other affairs first and perhaps in a year, give or take, you'll be able to meet. I know you'll like him. You have his eyes and drive. He's a very important man in the federal government today. His wife is terminally ill now too. The trouble you are going through is mild in comparison to his wife's illness and his desire to tell you for your whole life he's your father. Don't hate him for not being there for you Billie."

"I won't mom," Billie said as he leaned forward and kissed her cheek. "I promise."

Billie literally floated back to his airboat. All his life, Solomon and others like him had called him a half breed. He wasn't, and one day they would all find out. Is this what the Medicine Man referred to? Did he know already? Life was a funny thing. Maybe he should hate his mother, but she had never lied to him. She just hadn't revealed the story, mostly for his father's sake. Billie could see it so clearly now. To live with the shame, longing, and love for as long as he had been alive, Mabel must love his father very, very much. As excited as he was, Billie was also disappointed because he wasn't sure when he would see his father. "Well," he thought, "it's just added incentive to work things out with Christina and get the questions concerning the landfill operation behind him." Billie cranked his airboat and headed away from the docks. He was ecstatic. Life was great he thought as he gunned the engine and sped across the sawgrass, the wind in his face made him feel more alive. Never had he felt so exhilarated. But now he had another problem. He loved Christina, but he was hooked on Monique. How had he let this happen and how could he resolve the situation? It would take a great deal of thought and would not be easy.

As Billie sped away, Mabel watched him from the chickee. She hoped she had done the right thing and then decided she had. Billie had understood and she had wanted to tell him for so long. A great burden had been lifted from her shoulders. Time would tell how things would work out between them and Billie's father. It was still possible that they could be married. While Mabel hoped her lover's wife would recover, she knew there was no chance. She would be there to comfort him. Billie would be there too.

The shade was a welcome respite to the hot sun. Christina was glad that she and the other teachers had decided to bring the kids down for a swim in the spring. They had so much energy in class today. This would serve as therapy for the rambunctious little devils. It always surprised her how much noise a group of third graders could make when you gathered them into one place. As the children frolicked in the spring, Christina watched their happy faces. Despite their ability to cause trouble, they were the closest thing she could think of to angels. Now, with smiles on their faces and some of them napping on their blankets, they were the Great Spirit's little angels. It made her long for her own children. She was well aware of her ticking, biological clock. Because she taught Billie's son James, she felt close to Billie and though she wondered why Billie hadn't talked to her yet, she really loved James, as if he was her own son. They always ate lunch together and she had become accustomed to his lively mood and silly questions. He was indeed a happy boy.

Thinking of the good times they had made her think more about Billie. Wanting to put thoughts of him aside for the moment, Christina decided it was time for lunch. She began looking for James's face among those of the other children in the spring. He wasn't there. A nervous feeling began to grip her stomach as she noticed that several other children also were missing. She looked for them on the rope swing where children were taking turns swinging out over the spring and dropping into the cool water. There was no sign of them.

She rose and hurriedly walked through the nearby woods. Christina began to panic and was ready to enlist the aid of the other teachers in her search when she heard faint laughter coming from an adjacent feeder canal that carried water through the entire reservation and bisected Snake Road, which ran by the landfill site. She hurried toward the sound, which grew louder as she approached. Although she had been apprehensive and somewhat angry, Christina was relieved to see the missing children playing in the canal. About a dozen troublemakers she thought.

She was ready to let them have it when she walked up and saw them spitting canal water at each other.

"Just what do you think you're doing?" Christina shouted. The school children looked up, surprised to see her standing there. "Get out of there this minute. James, you should be ashamed of yourself. You're supposed to set an example."

"He pushed us in," James said, pointing to another student. "Since we were wet, we decided to stay."

"I'll deal with him later," Christina said. "Right now, I want all of you out of there, on the double. Move it, move it, move it."

The children began scrambling out one by one, up the canal bank to where she stood.

"Good," Christina said. "Now get back to the rest of the group. Scat. I don't want grass growing under your feet. James, you stay."

The children scampered off giggling and laughing like nothing had happened; all in a day's fun.

"What's that in your pocket?" Christina pointed.

"I don't know," James said as he gave the typical response of a child. Maybe she should try that some time Christina thought as James pulled a fish out of his pocket. Life would be so easy if you could say "I don't know" to everything someone asked you.

"Ooooh!" James exclaimed. "It's dead." He tossed the fish back into the canal.

"Next time I go fishing," Christina said as she laughed, "I'll take you instead of my pole. Maybe I'll use you for gator bait too. Come on, let's go back." They turned to walk back to the group. James thought he was in big trouble.

"You're funny," James blurted, giggling. "You and dad are a lot alike. Do you like my dad?"

"Yes, I do," Christina replied. "But I'm not sure if he feels the same about me."

"He does," James said cheerily. "He talks about you all the time."

"Really, I mean I'm sure you have other things to talk about," Christina said, trying to hide her excitement. "He seems so busy now and he's barely spoken to me."

"It's just this business thing about the site," James said. "I bet he'll talk to you lots when it's over."

"I wish I had your optimism," Christina said. "So, tell me, your birthday is coming up next month. What do you want for a present?"

"It's something dad says I can't have right now," James replied sullenly. "He says he's working on it, but it will take a while and didn't know if he could make it happen."

"What is it?" Christina asked. "You can tell me. Maybe I can help."

"I want a mom," James said sadly. "Everyone else has one. Why can't I? Could you be my mom? Could you?" The hurt and pleading in his eyes made Christina want to cry one minute and take him home the next. He was such a cute kid. It was hard for her to see him in such turmoil. She had never realized how difficult it must be to grow up without a mother. But, thinking about her own mother's death, Christina could empathize with him.

"Maybe," Christina finally responded. "It depends on how well your dad and I get along."

"You just have to try hard, like when you taught me how to swim," James proclaimed with a matter-of-fact tone. "I know you can get along real well. I'm gonna talk to my dad about it." Before Christina could utter a word, James bounded ahead to the rest of the group.

"Wow!" she thought. "What have I gotten myself into? I hope Billie doesn't get too angry with him, or me. On the other hand, maybe he's just the catalyst Billie needs to help him make a decision about us."

L ater that afternoon, Genesis was out of breath as he barged into Billie's office carrying the shredded remnant of a tribal police shirt in his hand.

"Good, you're both here," Genesis panted. Billie and Jacob looked at him quizzically as he stood in the door gasping for breath.

"Look at this," Genesis said. "It's part of Freeman's shirt. His badge was still attached to it." Genesis was holding out the badge in his hand as if to say, see, I told you so.

"Where did you find it?" Jacob asked.

"One of the elders found it in the old gator hole in Osceola's cypress head." Genesis replied. "And that's not all. Look at these marks. At first I thought they were teeth marks."

"An alligator?" Billie asked.

"No," Genesis stated flatly. "These and some of the others are clearly a cut made by a knife. Right in the area of the heart, there's still a faint trace of blood around the hole. But it's definitely from a knife."

"How do you know that?" Billie asked.

"Hell Billie," Genesis said. "Have you forgotten I taught knife fighting for the LRRP in Afghanistan and at Ft. Bragg? I'm certain of it."

"I haven't forgotten," Billie replied. "I just didn't want to believe someone out here would do such a thing."

"This was not done by one of our people," Jacob argued. "It had to be those thugs at the landfill. I'll have to side with Genesis on this one."

"You're most likely right," Billie said. "Have you found anything else to back up your theory?"

Just as Genesis opened his mouth to reply, the secretary interrupted on the intercom. Jacob was smiling at Genesis who looked like he was trying to catch flies. Realizing his awkward appearance, Genesis snapped his mouth closed.

"Billie," the secretary said. "You have an urgent call."

"When it rains, it pours," Billie exclaimed as he picked up the telephone receiver. "Yes! When? I'll be right over." As he looked up, Genesis and Jacob could tell Billie was noticeably shaken. "It's my son. He and several other kids are very sick. They've been taken to the clinic. Come with me."

The small clinic on Big Cypress was in turmoil as the three rushed into the building. Billie had never seen so many people in the place at one time. The phones were ringing off the hook; people were yelling and shouting, asking where their son or daughter was. The nurse at the receptionist's desk seemed overwhelmed when Billie approached. So frustrated, she didn't utter a word, just pointed, motioning them down a narrow hallway. The three men hurried down the hall and barged into a small treatment room past several more nurses to find the doctor bending over a young patient. He looked up at them disapprovingly as he continued his work.

Christina, who had brought the children in, was standing quietly out of the way. She was glad Billie was there. It relieved her to think she was no longer alone in her feelings for the life-threatening predicament the children seemed to be in. Billie noticed her and made an attempt to smile, but concern clouded his face. His gaze darted from bed to bed, spotting James, he quickly walked to him. Billie leaned over his son trying to coax a response from the young boy who was curled into a fetal position, obviously in great pain. James could not speak. Painful groans were the only sounds that escaped his lips. Billie had a sudden attack of panic. Christina gently tugged at his arm and pulled him away.

"Let the doctor work," Christina whispered. "There's nothing you can do."

"What happened?" Billie asked.

"They fell ill a few hours ago," Christina replied. "At first, it seemed like an ordinary stomachache, but then became much worse. I called the doctor and here we are."

"You don't have any idea what may have caused it?" Billie asked.

"Well," Christina said. "We took the class to the spring today and everyone is fine except for them. They all ate the same thing, went swimming and played around; nothing out of the ordinary. Wait, come to think of it, these kids went swimming in the canal. Yes, almost all the kids who swam in the canal are sick, the one's that didn't aren't. Maybe it was something in the canal water."

"That may be an explanation," Billie said. "Does the doctor know what caused it?"

"Not yet," Christina replied.

The doctor glanced up at them as he examined a young girl. He rose and walked over.

"I need you to wait in the lounge until I've finished my examination," the doctor said tersely. "I'll continue working with them, run some blood tests and keep trying to figure out what's happened. Meanwhile, I want to call an expert in New Hampshire who may be able to assist me with an initial diagnosis. We can't afford to jump to any conclusions at this juncture."

The doctor held out his hands like a mother hen rounding up her chicks and escorted everyone out of the room except the nurses.

As Billie and his entourage left the treatment room, they entered a small lobby and lounge area just outside the door. The parents of the children had arrived and were in heated discussions. The room buzzed like a hive of wasps. As Billie and Christina approached, several of the parents confronted them.

"This is all your fault," yelled one parent. "You and that damn landfill."

"Look," Billie said exasperated. "We don't know what's wrong with them yet. It won't do any good to start throwing around accusations."

"Then how do you explain this," the parent queried.

"I can't," Billie said. "Until the doctor can run some tests, I'm as in the dark as you."

"We're holding you responsible Billie Panther," said another parent. "You better pray to the Great Spirit our kids don't..."

"Don't think about the worst," Billie interrupted. "They'll be okay. You'll see."

"For your sake, they had better be," the parent continued.

Jacob had taken about all he could. He walked up to Billie. The parents, sensing they were unwanted, backed away.

"Billie," Jacob said curtly. "There's no telling how long we'll have to wait, so Genesis and I are going to pursue the matter we discussed earlier. Keep us posted, will you?"

Billie nodded his head and sat down. Christina sat on a sofa opposite him, a small table serving as a barrier, almost as if they were opponents who would square off against each other at any moment. Feeling a bit awkward, Billie blindly picked up the closest magazine and began flipping the pages. Christina did likewise and as the next few minutes passed, they eyed each other warily over the tops of the pages. Finally, Billie couldn't take it anymore. He rose quickly to his feet, walked around the table and planted himself beside Christina.

"We need to talk," Billie blurted out, surprising Christina who immediately regained her composure.

"You start," Christina said smartly.

"Okay," Billie said. "This is hard for me. You know I have feelings for you. I would like to uh, uh, keep seeing you and have a more permanent relationship."

"Billie," Christina said. "Why didn't you tell me this before? I've been waiting for so long. When you kept avoiding me and promising to talk, then didn't, I wasn't sure about us anymore. I was beginning to make other plans."

"I understand," Billie said. "But every time I wanted to talk, something else seemed to come up. However, just so you know, I feel better about things now. I think I have everything sorted out."

"You know I love you Billie," Christina said. "I'm going to have to think about..."

Christina was interrupted by the doctor as he seemed to appear from nowhere. The noisy conversations came to an abrupt halt. The only audible sound was the anxious breathing of the parents as they awaited the doctor's report.

"I don't know how to tell you this," the doctor began. "James and the other children are seriously ill. I conferred with the specialist in New Hampshire. After discussing their blood tests and other symptoms, well..."

"Well, what?" Billie asked sharply.

"We've come to the conclusion that they've ingested a toxic chemical of some sort," the doctor said. "It looks like an industrial chemical, perhaps a gasoline derivative. Whatever it is, it's slicing through the body's cells like a hot knife through butter."

"What can you do?" Billie asked.

"We don't have adequate care facilities here for something of this nature," the doctor said. "They'll need to be taken to Miami General and given blood transfusions. It's their only hope."

"Hell fire!" Billie shouted, frustrated. "Is there anything we can do to help?"

"Nothing on the medical end," the doctor said. "But, if I were you, I'd check the water supply. It's almost a certainty that's where it came from. You need to warn all residents not to drink the water until it can be tested. I'll have the children transferred to Miami immediately; Flight-for-Life helicopters are already on their way and should be here within the half hour. Sorry, I can't tell you more, but I'll keep you informed about their condition."

"See," a parent shouted at Billie. "I told you it was that damn landfill."

"Blaming Billie isn't going to help us now," said the doctor, compassion in his voice. "We need to stay calm."

"That's easy for you to say," said another parent. "It's not your kids."

"The doctor's right," Christina said. "Let's not blame anyone. We need to cooperate."

"Christina, will you call the water plant?" Billie pleaded desperately. "Tell them to shut down the water supply. Then, call the dispatcher. Have her send out the deputies and warn everyone not to drink the water and to have Genesis and Jacob meet me at my office. Begin the tribal calling tree; warn everyone as quickly as you can. I'd like to stay and finish our discussion, but I have to go."

"I understand Billie," Christina said. "We can finish it after this is over."

"I promise we will," Billie said as he rushed out the door.

Pandemonium had broken loose on Big Cypress. Every police officer had been recalled from off duty status. Climbing into their cruisers, they were quickly warning the residents of the community not to drink the water. They traversed every street and went to every outlying house and chickee, their lights flashing and sirens blaring intermittently.

"This is a police department warning — do not drink the local water. It may be contaminated."

The message was repeated on every block, on every street. Telephones were ringing incessantly at police headquarters as residents flooded the station with calls to confirm the news. The police said it was true and to please warn each neighbor. At the water plant, a technician furiously turned valves and switched off SCADA (supervisory controls and data acquisition) controls, the controls that turn on and off all water conveyance and electrical supply mains in an attempt to cut the local water supply as quickly as possible. Within minutes, water supply to local residents was severed and everyone who could be, had been warned. An atmosphere of paranoia and panic prevailed.

CHAPTER 9

Billie rushed straight to his office. There was no time to lose. The suspicions Genesis and Jacob had about the landfill site were likely true. There was no other source on the reservation that would leak a gasoline type contaminant into the water. From what Christina had said, the only kids that had gotten sick so far were some that had been in the canal, but the landfill was some distance from that canal. Given the time the landfill had been in operation, there was no way a contaminant could leak to the groundwater fast enough to travel that far.

There was only one thing to do Billie surmised as he walked into his office. They would need to sample all the wells on a grid below the landfill site and the community water supply. Water from the canal where the children had been exposed would also be sampled. Billie knew that time was the enemy as he picked up the telephone and dialed a friend who owned an environmental laboratory in Miami.

"Sarah, this is Billie," he said. "Yes, I'm doing fine. Look, I've got a problem here. Several children have been exposed to some sort of toxic chemical. The doctor said it was likely ingested, probably water borne, and a gasoline type derivative. The children are in serious condition. We need to analyze some samples right away. It's a matter of life and death."

"We're pretty full up," Sarah said. "But, for you and the kids, we'll drop what we're doing and perform the analysis immediately."

"Great," Billie said. "I don't know what I can do to repay you, but thanks."

"How about a hot date?" Sarah asked laughing, "Seriously though, how soon can you have the samples here?"

"We'll have the samples there first thing in the morning, about 9:00 a.m.," Billie said. "We'll need to sample all night. How soon can you have an analysis?

"About twelve hours, maybe less I should think," Sarah replied.

"Great," Billie said. "Do whatever it takes. Right now, about six kid's lives are at stake. They're on their way to receive blood transfusions at Miami General."

"You just get me those samples," Sarah said. "We'll do what it takes to find out what's in them for you."

"Great," Billie said. "I'll see you in the morning. I really appreciate this."

Billie felt a little better as he hung up the phone, but the contaminants still puzzled him. He was about to say a silent prayer when Genesis and Jacob rushed into his office. He held up his finger for silence as he dialed another number.

"Timmy, this is Billie," he said. "I need you to load my sampling supplies onto the swamp buggy. Yes, the two red ice chests and the three white wooden boxes, along with the other gear lying next to them. I'll be there in a few minutes with Genesis and Jacob to pick it up. Great. See you then."

"You look concerned, give it to me," Billie said.

"Several more children have gotten sick," Jacob said. "That brings the count to ten and from what Christina told us, that's all the kids that were in the canal. None of the others show any symptoms."

"What the hell is going on?" Billie asked, frustration in his voice. "We've never had any problems like this before."

"Remember those trucks I told you about?" Genesis asked. "They must have been dumping something. Jesus, I should have checked it out."

"If anything, it's my fault," Billie said. "But the puzzling thing is that if the trucks you saw were dumping something at the site or if they've dumped something there before, there is no way it could have traveled that distance so quickly. Groundwater flow is far too slow."

"Something had to cause it," Jacob said.

"We'll have to worry about that later," Billie replied tersely. "Right now, we need to do all we can to identify the chemical."

Billie walked over to a file cabinet and pulled out a large piece of rolled paper. Before Genesis or Jacob could ask what it was, Billie startled them by walking to the conference table and brushing everything onto the floor as he unrolled it. He was in such a frenzy they thought he had gone mad. The paper was a map. It showed the entire reservation, but there were some blue dots in a grid pattern that neither Genesis nor Jacob recognized. Before they could ask, Billie was in mid-sentence.

"We'll collect a sample from the local water supply," Billie began. "Then, we need to check these wells, represented by the blue dots, to see if the area surrounding the landfill is contaminated. Note that they're on a grid pattern. If a chemical has been dumped, we'll know where by the concentration plume. We should be able to sample the wells without being seen. Hurry, there's no time to lose."

"I don't' mean to sound ignorant Billie," Genesis said. "But what is a plume?"

"Suppose you put a few drops of food coloring in a tub of water, at first they're small and brightly colored," Billie said. "However, as time passes, the droplet spreads and the color lessens, but you can still see the outer edge of the drop and a distinct boundary with the clear water in the tub. That outer edge and all within it is the plume. It shows you how far the drop has spread. But, in groundwater, because of continual flow, the droplet can spread significantly. Also, you can't see it, so you need to take water samples and compare the concentrations of the chemical found in one sample with that found in another sample. Understand?"

"Yeah," Genesis said. "Does that make me a hydro whatever now?"

"A hydrologist," Billie said laughing. "And yes, it does. Let's go."

The three raced outside, climbed into Billie's truck and sped off to meet Timmy. Concern about the children showed on their faces. None spoke as Billie concentrated on driving. So stoic were their countenances, they appeared to be perfect candidates for wooden Indians in a cigar store. Within a few minutes, Billie was pulling off the highway onto a dirt road that led a short distance into a cypress head. The glare from the headlights was in stark contrast to the blackness of the

Florida swamp as they shot like laser beams into the tangle of dwarf cypress trees and sawgrass.

Billie rounded a sharp curve, barely missing a fallen tree that jutted out onto the edge of the road. Suddenly, they had arrived at their destination. Timmy already had the swamp buggy loaded with equipment, the motor idling. He knew when Billie said he was in a hurry; he was in a hurry and Timmy had heard the news about the children. He also knew that every second counted. He scampered over to the truck as it rolled to a stop and Billie killed the lights and motor.

"Everything is ready," Timmy said. "Your equipment is on board and the buggy is full of fuel. It should be more than enough to last the night. I also have some gas cans tied to the back, just in case."

"Thanks Timmy," Billie said. "Having everything ready will save us a lot of time. It could mean living or dying for those kids."

"Anytime," Timmy said. "There's a satellite cell phone next to the driver's seat in case yours doesn't work when you need it. I'll get another buggy ready as a standby. Take these."

"What a man," Genesis said. "You think of everything. We'll certainly give you a call if we need to."

Billie climbed into the driver's seat and switched on the lights of the swamp buggy. To someone who hadn't seen this one, it looked like it should be used in a Mars landing. It was a stripped down, 1958, long wheelbase, Willy's Jeep with a flat head, super charged six-cylinder, Super Hurricane engine as a powerhouse. The metal body had been completely removed and replaced with a lightweight wood and fiberglass composite. The tires were four and one-half feet tall and two feet wide. The weight to tire ratio made the buggy so light it could actually float. Where it was going tonight, it would likely need to. The lights were 500 watts or as the old timers would say about 470,000 candle power each. In lay terms, enough watts to light up the whole damn swamp. Two were positioned in front, above the bumper for on and off-road use and four more were mounted above a roll bar about a foot ahead and elevated in front of the driver. There were also two portable spotlights on either side. Even though the Florida night was often so black you couldn't see your hand in front of your face, the lights would penetrate one-quarter mile into the darkness as if it were day.

The buggy pulled away from the compound and through the cypress swamp. The grinding of the transmission and humming of the four-wheel drive could be heard for some distance. Occasionally, they would jump white-tail deer on the edge of some of the pine islands and cypress heads they skirted. Their bodies clearly visible in the lights, eyes reflecting emerald green. It was like watching a National Geographic safari in Africa. Abruptly, they encountered a large bog where the sawgrass butted up against a cypress head. Billie knew it would be rough. He shifted into four-wheel low; the grinding sound of the gears became deafening as he gunned the buggy forward. As they eased ahead at a continuous pace, the buggy literally fell into the bog, as if it had fallen from a cliff. Only two or three inches of the tires protruded above the black ooze of the swamp. Mud was being slung everywhere; the headlights suddenly dimmed; the three men were coated from head to foot in black muck. As quickly as it started, they were through. Billie shifted back into four-wheel high and kicked the buggy into overdrive. Jacob and Genesis had grabbed a couple of rags and were cleaning off the lenses of the lights and their faces, hanging on for dear life as Billie hit an occasional rotted stump or submerged log.

The buggy coasted to a stop in front of the first well, which Billie kept illuminated with the portable spotlights. The three men had hit the ground running.

"Genesis," Billie yelled. "Take the cap off the well while Jacob and I get the equipment. Billie and Jacob rushed around to the back of the buggy and grabbed sampling bottles, a bailer, Sharpie marker, writing tablet, and rubber gloves. By the time Genesis had gotten the cap off, Billie and Jacob were right on top of him.

"We have to take three samples with the bailer, discard them, and save the fourth sample for analysis," Billie said. "I'll bail, Jacob will put the sample in the bottle; Genesis, you label the bottles and write down the well number and time. Do you understand?"

"Understood boss," Genesis said.

"Good," Billie replied. "We will perform the same protocol at each well. Let's get started."

Billie dropped the bailer down into the well. It was a simple mechanism, essentially a piece of PVC pipe whose outside diameter barely fit into the inside diameter of the well. A yellow nylon rope was attached to the upper end so it wouldn't be lost inside the well as Billie dropped it down. Once dropped, only a few seconds were required to fill it and pull it back to the surface. Thanks to the high-water table, being only several feet below land surface, the bailer didn't require a long drop as it would in desert climates. Billie discarded the first three samples by turning the bailer upside down and letting the water run onto the ground. He poured the fourth into a Nalgene sampling bottle held by Jacob, which Genesis had already labeled as well number one.

As they worked, thousands of insects, attracted to the lights, began descending upon them. The insects were in their hair, pockets and under their shirts. Mosquitoes had also joined the fray. They were so thick the men could literally reach out and grab several with one hand while in midflight. They were uncomfortable, squirming back and forth through the ordeal like little kids who were holding themselves until they could find a toilet. As bad as the insects were, the urgent nature of their work kept them from complaining. They went from one sampling well to another, like robots on an assembly line, each fulfilling its task perfectly. As if possessed by demons, they worked in a frenzy at each well.

B layde was standing outside the door of the landfill office. Everyone gone for the night, he had brought out a few of his favorite movies to pop into his VCR. They were the kind no respectable man would be caught watching. Having watched several, he had decided it was time for a nicotine break. He blew circles of smoke into the air toward a sliver of a moon. The light outside the office door made it difficult to see, so he reached his hand inside the door and flicked it off. That's better he thought as he watched a star-studded sky. Watching the moon through perfect circles of smoke he blew from his coffin stick, he compared the view to that of the sky in New York. For as long as he could remember, he had never seen the stars above New York except for an early one now and then which came out before the Big Apple lit up. What an amazing sight. Not having much of an education, he could identify the Milky Way, the big and little dippers, and several other constellations. He was really getting into it. Nature was not one of his strong points, but the peace and quiet of Big Cypress had already left its mark on him. Once visited, it would always be remembered.

Blayde reached into the office and picked up his binoculars. Pretending he was a world-class astronomer, he began looking at each single star, the sliver of the moon and an infrequent plane as its strobe light moved smoothly through the darkness. It had been years since he had felt this young. He lowered his binoculars and focused on stars near the horizon. Without warning, the stars in his binoculars became tenfold larger. "What the hell," he thought as he focused on the large lights. Removing the binoculars from his eyes, Blayde could see the swamp buggy in the distance. It was too far away to hear; only the lights on the roll bar were visible. Blayde watched the swamp buggy for over an hour as it stopped for a few minutes and then moved on. The pattern repeated itself over and over. He tried to see what was happening through the binoculars, but the distance was too great. Once in a while, the figure of a man could be discerned, but the identity and the reason for the vehicle being there remained a mystery.

Blayde decided the best thing to do was to call Mike.

"Hey Mike," Blayde spoke into the receiver. "It's Blayde."

"Are you crazy?" Mike asked. "It's two thirty in the morning."

"I know," Blayde replied. "But something's going on out here. A vehicle is moving south of the site. It's lit up like a damn Christmas tree. It stops for a few minutes and then moves to another location."

"Maybe it's just some Indians wandering around," Mike said.

"I thought it might be too," Blayde said. "However, the movement doesn't appear to be random. They appear to be running on a straight line."

"You mean like a grid type pattern," Mike stated flatly, suddenly wide awake.

"Yeah, yeah, that's right," Blayde said.

"Keep watching them," Mike said. "I'll call Mr. Lorio. Let us know everything they do."

"Sure thing," Blayde replied as he hung up.

He walked back outside and moved four fifty-five-gallon drums together into a diamond shape. Blayde pulled out three insect repellant ropes from his pocket, put one on each of the three outside drums and lit them. Pulling himself onto the fourth, he found a small reprieve from the mosquitoes and settled in for his vigil.

Billie and his companions were sampling the last well. Dog tired, it was hard to focus on what they were doing. Almost with super-human strength, they pushed themselves to the breaking point. The long night had extracted a measurable toll.

"This is the last of them," Billie said. "As soon as we get back to the road, get those damn police lights flashing. I want these samples to the lab in Miami ASAP."

Genesis glanced at his watch. "We'll have them there by 9:00 a.m." he said.

"I hate to sound dumb Billie, but I didn't know we had these sampling wells and I've been on the board for ten years," Jacob said.

"No one else does either," Billie said. "I put them in just in case something like this ever happened. You know the water problems we've had with the adjoining farmers and ranchers. We all claim someone else is polluting the water around and on the reservation. I just had to have a way to prove water quality if the need arose. I've taken a sample here about every six months so we can have some kind of background record."

"Damn," Jacob exclaimed. "And you say you're not political. Well, your secret's safe with us. It's best that no one else knows about the wells anyway. You may have just saved ours and those children's bacon."

"Too little, too late I'm afraid," Billie said. "Those guys have a hundred-year lease on the landfill now."

"Only if they abide by the terms of the contract," Genesis said. "If we can prove they're dumping toxic chemicals, the contract is void. And, if they see us out here, they'll come looking. All hell may break loose."

"We'll worry about that when the time comes," Billie said. "Let's get these samples to the lab."

As the three climbed onto the swamp buggy, the red glow of the rising sun was tinting the eastern horizon. The morning was still and quiet except for the roar of the engine. Billie pressed the accelerator pedal all the way to the floorboard as the buggy ripped across the sawgrass swamp. He was relentless in his effort to get the samples to the laboratory in Miami. By the time they reached the compound, the manifold on the six-cylinder engine was glowing cherry red. Genesis had called ahead for his cruiser. It was waiting for them when they arrived.

Without hesitation, they jumped from the buggy, unloaded the samples from it into the back of the cruiser and were climbing in when Timmy ran up, sandwiches and a hot thermos of coffee in his hands.

"I thought you might like these before you leave," Timmy said as he handed them to Jacob through the passenger side window.

"You're a saint," Jacob said. "We'll eat them on the run. Thanks a million."

With that, the three were off. Genesis turned on the flashing lights as he intersected Snake Road and within seconds was traveling 90 miles per hour.

Paul Lorio's car came to a skidding stop in front of the landfill office just as the sun broke the eastern horizon. Jumping out, he raced to where Blayde and Mike were standing by the office door.

"I got here as fast as I could," Paul panted out. "What's going on?"

"Blayde saw a bunch of lights out there," Mike said pointing to where Blayde had spotted the swamp buggy during the night. "They spent the entire night going from place to place."

"Yeah," Blayde chimed in. "They'd stop every little bit for ca few minutes and then go again."

"You got me out here for this?" Paul asked incredulously. "It's probably just some drunken Indians fire hunting."

"Fire hunting?" Blayde asked quizzically.

"Hunting deer at night with a light dumb ass," Paul stated. "I can't believe you called me about such worthless nonsense."

"It may not be so worthless," Mike said. "I heard the water supply at the reservation has been turned off. They're having it tested. Also, the pattern the swamp buggy was on last night was not random. From what Blayde told me, it was a grid pattern, characteristic of water sampling protocol on a large scale."

"Hmmm, this could be a big problem," Paul said. "But those chemicals we dumped couldn't have leaked into the aquifer yet could they?"

"Look," Blayde blurted out. "There's a police car. Man, that baby is moving."

"They may have been sampling wells to perform a water analysis," Paul added frantically. "Follow that car and see where they're going. Call me when you find out. Move!"

Mike and Blayde ran to their car and high-tailed after Genesis's cruiser. With their lights off, keeping their distance, Genesis didn't notice they were tailing him.

Paul sat down on the seat of his car. He was daydreaming as he watched the pink glow of the sunrise turn to an orange ball, which rose above the bald cypress east of the landfill. As a backdrop, it highlighted the Spanish moss, draped like a thick carpet over the cypress branches. He cursed himself and the tribal police for not being able to enjoy it more fully. It was the first sunrise he had watched in many years. What could be wrong? Paul had gone over the aquifer and soil properties himself. There was no way any chemicals could have polluted the water in such a short time. There had to be another explanation. Satisfied it had to be something else, Paul pulled a McDonald's bag off the seat and planted himself on the hood of his car to admire the sunrise as he drank orange juice and finished a Danish pastry.

When the police cruiser pulled into the laboratory parking lot, the morning was already sweltering, the temperature in the mid-eighties. Genesis steered the car under the shade of a group of large oak and palm trees. On the outer fringes of the bustling metropolis, only enough trees and shrubs from the natural habitat had been cleared to make room for the laboratory and parking lot. Heat waves were already beginning to rise from the black asphalt as the three men rushed to the building entrance carrying two sizeable cardboard boxes. Above the entry, the words CYTECH ENVIRONMENTAL sprawled across the building in an arch in large silver, block letters. The three had barely made it into the foyer when Billie noticed Sarah emerging from a hallway on the far side of the lobby.

"Sarah," Billie shouted as he hurried across the lobby smiling. He paused long enough to pull her into his arms and give her an affectionate hug. Not the kind a mere friend would give, but the type two old lovers would extend to each other. "God, it's good to see you again."

"Too bad it's under these circumstances," Sarah replied. "I remember better days during college when you and I, well you know. Anyway, I'm sorry to hear about your son. Is there anything I can do to help?"

"Yeah," Billie said. "Analyze these samples for us by yesterday."

"No problem," Sarah replied laughing. "The impossible just takes a little longer. Bring them back to the main lab. We have everything set up." She led them down a narrow hallway to a large laboratory where several technicians were hovering over pieces of equipment that looked like they belonged on the space shuttle. "You can put them on that counter over there."

Genesis and Jacob were obviously impressed as they studied the equipment set up in the laboratory. They didn't have the slightest clue as to what they were looking at. Sarah noticed their expressions and began to explain.

"I can see you're wondering what some of these futuristic looking machines are," Sarah began as she started pointing out various instruments. "That's a scintillation counter, gas chromatograph (GC), high pressure liquid chromatograph (HPLC), and a specific surface area measuring device. You know, that's what pharmacists use to help determine dosage rates for pills based on body size. Each compound has a specific surface area, usually listed in meters squared per gram of compound."

"Sounds like Greek to me," Jacob muttered.

"It's really simple," Sarah said. "For example, if you could spread one gram of sand out on an even surface, it would cover about eighty square meters. Anyway, we also have pressure chambers, atomic absorption spectrophotometers and a host of other equipment. We can analyze almost anything, organic or inorganic."

"What about these samples?" Genesis asked.

"Based on what Billie told me last night and what the water plant manager relayed to me this morning, we've set up the GC to check for volatile organics," Sarah said. "We've also set up the HPLC and a Photovac with a flame ionization detector to check liquid samples for organic contaminants. We assume organic since the doctor believes the pollutant is a gasoline derivative. If that's what it really is, we'll find and identify it. The HPLC can actually analyze for 35 compounds at once and we have set it up for the suspected chemicals. Hopefully it is among the group we think it is and just maybe we'll get a break more quickly than anticipated."

"How soon can you have them analyzed?" Billie asked.

"We've dropped everything else to work on this," Sarah said. "It may take us up to twelve hours. So, if you'll take yourselves out of here and let us work, we'll get right on it."

"We really appreciate this Sarah," Billie said.

"Yeah," Jacob said. "If there is anything we can do to repay you, just name it."

"Don't mention it," Sarah said softly. "I would do the same for you. Now get out of here and go see those kids. They will need some cheering up."

About a block down the street, under the shade of a large oak, Mike and Blayde had pulled their car off the side street and watched Billie and his companions as they emerged from the laboratory. They had seen them carry large boxes in and now were leaving without them. There was no doubt in their mind that samples had been delivered for analysis. When the police cruiser sped out of the parking lot, Mike picked up his cell phone and called Paul.

"Where did they go?" Paul asked.

"We're at some place called Cytech Environmental," Mike replied.

"That has to be a water quality and analysis laboratory," Paul said. "Did they take samples in with them?"

"They delivered two large boxes," Mike said. "It had to be quite a few samples."

"Damn," Paul whispered. "This has put a monkey wrench into things. Look, we've got too much money at stake to risk anything going wrong now. We've already collected about four million. What to do, what to do. There's no other choice. The analysis of those samples must not leave that laboratory. Wait until dark and do what has to be done. Call me when it's taken care of."

"We'll take care of the problem boss," Mike said as he hung up the phone.

"What's up?" Blayde asked.

"Lorio wants us to eliminate a potential problem," Mike said, pulling a small case from beneath his seat. Inside the case was a silencer for his 9mm Beretta pistol. He lovingly caressed it as he withdrew the gun metal blue object and began screwing it on. Blayde, his fetish for sharp instruments ever noticeable, flipped out his switch blade and began softly dragging the cold blade across his tongue. He removed the blade and began to polish it on the leg of his trousers, an evil grin on his face.

Mike watched Blayde carefully. He had to be the craziest son-of-a-bitch he had ever run across. There was nothing Blayde liked better than to kill some hapless victim. Maybe that's why Lorio and some of the other bosses called on him so often. They knew they could always count on him because of his love for the kill. Mike wondered what would happen if someone ever fought back. Would Blayde, as cocky and pretentious as he was, be able to handle the situation or, would he come running for help? It was going to be a long day. They waited for darkness to fall.

Jagged Grass

At Miami General, a large room had been modified and equipped so the sick children could be tended together. Because they were all getting blood transfusions, a central room allowed both the doctors and nurses to efficiently carry out their duties. The Indian children were lying in beds. Every one of them had a needle in the arm; fresh blood was being pumped into their veins. Their faces and skin were not the lustrous brown of the mighty Seminole, but the pale, bluish color of those about to die. As the three men stood looking at them, they realized time was running out. Their only hope was that Sarah could identify the toxin today. Tomorrow would be too late. Despite the fact that they had been up for over twenty-four hours, the three quickly moved about, from bed to bed, trying to comfort the children, along with several parents who were there.

Billie approached his son James who tried to give a weak smile. Billie's heart was being torn apart inside; first his wife and now possibly his son. He didn't know if he could take it. His son meant everything to him. There was nothing he wouldn't do for him. The fishing trips and airboat rides, working in the Glades in all types of conditions, James had been with him many times. He was a part of his life, even more than his wife had been. They relied on each other. "I have to be strong," Billie thought to himself. "This is no time for self-pity. Only confidence and reassurance must reflect from my face."

"How do you feel son?" Billie asked gently.
"Okay," James hoarsely whispered. "Are you still taking me on an airboat ride on Saturday?"
"Wouldn't miss it for the world champ," Billie said. "But you have to get better first. What do you want for your birthday?"
"Well, could Christina be my new mom; I really like her?" James asked as he forced another smile.

"Hmmmm," Billie responded. "Tell you what, I'll work on it."
"You promise," James whispered, his eyes widening in excitement.
"Cross my heart," Billie said. "You know how the song goes. *I got women that can cook, I got women that can clean, I got women that can do most anything.* If Christina won't do it, one of the others should be willing to be a mom." The two laughed aloud as Billie continued to hum the Hank Williams Jr. song. A nurse hearing the commotion, walked to the bed.
"He needs to rest now," the nurse said sternly. "You must come back later."
"Okay," Billie said. "I'll talk to you later son." Billie lingered for a moment to squeeze his son's hand then, quietly walked away, a great burden of anguish riding his shoulders.

Finishing rounds on his last patient, the doctor motioned for Billie, Jacob and Genesis to wait for him in the hallway. They were sitting on a small sofa when he walked out of the room.
"How are the children doing?" Billie asked.
"The transfusions are helping," the doctor replied. "The kids are improving, but they are still in critical condition. We won't know for sure if the transfusions alone will be enough, at least for several more hours. But I must warn you, it is doubtful. We must determine what they're contaminated with."
"We'll have that answer for you tonight," Billie said. "The water is being analyzed as we speak."
"Commendable," the doctor said as he turned to go back to his patients. "Let me know as soon as you can. I'll keep you informed about the children's condition.

"Genesis," Billie stated matter of fact. "I want the son-of-a-bitch that did this. I don't care what it takes or who it is."
"We'll find them," Jacob said. "Maybe we should turn them over to the parents when we do."

"That would be too easy," Billie said. "They don't even deserve to breathe."

"Look," Genesis blurted out interrupting them. "We all know who it is. Let's get the proof we need and put their ass in jail."

"Speaking of proof, let's take a short nap and then get back to the lab," Billie said.

The hot day had been a long one for Mike and Blayde who kept a silent vigil on the environmental lab. They were getting on each other's nerves as the sun's last orange rays faded to night. Even with the windows down in the shade of the oak, it had been hot and suffocating. Sweat had oozed out of every pore all day, making sitting in the car extremely uncomfortable; damp clothes clung to their bodies like a skin rash. Since night had fallen, most of the cars in the lot had departed one by one. Several workers were leaving the building as Mike and Blayde readied for the task at hand. Blayde retrieved his silencer equipped pistol from a bag on the rear seat. Both checked their guns to make sure they were loaded and then picked up several books of matches and a couple of flares. As the workers drove out of the lot, the two exited their car.

Although the lights in the parking lot shown forth with a bright, harsh glare, they were confident of not being seen because of the dense trees. They strolled across the still hot asphalt as though out for a stroll along the beach. The main door, unlocked, was silently opened. They stood in the lobby for a couple of minutes to accustom their eyes to the darkness, the air conditioning a welcome relief from the heat of the Florida summer. The building was dark except for lights at the end of the hall in the main lab. Like big cats stalking their prey, the two assassins stealthily crept down the hall toward the sound of voices.

Sarah and two technicians were at their instruments, checking and recording data measurements. When Sarah glanced up to see the two men standing in the doorway, she should have sensed something was seriously wrong. Instead, she was just surprised to see them. Years of commonplace occurrences had dulled her survival instincts. Had she been in a dark parking lot, a red flag would have certainly went up but for some reason, in the would-be safety of her office, with her coworkers, she felt safe.

"May I help you?" a startled Sarah asked.

"Billie sent us to pick up the analysis of the water samples brought in this morning," Mike said.

"He said he was going to get them himself," Sarah replied as the two technicians looked on. "Did he change his mind?"

"Well," Mike replied. "He's just dead tired from being up all day and night. We offered to pick them up for him." Sarah seemed relieved. Mike's explanation had made perfect sense. She knew Billie, that he was always pushing himself beyond the normal limits of individual staying power.

"Alright, let me get the results from my office," Sarah said as she hopped off her stool. "We won't have all the results for about four more hours, but these should help the doctor treat the kids."

As she made her way past the two men, Sarah began to get an uneasy feeling. Looking at Blayde, there was something inherently evil about him. His eyes, so flat and black, inset on a face that showed no emotion or life. Suddenly, she noticed a bulge under his sport coat. She knew without looking it was a gun and these were not cops. Walking down the hall to her office, the hair on the nape of her neck began to tingle. From her office, she could see into the lab. Unfortunately, Blayde could see her as well. Sarah quickly picked up the phone and dialed 911. She heard the phone ring on the other end but was unable to wait for an answer as she dropped the phone in panic and fear.

"They're onto us Mike," Blayde yelled as he ran toward Sarah. Mike, who had been keeping his eye on the two technicians, pulled his gun. Panic stricken, like cornered mice, the technicians tried to escape. Mike shot one in the back of the head as he reached the exit door. The man fell into a lifeless heap upon the floor. The other technician ducked behind a lab bench while Mike fired several rounds at her. Mike ran around the bench and cornered her. With no place to run or hide, she stood to face her executioner.

"It's just business," Mike said emotionlessly as he shot her twice in the chest.

Sarah, seeing Blayde running toward her office, tried to escape out the window. She had almost made it when Blayde rounded the corner and shot her in the back, the bullet striking just above the left kidney. Sarah felt a hot pain shoot up her spine as she fell like a sack of flour atop the shrubs outside the window. Satisfied, Blayde returned to the main lab.

"I killed the bitch," Blayde said, elated. "She wasn't fast enough."

"Hard to outrun a bullet," Mike retorted. "Let's torch this place and get out of here."

"Hey, there's a chemical cabinet over there," Blayde said. "Take a look see."

Mike opened the cabinet and found several flammable chemicals as well as concentrated acids.

"Here's some acetone," Mike muttered aloud. "That should do the trick."

They took several cans of the acetone and poured it all over the floor of the lab. On their way down the hall, Mike threw and broke several bottles of concentrated sulfuric and hydrochloric acid onto the counter tops. As they passed each office, Blayde poured acetone into each one. Finally, in the main lobby they stopped. Out of breath, they panted until the fumes from their handiwork made it impossible to stay longer. Blayde walked to the door and looked outside. Not a soul in sight, he motioned to Mike who pulled out a flare and threw it towards the end of the hall to the lab. While the flare was still in the air, Mike and Blayde were out the door, scurrying across the parking lot to their car.

Halfway to their goal, the lab exploded into flames. Multiple explosions ripped the building apart as the chemicals inside reached critical heat points. Climbing into the car, Mike hurriedly started the engine and pulled out, lights off until they rounded a few street corners. The glow from their handiwork was visible in the rearview mirror. Flames licked the night sky as they calmly drove away, avoiding bringing suspicion to themselves. Mike, breathing a sigh of relief, called Lorio.

"It's done," Mike said. "We'll see you in a couple of hours." Mike hung up and concentrated on his driving.

Billie, Jacob and Genesis arrived to find the parking lot and street packed with fire trucks, police cars and ambulances. "What the hell," Billie managed to blurt out as he braked the car in the middle of the street. Without thought of the car, all three were racing full speed across the street to the grisly scene before them. The first thing to catch Billie's eye was two paramedics pushing a stretcher to an ambulance. He had a sinking feeling in his stomach, a nauseous wave washing over him. Like a two-hundred-meter hurdler, he leaped over equipment, fire hoses and cars in his effort to reach the stretcher. Upon reaching his objective, his worst fears were confirmed. It was Sarah. Billie knelt down to speak to her.

"Who did this?" Billie asked helplessly.

"Two men...wanted samples," Sarah said struggling to reply. "Didn't get. Samples contained benzene and tri-chloro eth..." She gasped her last breath, eyes open, she was gone. Billie hugged Sarah tightly, tears filling his eyes. Everyone he knew was being hurt and killed. The sadness he felt gradually turned to anger, swelling like a tidal wave until it crested. Billie stood up as the paramedics pried him away from her body. He was in a rage when Jacob and Genesis reached him.

"Whoever did this, I want them," Billie screamed. "I'll kill the bastard's myself, with my bare hands. Leave now for the landfill site. See what's going on out there. It had to be them." Jacob and Genesis had seen Billie like this once before when his wife died. They knew better than to try to comfort him. Without uttering a word, the two jogged off, climbed into the cruiser and hit the highway. Billie approached a nearby patrolman.

"May I use your radio to patch a call through to Miami General?" Billie asked.

"Sure," the patrolman said. "Use that car over there." Billie walked to the car the officer had pointed to and slumped into the seat. He picked up the radio and depressed the send/receive button.

"Yes, I need you to patch a call through to Miami General," Billie said. "It's an emergency. I need to speak with Dr. Arthur Bell."

"Roger," a voice replied. Within a minute, Dr. Bell was on the line.

"Dr. Bell, this is Billie Panther," he said. "The chemicals found in the water were benzene and tri-chloro ethane, commonly referred to in the environmental field as TCE."

"Very good," Dr. Bell said. "That will speed up the treatment. By the way, the children haven't gotten better, but they haven't gotten worse either. This information will help us a great deal."

"Will they recover?" Billie asked.

"Health is not a science," Dr. Bell replied. "But this information will give them a good chance. Thanks for your effort. I'll begin treatment based on what you've told me."

"Sure thing doc," Billie replied. "Keep me posted."

Billie sat back in the seat, watching the firemen as they got the blaze under control. He wanted to go to sleep, but there was too much to do. Jacob and Genesis would tell him if there was any activity at the landfill site. Until then, he needed to try to find out how the chemicals got into the water. The process of deduction and reasoning screamed at him to find out which samples had been infected. Was it the well samples, the community water supply, or the canal where the kids got sick? If it were the wells, he knew the source. If it were the other samples, well, there was a lot of work to do.

The day had been most unpleasant. Now, Billie was without a car. Thinking about his night of passion with Monique, he became aroused. Almost as quickly, he felt guilty for what had happened. Not wanting it to happen again, he called the only person he knew who could pick him up and take him where he needed to go. Hopefully, he wouldn't regret it. "I better think about his," he thought earnestly to himself. "It could make a bad day worse." He decided to think on it a few minutes as he walked to a nearby convenience store and gas station. Billie walked casually into the store and purchased a Pepsi, then strolled to a nearby bus stop and sat on the bench.

Billie thought deeply about how Christina had treated him the last few times they had met. She had been cold, almost mean. But Billie knew some of it was due to his spending so much time in the company of Monique. On the other hand,

Monique had built him up, made him feel good about himself. Totally the opposite of what Christina had done. However, if the contaminants were because of the landfill, it would have to be due to illegal dumping. If that were the case, did Monique know about it? Billie got that sinking feeling again. Was he being used?

Deep in thought, the bus startled him when it pulled to the curb. The happy chattering of a small boy drew his attention as the boy and his parents disembarked.

"That was great dad," the boy said. "Can we go see the Marlins play again next week? Please."

"If you're nice and do all your chores," the mother said. "We'll go again."

While they walked away, buried memories came flooding back. Billie could see the happy smiling face of his wife, her witty way and good looks. Like a thunderclap, it struck Billie how much she and Christina had in common. Billie did love Christina. He always had. His mother was right, anytime he could talk to her was the right time. Without hesitation, he walked to the pay phone on the convenience store wall and dialed her number. He crossed his fingers as the phone rang.

"Hello," answered Christina's pleasant voice on the other end.

"Hi, how are you?" Billie asked.

"I'm fine," Christina replied. "I was just thinking about you. Heard you were at the hospital today, guess I missed you."

"Yeah," Billie said. "We had to leave for the lab, pick up the results of the samples we took last night." Billie paused.

"And?" Christina queried.

"The lab was destroyed," Billie said. "Sarah was killed." Billie related all that had transpired the previous night and during the long day. Christina realized that Billie was in need of a friend.

"That's terrible," Christina said. "How can I help?"

"As a matter of fact, I'm sort of stranded at the moment," Billie said. "I don't have a car and wondered if you could pick me up?"

"Just tell me where," Christina said.

Billie relayed the necessary information.

"I'll be right there."

The convenience store was only a few minutes away. On the way over, Christina made a firm resolve to think before she spoke. Billie was a good man, and she hadn't treated him very well lately. He was calling her in a time of great need. That meant something. "I'll let him talk to me, get things off his chest," she thought. "I'm just a listener and friend tonight. No matter what he says, I'll hold my sharp tongue and be patient." Christina saw him seated on the bus stop bench with two Pepsi's in his hand. She was excited to see him and it showed. It would be the first time they had been together for over three weeks, a short date with drinks. Even in his time of need, he was thinking of others. Pulling to the curb, Billie hurried in and they were off. He could tell she was excited. It boosted his spirits immediately and without thinking, he leaned over and kissed her softly on the cheek.

"You should do that more often," Christina whispered softly.

"I know," Billie said. "I really would like to. This may not be a good time, but I'd like to talk to you."

"It's the perfect time," Christina said as she looked for a place to pull over. Coming up on her right was a lighted ball field. A city league softball game was in progress. Christina pulled into the parking lot and found a space. There were a hundred or so people attending the game, but there was more than ample seating. Billie escorted her to the far end of the seating area near a couple of palm trees. Sitting down next to each other, Christina was excited, turned on just to be near him. They watched the game for a few seconds. She knew he would speak when he was ready.

"Oh!" Billie said. "Almost forgot. Would you like a Pepsi?"

"You betcha," Christina said happily. As she unscrewed the cap, Billie rubbed her softly on the back for an instant and then leaned back against the tree.

"It's been a rough day hasn't it?" Christina asked.

"Yes," Billie replied slowly. "First the kids got sick, we spent all night sampling, most of the day at the hospital, then my best friend from college, Sarah, was killed. It seems like everyone that is close to me has been injured. If it's not someone else doing it, it's me. Hell, I can barely keep my eyes open."

"It's not your fault Billie," Christina said, her eyes glazing with tears as she saw the man she loved in such agony and despair. "We can't control everything in life. When it comes right down to it, there's very little we can control in our high-tech society."

"I know," Billie responded. "It's just that I would like some control or at least the opportunity to try. Anyway, that's why I wanted to talk to you. You've been very patient with me and I appreciate that. I don't know if I could have been as patient with you or anyone else for that matter. I feel if I don't get it out of my system, I'm going to bust."

"What do you need to get out of your system?" Christina asked, not sure what Billie was getting at.

"I've been thinking a great deal about our relationship," Billie added. "I don't know what you think about it right now or how you think is should go. Well, damn it. I don't know how to say it; I'm too tired to think."

"Don't think Billie, just say it," Christina replied softly. "I'll understand."

"I love you," Billie blurted out. "There, I said it, not as hard as I thought. I love you Christina. I always have."

Christina looked at Billie, staring deeply into his blood shot eyes. She knew he was telling the truth. Like him, she had felt the same way for so long. Joy flooded over her. For the first time in her life, she was speechless.

"To be fair though, there's something else I need to tell you," Billie began. "It's about Monique. I tried to fight it, I just..."

She put her finger over his mouth, not wanting to hear.

"I know," Christina said. "Women seem to have a knack for such things. We won't speak of it again."

Christina jumped over and pushed Billie to the ground. Climbing on top of him, she kissed him passionately. She was not about to let the ecstasy of the moment be clouded by the memory of either a dead or living woman. Billie responded in turn. They rolled back and forth on the grass like two school children.

Christina sat up for a moment to catch her breath. She was so aroused she wanted to strip Billie's clothes off right then and there. Watching the game briefly, tears streaming down her cheeks, she was elated, filled with an unspeakable joy.

"We have a great life ahead of us Billie," Christina said. "We can control what we want to do. What about..." Turning her head over her shoulder, she discovered Billie was asleep. Being up for almost two days had taken its toll. Not to be deprived of her happy feelings, she snuggled next to him and laid her head upon his chest. Christina would let him sleep for a couple of hours and then take him home. Whatever happened tomorrow, Christina was determined to make the best of it.

CHAPTER 10

Insects were swarming by the hundreds in the light surrounding the office of the landfill site. Mike and Blayde hurried through the door to make sure the insects stayed outside. Monique and Paul were waiting for them.

"Give me your report," Paul said before they had a chance to sit down.

"There were three people in the lab," Mike said. "They're speaking with Jesus now. I don't think they passed on any information about the samples. The lady at the lab was waiting for Billie to come get it."

"Are you sure they didn't get the information to Billie?" Paul asked.

"Pretty sure," Blayde said. "She definitely indicated she was expecting Billie, and was surprised to see us, real surprised.

She's dead and there's nothing left of the place. No witnesses. No information."

"Good," Paul replied. "I want you to lay low for a while. Hang out in Miami until I call for you. I want you both well away from here in case we have visitors."

"But," Mike began as he was cut off.

"But nothing," Paul exclaimed. "Get out of here now. You can't be seen here tonight."

"I'd rather hang out in Miami than this mosquito infested shit hole any day," Blayde said. "Let's go Mike."

Paul watched the taillights of their car disappear down Snake Road then, turned to Monique.

"This situation may call for more drastic measures than I planned," Paul said. "How is your relationship with Billie?"

"He likes me fine," Monique said. "But he's in love with Christina. I actually had to drug him to have sex with me. It was the only way. He feels bad about it but doesn't know he was duped."

"Can you make it work?" Paul asked, concern in his voice.

"I thought it would," Monique replied. "But, now it's doubtful, especially since his son is sick. He'll be seeing more of Christina than me; just my intuition. God Paul, what did you dump anyway?"

"I didn't dump anything and that's what worries me," Paul replied sharply. "None of this should have happened. So, he cherishes Christina. That may come in handy after all. She trusts me, so it'll give me an edge if we must, shall we say, neutralize them."

"Do you want me to keep after him?" Monique asked.

"Only if you want your three hundred grand," Paul said sarcastically. "I don't care what you do; drug him again if you need to. Just don't let him come up for air. Be his friend. He has a lot on his mind right now."

"Christina will be stiff competition and so will his son," Monique said.

"I'll take care of Christina," Paul said. "I think she's falling for me."

"Don't bet on it," Monique said. "I've seen the way she looks at Billie."

"I have her where I want her," Paul said confidently. "If she doesn't cooperate, well..., but first things first. I must speak to Billie, make up something to calm the troubled waters."

Billie was late to his office, but glad he had taken the opportunity to talk to Christina. She was more understanding than Billie had expected. At least he had told her how he felt. They had agreed to continue discussing their relationship tonight over dinner. Billie was looking forward to the prospect as he picked up the phone and dialed Miami General.

"Yes, may I speak with Dr. Bell please, this is Billie Panther?" Billie asked.

"One moment," a female voice said politely. Billie was becoming preoccupied with his feelings and thoughts of Christina when he was startled out of his daydreaming.

"This is Dr. Bell."

"Did the information I gave you help Doc?" Billie asked.

"Yes," replied the doctor. "There is a slight improvement in the children as we speak."

"That's wonderful news," Billie said. "I'll pass it on to the other parents. How long before we know for sure?"

"We should know in a few more hours," the doctor said. "More blood tests are being run now. That will be a good indicator of how fast they'll recover. Why don't you wait before you tell the other parents? Perhaps we'll have even better news to give them."

"They've been waiting what seems an eternity now doc, but I understand." Billie said. "I want to know the minute anything changes."

Paul had convinced himself that it was impossible for the landfill to have polluted the water. Having studied the geology of the site once more, he was prepared to defend his reasoning to Billie as he reached his office door. Billie was just hanging up the phone as Paul tapped lightly on the door.

"Come in," Billie said.

"I heard you have several sick children," Paul said. "Is there anything I can do?"

"Can you perform a miracle?" Billie asked, frustration in his voice.

"That bad huh?" Paul mused. "What happened?"

"We're still trying to figure it out," Billie said. "The doctor said they likely drank some contaminated water. After what happened last night, I'm inclined to agree."

"You lost me," Paul said, raising his eyebrows. "What are you referring to?"

"We took some water samples to a lab for analysis," Billie replied. "The lab was destroyed, three people killed."

"Was it an accident?" Paul asked.

"Let's be frank," Billie said. "Genesis thinks your thugs did it. I'm not convinced yet, but I have to admit, things do point to the landfill operation."

"Now wait just a minute," Paul said, raising his voice. "I know we're the new guys in town, but you can't accuse us without proof. What evidence do you have? If it is some of my men, I need to know."

"We don't have any solid evidence, just coincidences," Billie stated.

"Such as?" Paul queried.

"A deputy is missing and likely dead." Billie began. "His shirt was found on the edge of a gator hole near the landfill site. It has a puncture hole in it made from a knife. Not long after the landfill became operational, about a dozen kids are suddenly seriously ill. The laboratory we took water samples to has been destroyed, and three people murdered."

"I fail to understand how that implicates us," Paul said, trying to allay Billie's suspicions. "Anyone could have done what you say. This deputy could have skipped on you because he's tired of the place or hates his wife or girlfriend. He could have been killed by the drug smugglers you told us constantly use the deserted roads on the reservation for night runways. As far as the kids are concerned, you have my sympathies for them and their families. But you know as well as I, even if we were dumping illegal chemicals on the site, which we are not, that there is no way any water could have been polluted given the short time we have been in operation. Someone else could have a vendetta against the lab. You know how serious environmental crimes are today."

"What you say is all true," Billie said. "But who would have a vendetta against our children or our small community?"

"It's certainly not us!" Paul exclaimed. "We didn't enter into a partnership to kill your people. You will agree we did it for mutual profit, which I might add has been going well for all of us. So, where's our motive?"

"Right now, Genesis is looking into it," Billie said. "Since it happened on sovereign land, the FBI is also on the case. I should warn you that the landfill site will be closely watched and possibly searched."

"We have a hundred-year lease," Paul said. "The site is essentially ours and unless you have proof, you'll never be allowed to search it. I'm warning you. Don't meddle in my business."

"Your business!" Billie said. "I thought it was our business. I have a dozen sick kids that could die, and you're worried about business. Who the hell do you think you are?"

"Someone you don't want to fuck with," Paul stated, his voice rising.

"We'll see about that," Billie said. "We are our own nation. We have our own law enforcement personnel who conform to what is best for tribal citizens. If Genesis finds proof of any kind, you can expect him and several deputies at your office soon. They will make a thorough search."

"So, it's come to this," Paul said as his eyes narrowed. "I can play rough too, half breed."

Paul turned and stomped out the door in a rage. Recalling the last words he had spoken, Billie was in a rage. Both men had stood toe to toe, literally screaming at each other. Heads were stuck out of several offices up and down the hall as fellow co-workers listened in on the conversation. There was no need to listen hard; the argument had been so loud it was as if the two men had been using bull horns. When Paul stormed out, the heads quickly disappeared into the doorways, like field mice scurrying from a hawk. Several phone calls were being made. Within minutes, almost every member in the community had heard what happened. Nothing spoken aloud could remain secret on Big Cypress for long.

Paul realized that they were in trouble. It didn't take a genius to figure that out. The police on the reservation didn't need much of an excuse to search the facilities, with or without a warrant, and if they did search the landfill, they would certainly find the hidden underground tanks. Further inspection would reveal hazardous, illegal chemicals. It would be in strict violation of federal environmental regulations and would likely result in twenty years in a federal prison. The fact that the landfill was also on an Indian reservation would result in more federal charges. There was no way Paul would spend time in prison. He made a few quick calls then, ran a couple of errands.

Upon arriving at the landfill office, he was relieved to find that Monique, Blayde and Mike were all present, sitting in the cramped office. As if to accentuate the predicament they found themselves in, the air conditioning had gone out, making the office a steam bath. The temperature increased with each passing minute as the relentless rays from the hot afternoon sun beat down. Paul, already irritated, couldn't stand it. The four left the office and sought relief in the shade of the nearest tree.

"We're in trouble," Paul began. "The Indians think we had something to do with the water being poisoned. They are threatening to search the site."

"They won't find anything," Blayde said. "Let them come."

"Oh no," Mike responded. "They won't find anything but the hidden tanks. You want to go to jail for the next twenty years or so? If they find those, it'll be easy enough for them to piece the rest of the puzzle together."

"What are our choices?" Monique asked.

"Slim to none I'm afraid," Paul said. "If we get searched, which is almost a certainty, they'll discover the tanks. Whether we made the children sick or not, we'll be blamed for it. They won't bother to look further since we'll be the proverbial smoking gun. That's just for starters. If they dig around, the lab will be linked to us and likely the deputy's death as well."

"I've been involved in these things before," Mike stated. "We would face charges on environmental counts, reckless endangerment of the public, arson, breaking and entering, murder, and if you're me, you could add resisting arrest."

"You can't be serious," Monique said. "I didn't agree to any of this."

"We all agreed to it when we signed on," Blayde said. "Besides, it doesn't look like we have much of a choice now. If we wait here, they'll be on us by tomorrow. I say we make a run for it."

A quiet hush fell upon them as the four sat around the tree, everyone thinking of an easy out. Being aware of the modern forensic technology that could be directed at them, it was a foregone conclusion that they would eventually be linked to the lab deaths. Because they all knew about it, conspiracy to commit murder would be the highest charge for Monique. The most reasonable thing to do seemed to be to run while they had the chance.

"I gather we're in agreement then," Paul said. "It's not a total loss. We have made over five million during the course of the operation. And, if we can make it back to New York, Don Cilatro will give us protection. The cops would never find us."

"What are we waiting for then?" Mike asked. "Let's get out while we have the chance."

"Some sort of insurance would be nice," Blayde said.

"I have just the thing," Paul said, glancing at his watch. "Let's go pay a visit to our lovely schoolteacher. Her class is about to let out, permanently."

The school parking lot was vacant when the four arrived. All the children had left, but the main door remained open. Paul knew Christina's habits well. She always stayed to close the small school. A hard worker, she believed in what she was doing and spent a great deal of time trying to improve the lives of the children she taught. They looked around before exiting the car. Sure that no one was nearby they casually sauntered into the building. Monique followed the three men as they silently walked from one classroom to the next, seeking their prey. Christina was finally discovered, talking earnestly to Solomon Osceola.

"He ...," Solomon stopped when he saw them. "Well, good afternoon gentlemen. What brings you to our fine school?"

"We're here to take Christina to an appointment," Paul said.

"I don't have an appointment," Christina stammered, surprised by Paul's behavior.

"You do now bitch!" Mike said as he grabbed her arm. Before she could yell out, Monique stuffed a rag in her mouth. Her muffled sounds would not be heard outside the room.

"You're making a big mistake," Solomon said, jumping forward to help Christina. "Billie will hunt you down for this."

"Good," Paul said. "I'm counting on it."

"Back off dick weed," Blayde said, pulling his switch blade. "You're making the big mistake."

Blayde had a smile on his face as he approached Solomon.

"Make it fast Blayde," Paul said. "We'll be in the car."

Blayde's cohorts in crime dragged Christina from the room. A strange silence settled on the scene like a thick fog. Being old, Solomon knew he didn't have much of a chance. He tried to get around his antagonist and out the door in the hopes somebody might hear him yell for help. He wasn't fast enough. Blayde began to slice him. Just a little at first to get his attention. The shining metal blade swished through the air, back and forth, as it cut into the flesh of Solomon's arms, chest, legs, back and head. Blood was flying everywhere as Blayde closed in for the kill. Slicing Solomon several more times, Blayde stabbed him twice in the abdomen.

Solomon dropped to his knees then, fell onto his side in a pool of blood. Blayde stood over him, like a vulture. He was admiring his handiwork.

"It's been a pleasure," Blayde said. "And, you know what they say, the only good Injun' is a dead one."

Blayde spun on his heels and hurried to the car. Pausing at the main entrance and glancing furtively about, he climbed into the back seat. Mike eased the car out of the lot and onto the highway heading back toward the office to make final plans.

Genesis had been watching the landfill site for several hours as he sweated it out in his cruiser. Glancing at his watch, he realized it was going to be a long day. The crackling of the radio jolted him out of his seat, nearly scaring him to death as he began to doze off, the heat of the afternoon sucking the oxygen out of his blood.

"Genesis, this is dispatch. We have an emergency at the school. A stabbing has occurred."

"I'm on my way," Genesis said, cranking the engine and speeding off. His lights and sirens going, the cruiser was literally flying down Snake Road at over ninety miles per hour. The speedometer was buried as Genesis held the pedal to the metal. Upon entering the community, he slowed the car to about fifty, his destination in sight.

Two police cruisers and an ambulance were already on scene as Genesis skidded his cruiser to a stop in a cloud of dust in the limestone parking lot. A crowd of onlookers were beginning to gather. Genesis rushed past them and inside to find Billie, Jacob, several deputies, and a couple of paramedics. The scene was gruesome. It was as if some children had gone wild with a can of red spray paint. Genesis hadn't smelled blood like this since Afghanistan. He almost threw up when the pungent aroma hit him, like a fast jab to the gut. He slowed to a walk as he approached the paramedics.

"What the hell happened?" Genesis asked.

"It's Solomon," Jacob said. "He's still alive, barely."

Solomon was whispering.

"I tried to stop them. Billie, they took Christina."

"Who?" Billie frantically asked, who had just hurried in. "Who took her?"

"Lori.." Solomon gasped as he passed out.

"That bastard!" Billie screamed in anguish.

The paramedics pushed everyone out of the way as they loaded Solomon onto a stretcher, an IV in his arm. They were followed outside by Billie, Jacob and Genesis who watched silently, helplessly as the stretcher was loaded into the ambulance. The driver rushed to the cab, jumped inside and spun off in a critical race against time. The time it takes for a man's life blood to ooze out of his body. The sirens screeched against the windless calm as the flashing lights penetrated the now dark, evening sky. The Flight for Life helicopter was just landing as they pulled up and unloaded Solomon.

There was a look of grave consternation on Jacobs face. "Billie, we've had enough of this. What are you going to do?"

"I told Lorio that Genesis might be out to search his place soon," Billie replied. "It's my fault this happened. I made a mistake, now it's time to correct it."

"Not you Billie, all of us," Genesis chimed in. "We all wanted the jobs, just as much as you. The opportunity presented itself and we all pounced on it, like a cat playing with a mouse. No one knew something like this would happen."

"Then, we know what has to be done," Jacob said. The three men nodded in agreement. In unison, they walked to their vehicles and raced to police headquarters.

Genesis nodded to the officer on duty as the trio walked into his office. He closed the door behind them and locked it. "Help me with this," Genesis said.

Billie and Jacob helped him push several file cabinets out of the way and remove a four by eight-foot painting of the Florida Everglades from the wall in front of them. A hidden door was revealed. Genesis removed a key from his pocket, inserted it into the lock and turned. An overpowering odor of staleness exuded from the small, concealed, dark room.

Just inside the doorway, Genesis pulled a light chain illuminating the contents of his secret hiding place. The room was filled will all kinds of Afghanistan military weapons; M-4's, grenades, M-79 grenade launchers, M-60 machine guns, pistols, knives of all kinds, several sniper rifles, flares, clothing, a couple of mortars, and boxes of ammo stacked from floor to ceiling.

"Holy hell!" Jacob exclaimed. "You brought the whole damned war home with you."

"I hoped we would never need to use this kind of equipment again," Billie said. "I stopped hunting a long time ago."

"We all did after Afghanistan, Billie," Jacob whispered in the stillness. "It just wasn't the same when the quarry quit shooting back."

"You both knew the time might come again given the attitude of others towards the Indian," Genesis said. "I'd hate to be unprepared."

"That's an understatement," Billie said. "But we can't just go gun them down."

"You're right," Genesis said. "We will do it legally. Raise your right hands. Do you solemnly swear to uphold the laws and the constitution of the Seminole Tribe of Florida, to act in a professional and ethical manner, to use only the force necessary when dealing with a fugitive?"

"I do," Billie and Jacob said in unison.

"You're now official deputies of the Seminole Tribe of Florida Police Department," Genesis stated. "Act accordingly."

The three men began strapping on equipment. Genesis selected a .45 caliber pistol and web belt. He fondled the pistol as though it was a long-lost friend, or perhaps it was remembrance of war days in Afghanistan when he had to take the life of the enemy to save his own and those of his squad. His feelings had deep root from serving dual duty as a member of a LRRP unit and special ops group. After checking the magazine, action, and barrel, Genesis placed the pistol in the holster now buckled on his hip. Sorting through the myriad knives on the wall, he selected a long-bladed combat knife along with a flashlight.

The first items selected by Billie and Jacob were camouflage shirts and pants. Billie also selected a .45 pistol, knife and an M-4 carbine with an M203 grenade launcher attached beneath. It had been his guardian angel in Afghanistan, keeping insurgents from overrunning his position. After checking his pistol, he hoisted a bandoleer of ammo onto his shoulder for the grenade launcher. Jacob's choice of weapons was simple, a .45 caliber pistol and an M-4. Except for the modern weapons they were carrying, the group had they resembled bandits from the old west; a motley looking crew.

"Well," Genesis said, "Looks like we're ready."

"Let's go then," Billie snapped.

"That wouldn't be too prudent," Genesis said. "We need some backup. They have twenty to thirty men there. Given our suspicions, I'm guessing they're all well-armed. There is not much we can do in the dark. We'll need to wait for first light."

"But, Christina," Billie started.

"Genesis is right Billie," Jacob said. "If we go in the dark, Christina will be in jeopardy. You don't want to risk that do you?"

"No," Billie replied glumly. "What can we do?"

"I'll start calling law enforcement in the surrounding area," Genesis said. "I'm certain help will be here before they can move on us."

Christina sat in the corner of the office, thrown on the floor like a basket of dirty laundry. She had silver duct tape around her mouth to keep her quiet. Her hands had been tied behind her, along with her feet; she felt utterly alone and helpless. She could not recall ever having been in such a state. Scared as she was, a feeling of rage began to wash over her. Somehow, she knew Billie and others would be coming after her. Hopefully, they wouldn't arrive too late. She sat patiently as her kidnappers made plans for their escape.

Realizing events were moving too fast and perhaps beyond his control, Paul had to make quick decisions about the best way out of his predicament.

"My guess is they've just discovered Solomon," Paul said. "Likely, they won't show up until later tonight and then try to force their way onto the site at dawn. They'll need to wait because they will need back up."

"That gives us a few hours," Mike said. "We can prepare for them by then."

"Except we won't be here," Paul said with authority. "How many men do we have?"

"Thirty-two," Blayde answered. "Why?"

"You and Mike tell them to get ready," Paul explained. "They'll defend the facility while we make our escape."

"Are you sure that's wise?" Mike asked.

"That's what I pay them for," Paul said. "If we stay here, we'll be pinned down, wind up in jail. Yes, it's the right thing to do. Now go."

Paul watched for a few minutes through the office window as Mike and Blayde rounded up the men. Many carried automatic weapons. The rest walked to a nearby storage shed and began retrieving pistols, rifles, heavy barreled machine guns, and a couple of mortars. Paul picked up the telephone, looking smugly at Christina in the process.

"How are you doing babe?" Paul asked smiling. "I have something for you when this is over. We'll finish what we started a few nights ago."

Christina eyed him angrily as he dialed.

"Yes," Paul said. "This is Lorio. I want you and your chopper at Shark Key tomorrow. Do you remember that hammock we scouted out earlier? Good. Be there at noon. Don't be late."

"You don't think you'll get away with this do you?" Monique asked.

"Most certainly," Paul replied. "I have what he wants most. He won't try to take her in the dark for fear of risking her life. So, we'll lay low near Shark Key for a day then disappear. When they don't find us here tomorrow, they'll think we made a clean getaway. Sure, they'll put up a few roadblocks for a while. Without early success and other pressing priorities, the state police and other cops will stop looking for us."

"What about her?" Monique asked, nodding her head in Christina's direction.

"Once she's served her purpose, she'll be taken care of," Paul said. "Perhaps I'll send her to my hacienda in Mexico and retain her there as my personal slave."

"Just so you don't kill her," Monique said. "I won't be a party to murder. I did what I was supposed to do, so give me my money and I'll be out of here."

"You're already implicated," Paul said. "You are up to your ass in it and I'm not giving you one damn dime until we're out of this mess."

"Fuck you Paul," Monique screamed. "I'm leaving."

As Monique tried to get past Paul, he slapped her viciously across the face, knocking her against the wall. She slumped to the floor onto her backside and began sobbing. Christina had been listening with great interest. It was now clear to her what Monique's purpose had been. She wasn't an associate; she was a paid prostitute to occupy Billie's time and affections. No wonder Billie hated most whites. If she did get out of this, she wasn't about to tell Billie he had been played for a sucker from the beginning. Although Christina had no love loss for Monique, she felt she was deserving of what she had just received, but also felt pity for her. A woman who could have any decent man she wanted if she would simply clean up her act, Monique had wasted her life with scum.

"Try that shit again," Paul stated ominously, "and Blayde will carve you like an Easter ham."

Mike and Blayde stepped inside the door just as Monique slammed against the wall. They were curious about what was going on but thought it best not to ask.

"It's all set," Mike said. "The men are ready."

"Good," Paul said. "Pick up those two and let's get out of here."

Exiting the office, Paul could see that preparations were going well. Several heavy machine guns had been set up inside groups of fifty-five-gallon drums along with two mortars. The men were in the process of shoving fill dirt against the outside of the drums to increase resistance against incoming rounds. Paul smiled in satisfaction at the scene before him. When the cops did come, they would be greatly surprised; they would be met by a bristling band of men armed to the teeth. Since most of them had prison records, they would not give up without a fight. Harm would come to many this day. Taking one last look around, Paul climbed into the car. Mike gunned the engine and sped off into the early morning darkness.

The orange glow of the sun was just cresting the eastern sky across the vast flatness of the sawgrass swamp when Paul and company arrived at the airboat docks. Mike parked the car in an inconspicuous part of the lot next to several others whose occupants were likely out fishing or frog gigging. Blayde opened the trunk and pulled out two long canvas bags. From their weight and shape, it was obvious they were filled with weapons of all kinds. Blayde hoisted the bags to his shoulders while Paul and Mike pushed Christina and Monique ahead of them.

Selecting two airboats, Mike and Blayde checked for keys in the switch, finding none, they hotwired the boats. Paul climbed into the driver's seat of one while Mike forced Christina and Monique to sit in the hollowed bow. He then ran to the other boat and climbed into the driver's seat. Blayde jumped from the dock into the front. Mike was beginning to gun the motor when Blayde signaled for him to wait. He jumped out and went from boat to boat pulling the wires off the magnetos and throwing them into the water. Unless inspected closely, no one would know anything had been done.

Almost before Blayde had planted himself into his seat, Mike and Paul gunned the airboats forward. Within seconds they had picked up speed and were gliding effortlessly across the mirrored surface. Paul breathed a little easier when the airboats crossed the boundary from open water to sawgrass. They were now in their own world, invisible to those who may pass on the highway, entering a haven of rest until the chopper could pick them up at noon.

Like most city dwellers, Paul's group was inexperienced with life in the swamp. What would normally be easily noticed in their city life went unobserved in the unfamiliar surroundings of the swamp. And so, it was that they passed the dugout canoe emerging into the open water in the early light of dawn. Had they noticed the canoe, it's unlikely they wouldn't have given the occupants a second thought; an old Indian with white hair and an unblinking, stone face with a youthful, muscular companion who silently watched the two airboats.

CHAPTER 11

Genesis, Billie, Jacob, along with three additional tribal deputies were gathered together outside the gates of the landfill. A large chain with a massive lock indicated visitors were not welcome. Genesis had a pair of binoculars pressed to his eyes. Taking them down, he let out a long sigh.

"This isn't going to be easy," Genesis said. "There's at least thirty of them. We'll wait a while longer. I have sheriff's deputies coming from Hendry, Broward, and Dade counties. They should be here any minute. I've also notified the FBI."

"We'll just hang loose until they get here then," Jacob responded as he lit a cigarette.

The other deputies had also taken binoculars and held a constant vigil on the site. Billie, unfamiliar with police tactics, sat on the ground, chewing a piece of Bahia grass. He couldn't get out of his mind how Christina had responded to him during their conversation. Even though she knew about him and Monique, she was willing to work things out. The thought of it made him feel even guiltier for what had happened. The anguish was overwhelming. First, James being in the hospital with a toxic chemical flowing through his veins, eating his body's cells, and now Christina kidnapped by these thugs.

Initially, the landfill had been worth the work and effort involved in getting it here. The tribe was already turning a profit and the self-esteem of those on Big Cypress who had been able to secure jobs at the site was soaring. That alone had lifted Billie's spirits and dispelled his fears, but now he wondered if the price that had been paid was worth it. Had his partners been honorable, it was, but now it looked doubtful. On the bright side, considering their actions, the landfill would become the sole property of the Seminole Tribe of Florida, but at an exorbitantly high price. No project was worth the lives or health of his people. Thinking about it was driving Billie crazy. He had to do something. At that moment, several sheriffs' cars rolled to a stop near the gate.

Police cruisers began rolling in one by one during the next few minutes until there were a dozen of them, each with two or more deputies. A black Chevy Suburban with government plates pulled up. Four men in casual clothes stepped out. It was the FBI. One of them walked to the gate where Genesis stood by himself. Genesis lowered the binoculars.

"Are you constable Motlow?" the man asked.

"Yes," Genesis replied.

"Good to meet you," the man said. "I'm agent Flynn with the FBI. We're here to help. Since we're on reservation land, you call the shots. What do you want us to do?"

"Get your men ready," Genesis said, "Looks like everyone is here, so we'll be moving in a few minutes. I have to tell you though, the men in the compound appear to be well armed.

You better have your men put on flak jackets and all the ammo you can carry."

"Roger that," agent Flynn said as he turned and began shouting orders at his men.

Each deputy began making last minute preparations to assault the compound. Many of them, including the FBI agents wore bullet proof vests. Donning their vests and flak jackets, the officers put on light jackets over the top. On the back in large letters were FBI, Sheriff, or Police depending on what agency they belonged to. All of them secretly hoped this would prevent them from being shot from behind once bullets began ripping through the air. Taking a last-minute look through his binoculars, Genesis reappraised his plans for the assault. He saw several of the thugs looking back through their own binoculars. They were waiting.

"Okay," Genesis said. "Gather round and let's go over our plans." He began counting them off; there were twenty-three law officers. "They know we're here and they're well-armed. I would like to make a three-pronged approach like this." Genesis laid a large piece of paper on the hood of the FBI vehicle as everyone gathered around him. He drew a small map of the landfill site.

"We can only approach them from the front and these two sides," Genesis began, pointing at the map. "The back of the landfill has a large canal and swamp behind it. One third of our group will be on the east, one third on the west, and the remaining third will make a frontal assault from the south. They have what appear to be heavy machine guns, here, here, and here, so watch yourselves. Once we bust through the gate, fan out to your respective positions and don't take any chances. If necessary, we have more backup on the way, but we cannot wait. Does anyone have anything else to add?"

"Be careful with the office," Billie said. "There's a kidnapped woman in there."

"Alright," Genesis said. "I'll try to talk the men inside the office out first, but I doubt we'll have any success." Genesis picked up a bullhorn from the back of his seat and walked to the gate.

"You in the landfill, this is the police," Genesis said. "You are surrounded. Lay down your guns, put your hands in the air, and come out. Let's be peaceful about this."

The reply was swift. Several bullets ricocheted off the posts and gate. Genesis and the rest of the deputies scurried for cover. Genesis scrambled back to his 4x4 and stood up.

"We have our answer," Genesis said. "Let's go."

Everyone nodded as they climbed into their vehicles. Jacob and Billie hopped in with Genesis. Genesis waited a few seconds until he was sure all motors were running. He stomped the gas pedal to the floor. The vehicle spun forward and crashed through the gate. The police cars behind him sped through one by one then, began making a circle around the site, like an old west wagon train trying to protect itself from attacking Indians. Every car had lights flashing and sirens wailing. No sooner had they started through the gate than mortar rounds began falling around them, ripping craters in the ground. Shrapnel whizzed through the air like bullets.

"Damn!" Billie yelled. "They've got mortars."

Billie jumped out the back door of the cruiser with his M203 grenade launcher and began firing. Several shells exploded around him as he hit the dirt. Several police cars had already been hit by the mortar rounds. Billie couldn't tell if the deputies had made it out or not. Two thugs began firing automatic weapons at him as he scrambled, zigzag fashion, to the nearest cover, a couple of empty drums. Firing his grenade launcher methodically, he was able to knock out the two mortars the thugs had, but machine gun fire was heavy. Billie jumped up to join several nearby deputies and was immediately struck in the upper arm. The flash of pain caused Billie to drop his grenade launcher as he continued running.

The thugs were now caught in a crossfire. Billie pulled out his .45 pistol and began firing, emptying one magazine after another. He and two deputies began working their way around the east side of the site. Thugs were dropping like flies. A butane tank outside the office was hit with multiple rounds and exploded into a fireball, taking the office with it.

"My God!" Billie exclaimed. He began running for the office, firing as he went. Seeing him, deputies from all sides followed his lead and a few seconds later the fighting had stopped. Several officers reached the exploded office before Billie and began searching the debris.

"There's nothing here," a deputy yelled to Billie. "It must have been empty."

The officers had rounded up all the remaining thugs. Genesis and FBI agent Flynn began questioning them as the remaining officers searched the entire area. No one else was found. Jacob plundered through the debris and the rest of the site. Satisfied that he had done all he could, he joined Billie.

"Looks like Paul and his accomplices have made a clean getaway," Billie said.

"Not if I can help it," Jacob responded as Genesis approached them.

"None of these bastard's know anything," Genesis said in exasperation. "I've instructed the sheriff's officers to put an all-points bulletin out on Lorio and his gang. We'll keep our fingers crossed. If they didn't make it out last night, our roadblocks will pick them up."

"We can't afford to wait," Billie said. "We've got to find them now."

"I know how you feel Billie," Genesis said. "We'll find them somehow."

The three stood watching as Lorio's men were placed in cruisers and taken away. Suddenly, Billie noticed a couple of odd-looking pipes protruding from the ground a few yards away.

"What's that?" Billie asked as he took off in a jog and got down on his hands and knees around the pipes. Genesis and Jacob, startled, pulled their guns, before they realized what was happening; reholstering them, they jogged after Billie.

"This isn't a normal part of a landfill site," Billie said as they approached. "Smells like toxic chemicals."

"What do you make of it?" Jacob asked.

"Looks like it may be a dumping place for trucks," Billie said. "I would suspect these pipes are attached to some underground tanks, probably with a few holes in them to let the chemical leach slowly into the soil. What a bunch of worthless bums. A money-making scheme on the side — an extremely dangerous but lucrative one."

"They'll pay for it Billie," Jacob said.

At that moment, the radio on Genesis's shoulder crackled to life.

"Constable Motlow," this is dispatch, "do you copy?"

"Roger," Genesis responded.

"There's been some vandalism at the boat docks near Shark Key," the dispatcher said. "The owner's screaming bloody murder. They need someone out there right away."

"We're sort of busy right now," Genesis said. "Unless it's an emergency, have one of the other deputies assigned."

"Well, I guess not," the dispatcher said. "Someone just ripped the wires from all the airboats and two more are missing. I'll call deputy Johns to look into it."

"That has to be them," Billie said. "Two boats missing, the others vandalized."

"Dispatch," this is Genesis, "we'll take care of that. Tell them I'll be there directly."

"Roger, Constable Motlow," the dispatcher said. "I'll let them know you're coming."

The three men jumped into a police cruiser. Genesis realized they would have to move quickly to apprehend the fugitives. He made several calls notifying other law enforcement agencies and had them on standby alert depending on what he found at the boat docks. An entire search team would be available within an hour if necessary. The FBI agents were right behind Genesis as they cruised down the highway, lights flashing.

The two airboats Paul and Mike were driving, slid to a stop, engines idling. They were about eight miles from the boat docks and hadn't seen anything all morning except miles of sawgrass and an occasional hammock. Paul was fairly certain they had made an undetected escape but decided nothing should be left to chance.

"Mike, I want you and Blayde to cover our backside for three hours," Paul yelled over the noise of the engines. "If no one shows by then, meet us at the hammock I discussed with you. You know what to do if you run into trouble."

Paul sped off. Glancing behind, he saw Mike and Blayde conceal their airboat in a group of gumbo limbo trees next to a very small hammock.

A smile was on Paul's face as he sped across the sawgrass. On the distant horizon, he could see the silhouette of the larger hammock that was his destination. It would be a welcome refuge until noon. The chopper would arrive, and they would be free. It was about two miles away. In front of him sat

Monique and Christina. Monique hadn't said a word since he slapped her at the office. She may want to go he thought, but she's stuck here like the rest of us. When push came to shove, she would do what she had to do because the money was more important to her than anything else. Christina, however, would be a problem. Although Paul was somewhat attached to her, he knew she could be his downfall. Now that he had kidnapped her, he knew they could not have a future relationship. "Too bad", he thought, "she would have made a great wife and lover." In that instant he made up his mind. If Billie made it this far, she would be bait in a trap. When all was done Blayde would have his turn, doing what he did best.

The airboat approached the hammock swiftly. About fifty feet from shore, Paul cut the motor. The boat glided like a pelican until it rammed to a sudden halt on the waterlogged soil. Without muttering a word, Paul jumped from the driver's seat, grabbed Christina by the arm and led her into the undergrowth. Not far away, he found a small clearing. Surrounded by thick water oak and palmetto, it had a large log in the middle. Paul tied Christina to the log and began searching the area. Having spent some time in the jungles of Columbia with several of his cocaine buddies, he was not a novice in the woods. He may not see everything, but he was adept as a woodsman. He always thought it was amazing how people made such snap judgments about city people. It would give him an advantage here. If Billie showed up, he would be surprised to find a woods savvy Lorio.

After a few minutes, he returned briefly to check on Monique and Christina.
"If Billie comes, we'll be ready," Paul stated.
"I don't want to be a part of this," Monique said. "I won't be a party to murder."

"It's too late to get out," Paul said. "We have no choice now. It's prison or escape."

Monique stomped off, contemplating what Paul had said. Paul scoffed at her, checked Christina's bonds and walked off in the opposite direction.

Monique wondered how she had gotten mixed up in this. It was one thing to be a pawn for Paul, selling her body to the highest bidder so she could become wealthy and they could have their control. She had liked Paul from the start but knew he would never marry her. All she wanted was a family, but the possibility of forever remaining poor overrode the desire. She wanted to do it on her own terms and Billie was the only client she had ever felt close to. She was determined if she made it out of this, her days with Paul and her current lifestyle were over. Monique had stashed a couple of million dollars during the past six years. The money would help her disappear and start afresh, a new life. Nothing would stop her from it now, not even Paul. And, even if she ended up in the jail, the money would be waiting for her when she got out.

Mike and Blayde sat lazily on the airboat, watching egrets and other birds as they flew by. In their position, they were used to this kind of boredom. Gazing toward the horizon in all directions, listening, they patiently waited.

"Think we'll make it out of this?" Mike asked.

"Yeah, don't you worry about a thing," Blayde said. "We can handle anything they throw at us."

"Don't be so cocky," Mike responded. "What if they come in with a helicopter or two?"

"Then, I have these," Blayde said as he uncovered an M-60 machine gun and several LAW's (light antitank weapons) capable of launching their two-foot rockets for several hundred yards.

"Has anyone ever told you you're a damn lunatic?" Mike asked, whistling.

"Yeah," Blayde replied. "But, when trouble comes, they always call."

"What do you think Paul has in mind for the Indian woman?" Mike asked.

"He'll use her to get what he wants then he'll kill her," Blayde said. "Keeping her would just be trouble unless he sent her to his hacienda in Mexico. He's got several women there now, slaves really. They can't escape. He makes them perform certain favors for his clients if you get my drift. If I were this Indian woman, I'd rather die here."

"You know Paul won't do it," Mike said. "It's easy for him to kill a man, but he'll never kill a woman."

"That's what I get paid for," Blayde said. "I believe in equal opportunity. Race or gender, it makes no difference."

"You're sick," Mike said.

"Maybe so," Blayde said. "But I'm happy with my work. I love it. Not many people can say that."

"Yeah, but most people aren't psychopathic killers," Mike said.

Genesis had been at the airboat docks for about ninety minutes. Having investigated the complaint of the owner, he and special agent Flynn had concluded that the vandalism done to the motors was not the act of a kid out for a night of pranks. As a result, he had called in the Calvary. A large contingency of law enforcement officers from surrounding counties had gathered to search the area for the fugitives at large. Airboats were being brought in for the search. Three FBI helicopters had landed and stood ready in the parking lot.

To the inexperienced, the scene appeared to be one of mass confusion, but everything was being done according to standard operating procedures. Each deputy had specific assignments. Communications, maps, and a makeshift command tent with open walls had already been set up. Several deputies were seated behind a long table manning radios and coordinating personnel. What appeared to be mass confusion quickly transformed into a perfect picture of order and professionalism.

"How long before we begin the search?" Billie asked.

"As soon as we repair some of the airboats that were vandalized and get some others here from Hollywood," Jacob said. "They left about forty-five minutes ago, so they should be here in the next ten to fifteen minutes."

"Good," Billie said. "Get Genesis to call everyone together and brief them."

Jacob walked over to Genesis who was speaking with agent Flynn. The two were just finishing their conversation.

"Billie wants you to brief the men as soon as possible," Jacob said. "He's anxious about Christina."

"I know," Genesis said. "Agent Flynn and I were just discussing some of the major points about the briefing. Genesis motioned to the command center. "Shall we?"

The two walked to the command tent where Billie was impatiently waiting.

"May I have everyone's attention?" Genesis spoke into a bullhorn. All the officers ceased what they were doing and gathered around the tent.

"Alright," Genesis began, lowering the bullhorn. "Agent Flynn with the FBI will help organize you into six teams. If you'll look at our topographic map, you'll see it's marked into six quadrants. According to your team number, you'll search each respective quadrant thoroughly. We'll maintain constant communication. The helicopters will search in a grid formation beginning in quadrant three, here, pointing to a specific location on the map. This will put them midway between all search areas. If they're needed for backup, they'll be only a couple of minutes away. Are there any questions?"

"Are we going to have to search every hammock on foot?" a deputy asked.

"Yes," Genesis replied. "But some are so small you can skirt the edge with your boat and see what's inside. However, if the perpetrators are holed up in one, it is likely an airboat will be hidden nearby. Look for tell-tale signs of undergrowth damage or any place they might hide the boat. Are there any other questions? Okay. If you run into heavy opposition, call in the choppers. The rest of us will swarm to you like bees on honey. Good luck."

"Wait," Billie shouted. "They have a female Indian hostage, so watch your field of fire. We don't want any innocent people hurt."

"Good point," Genesis commented. "These guys are dangerous and it's likely if we corner them, the hostage will be used as leverage. Since we have two hostage negotiators with us, don't make a move until they can respond. That's it then; take care out there."

The briefing over, all officers began making last minute preparations. Going over instructions with their commanders and double checking their weapons. Meanwhile, the remaining airboats had arrived and were hastily backed down the boat ramps and pushed off trailers into the water.

"We're ready," Jacob shouted into a bullhorn. "Man your boats."

The officers began hopping into various airboats. Billie and Jacob manned one airboat, Genesis and a deputy another. There was a crescendo of noise as the boats and helicopters started their engines. Within a few seconds, an armada of armed men was slipping through the sawgrass, the boat docks quickly disappearing behind them.

Monique removed Christina's gag, ripping the tape quickly from her face.

"Ouch," Christina blurted.

"Well, honey," Paul said. "Looks like Billie isn't going to make it. We'll lay low for another hour and then the chopper will be here to pick us up. If all goes well, we'll be in New York tonight. Fools! They thought they could beat me."

"You can't escape," Christina said. "Billie will come for me; he'll kill you."

"Ha!" Paul said, unable to contain himself. "I forgot. He's so loyal to you that he slept with Monique. Do you really think he'll be thrilled to see you or risk his life on your behalf? He's got too many other things to worry about, like his son in the hospital."

He may not do it for me, but he will do it for his son and his people," Christina said as she fought to hold back tears. "His revenge will be sweet."

"No..," Paul began as Monique cut him off.

"Shut up Paul," Monique said. "Just so you know Christina, I had to drug him into bed. It wasn't personal, just money. He never had a clue."

"So what, it's all irrelevant now," Paul said.

"You're a snake," Christina said. "I hope I can watch him kill you."

"If he comes, the trap will close and you will watch each other die," Paul stated flatly.

"You're always so cock sure of yourself," Monique said. "I hope I'm around the day you lose so I can laugh my ass off."

"I never lose!" Paul exclaimed.

Out on the sawgrass plain, the search was in full swing. Billie and Genesis's airboats were approaching the ambush set up by Mike and Blayde. As they neared, Mike and Blayde heard them and started their own boat, lying in wait like an alligator for its hapless victim. About a half mile away, Billie and Jacob cut away from Genesis to search a separate area within the quadrant. Genesis continued directly toward the ambush, a helicopter approaching his boat from the rear.

"Someone's coming," Mike said. "Sounds like a couple of them. Look, they have a chopper with them."

"Not for long," Blayde said as he pulled a LAW from his canvas bag. The helicopter was only a hundred yards away when Blayde aimed and fired. The chopper exploded into a fireball in midair as the mini rocket hit. When it exploded, it was directly above Genesis. His boat barely escaped as the chopper fell into the water like a wounded duck directly behind him. Genesis turned his head to look back.

"Damn!" Genesis exclaimed.

As he turned forward, Mike and Blayde had pulled their boat out of hiding. Genesis didn't have a chance to react before his boat crashed into the side near the rear of Mike's boat, glancing off and spinning sideways. Regaining control, Genesis, turned his boat sharply. Blayde was firing at him with an M-60 machine gun. Bullets ripped across the bow, spurting spray as Genesis gunned the motor to full throttle in an attempt to escape the trap. The deputy with Genesis began returning fire with his rifle.

"Turn to the right so I can get a clear shot before he turns us into Swiss cheese," the deputy yelled.

"I'll turn behind that small hammock," Genesis said. "When we come around the other side, be ready."

Genesis turned the boat sharply to the right, skirting the edge of the hammock. As he cornered, the rear of the airboat swung around until they were almost sideways in the water. Within seconds, Genesis had pulled behind Mike's boat. The deputy fired every round he could. His bullets were zeroing in on the target when Mike turned his boat and Blayde fired several bursts from his machine gun. One of the bullets struck the deputy in the arm, knocking him backward causing Genesis to swerve sharply and open the throttle. He somehow managed to lose Mike and Blayde between the small hammocks. After a couple of minutes, he stopped the boat in twelve-foot-high sawgrass and jumped down to tend to the deputy.

"Sorry, I'm not a better shot," the deputy said.

"This ain't the movies kid," Genesis responded as he began wrapping a tourniquet around the wound. "It's hard to hit a moving target."

"They outgun us, don't they?" the deputy asked.

"You could say that," Genesis replied. "But we have backup. Let's call them."

Genesis picked up his radio to make the call. It had been hit by a stray bullet and was useless. The deputy's face turned pale.

"Any other ideas?" the deputy asked, grimacing from the pain in his arm.

"We're safe for now," Genesis said. "Why don't we make a plan while we wait it out?"

Billie and Jacob had not heard the commotion behind them as they pushed forward into the swamp. After a few minutes, Billie slowed the boat and picked up his binoculars. He glassed several hammocks looking for signs of activity, hoping he would detect Paul and his captive. About a mile distant, a hammock, larger than the rest, rose majestically from the sawgrass swamp. It drew Billie's attention like a magnet. He cut the motor of the boat and braced the binoculars across the rudder control to steady them. The glasses moved slowly from left to right as Jacob looked on.

"There!" Billie shouted. "I can barely make out the outline of an airboat."

"Let me see those," Jacob said as he took the binoculars from Billie's hand and began glassing.

"Yes," Jacob said excitedly. "I see it. How do you want to handle this?"

"We need to come in behind them," Billie responded. "We're going to berth and come around the back side."

"That'll take at least thirty minutes," Jacob said. "We better call Genesis."

"No," Billie said. "Not until we're set. Too much noise and they may kill Christina."

"They won't kill her yet, they want you," Jacob said. "You do know that?"

"Yes, but I have no choice," Billie replied.

"Right, let's go then," Jacob said.

As they began making their way around the back side of the hammock, Billie had no way of knowing that Paul intended on using Christina as bait for his trap. Paul had never lost and if he left Billie alive, it would his first defeat. Billie realized they would likely find Christina alive, but what came after that would remain a mystery until their dangerous game played out. He had no way of knowing that Paul's skills were much better than he anticipated and that at that very moment Paul was getting a feel for the entire hammock. By the time Billie arrived, Paul would know every trail, thicket, and clump of palmettos.

The deputy and Genesis had made their plan. There had been no real choice in the matter; it was the only thing they could do. The two were sitting in the boat, engine idling when Mike's boat appeared in front of them, broadside. The two parties saw each other at the same instant. Blayde turned to fire with Genesis's boat hurdling directly at him like a freight train. Blayde and the deputy fired in unison, surprise and panic showing on both their faces. The deputy spun around as he took a bullet through the ribs, falling at Genesis's feet, his gun going off in the process.

The bullet from the deputy's gun struck Mike in the chest, killing him instantly. Almost instantaneously, the boats collided. The deputy and Blayde were thrown into the water, their guns following them. As the two men and their weapons plunged into the murky waters of the swamp, the protective cage around the motor of Mike's boat was knocked off, exposing the turning airplane prop.

Genesis cut the engine on his boat and hopped down to pull the deputy from the water. Blood was pouring from the wound in his side as Genesis lays him back into the boat. Out of the corner of his eye, Genesis could see Blayde crawling back into his own boat, looking for a gun. Everything had been thrown overboard. Almost with glee, Blayde stood and faced Genesis. The only sound that could be heard was the idling motor of Mike's boat.

"I've heard how good you are Injun'," Blayde said as he pulled a long-bladed knife from behind his back. "Let's play."

"You're a little outgunned," Genesis said as he pulled his .45 pistol.

"What's the matter, afraid I'll carve you like I did your deputy?"

Genesis seemed puzzled. It took a second for him to comprehend what Blayde had said.

"I knew it had to be one of you thugs," Genesis said hoarsely. "By all means, let's dance."

Genesis jumped from his boat into the bow of Mike's, directly in front of Blayde; the two squaring off against each other.

"I hope you know how to use that thing," Genesis said.

"Why do you think they call me Blayde?" he queried. "I've already killed two Indians, a would-be knife fighter and a dumb woman driver, you'll be the third."

Genesis's eyes widened as the last words sunk in. Blayde had killed Mary Jane. Blayde lunged at Genesis who easily side stepped to avoid the shining silver blade. Genesis dodged everything Blayde threw at him as the boat began to gently rock from their movements. It was like watching a cobra and a mongoose. Like a toy, Genesis manipulated Blayde. Abruptly, Genesis fell while stepping backward. Taking immediate advantage, Blayde jumped on top, stabbing Genesis in the shoulder. Genesis managed to fight him off and kick him back until both were again standing.

"Not so good after all, are you?" Blayde taunted.

"Opinions differ," Genesis said.

Blayde, knife weaving back and forth like a dancing cobra, lunged again. Genesis sidestepped, trapped his arm in a joint lock and deftly removed the knife from his hand.

"See, it is not so difficult to defang a snake," Genesis said.

Blayde frantically searched for another weapon, finding a four-foot-long frog gig in the bottom of the boat.

"Defang this asshole," Blayde said as he lunged at Genesis with the three-pronged spear head. Blayde struck Genesis in the same knife wound.

Genesis jumped behind the seat housing; he on one side, Blayde on the other. Blayde continually lunged at Genesis who was having a difficult time avoiding the long spear. Realizing he had the knife he removed from Blayde's hand in his own, Genesis began to slice Blayde at will. Every time he thrust with the spear, Genesis sliced him on the arm, not quite able to get a good cut. On his next lunge, Genesis sliced Blayde down the left forearm, from the elbow to the wrist. Blayde dropped the frog gig, screaming in pain.

Genesis started to jump around the seat housing to approach Blayde from the front, pulling out his handcuffs. He took a step forward and lost his footing on the wet floor of the boat. As he slipped forward, Genesis tried to grab the housing for balance. His hand fell on the throttle pedal of the still idling engine. The boat lurched forward knocking Genesis to the floor. At the same instant, Blayde was propelled backward into the prop and ground like hamburger as blood spewed across the swamp in a red mist.

Genesis saw what happened as he fell; rising to his feet, he cut the motor and then grabbed his wounded shoulder.

"That was for Mary Jane and Freeman, gator bait," Genesis mumbled as he cast his gaze on the red stain in the swamp, the only remains of his opponent. Dizzy from loss of blood, Genesis tried cutting the motor of the boat again before he realized the sound was coming from another boat. He looked up to see two airboats idling next to his.

"That was quite a show," a deputy yelled. "Sorry we didn't get here sooner to help you out."

"It all worked out for the best," Genesis yelled back. "Help me, my deputy is seriously wounded. He needs medical attention immediately."

Genesis and several other officers helped the wounded deputy onto a makeshift stretcher and lashed it down across the boats bow. The deputy was very pale, breathing shallowly. Without medical attention, he wouldn't last long.

"Call a chopper out here right away," Genesis shouted. "Every second counts."

"Roger," a deputy yelled as he made a radio call. After a few seconds he motioned for everyone to cut their motors.

"We got an incoming message," the deputy said as he turned up his radio.

"Base, this is Egret 3. We have a positive fix on fugitive location.

"Affirmative, this is dispatch, we copy. What is your location?"

"We are in search area three, approximately twelve miles northeast of the boat docks. We request backup immediately."

"Backup is on the way," the dispatcher said.

"Egret 3 out."

"That's Billie and Jacob," Genesis said. "Do you have a map?"

"Yeah, got one right here," the deputy said as he unrolled it on the bow of the air boat. Genesis and several deputies hovered over the map, intensely searching its topographical features, trying to find the location.

"That would be about here," Genesis said as he pointed. "There! It has to be this large hammock. If they have as much firepower as these two thugs, Jacob and Billie will be in serious trouble."

"The other search teams are coming in now," said a deputy. "How do you want to handle it?"

"Gather everyone together," Genesis said. "Let's plan the approach."

The airboats and other search teams arrived at the same time as several more helicopters. As the deputy was loaded onto one of them, all the airboats met bow to bow; Genesis began explaining the situation.

"This is the hammock where they're holed up. We are going to approach it from all sides. There are three friendly persons on the hammock, no telling how many perps. You'll have limited visibility due to thick undergrowth and palmettos, so watch your field of fire. If you need to shoot, make damn sure you see the target clearly. Let's roll."

The deputy rolled up the map as the officers climbed into their airboats. The sound was deafening as all boats surged forward, mist spraying in their wake.

James Tindall

CHAPTER 12

Paul, sitting on the end of the log to which Christina was tied, suddenly leaped to his feet.

"Do you hear that?" Paul asked.

"What?" Monique asked angrily.

"That," Paul responded.

From the distance came the faint sound of an airboat, growing a little louder with each passing second.

"Maybe it is Mike and Blayde," Monique said.

"No," Paul said sharply looking at his watch. "They wouldn't be here for at least another hour. It has to be Billie. They're coming around the back side of the hammock. Mike and Blayde would approach from the front."

"What are we going to do?" Monique asked, desperation in her voice.

"Gag her again," Paul said, nodding toward Christina. "We'll put our bait in the trap and see what comes after it."

Monique walked over to Christina and placed a strip of duct tape across her mouth. Wide eyed, Christina could do nothing, but watch.

"I only heard one boat, so there can't be more than two or three of them," Paul explained. They won't see her until they're right on top of the clearing. That's when we'll hit them."

"What do you want me to do?" Monique asked.

"Here," Paul said, tossing her a gun. "Shoot anyone you see."

"Don't tempt me," Monique responded, a grin on her face as she pointed the gun directly at Paul.

"Cute," Paul said. "When you're through fooling around, move your ass behind those trees over there."

"And?" Monique asked, staring at him.

"Now we play the waiting game," Paul replied. We don't move until we need to. Watch for my signal."

Monique thought she saw a movement but passed it off when she could determine what it was. Still, she felt she was being watched. Nervousness overcame her.

Paul walked to a large oak tree and positioned himself behind it. Looking about, he was confident they wouldn't be seen. The trio was nearly invisible in the midst of the thick undergrowth. Christina, sitting atop the log, bound and gagged, was looking out the opening of the clearing across the sawgrass. She had a look of longing, hoping Billie would come to her rescue, but at the same time fearing his death if he did. There's so much she wanted to tell him. Although they had never finished their discussion, it had gone very well. Christina had hoped he would ask her to marry him but knew too many other things were on his mind. Despite this, Christina had already come to her own conclusion. She loved

Billie and always had, and she knew he loved her. He had a lot of potential, two college degrees, a great personality, a lovely kid, and was a wonderful person whom she had come to treasure. If she did make it out of this and he asked, the answer would be an immediate yes.

Billie eased the bow of the airboat onto the edge of the hammock. He and Jacob dismounted and checked their pistols as they crept into the undergrowth. A tangled mixture of gumbo limbo trees, fern, sedges, and willow trees, slowly giving way to palm and oak trees and thick palmetto. It would not be a quiet or easy pursuit. The two men stopped, their gaze piercing as they swept the undergrowth.

"We'll head in that direction," Billie said, motioning ahead of them. "You circle left and I'll circle right. They'll likely hear us, so keep your eyes peeled."

Within seconds, the two could no longer see each other as they crept forward.

Prowling through the woods, Billie moved slowly, like molasses on a winter morning. He was using an old technique taught to him by the Medicine Man called still hunting. He would pick up one foot at a time, look in all directions and then slowly put the foot down, one foot after another. It was agonizingly slow, but hopefully, he would spot Paul first. Several times, Billie spotted movement, like a hidden warrior, but when he looked, he could see nothing.

"What was that?" Billie muttered to himself. "Nothing; I must be going crazy."

His nerves seemed to be getting the best of him as he half walked, half crawled through the undergrowth. Twice more, he thought he saw Indian warriors, but when he looked, there was nothing.

"Maybe it's our ancestral ghosts," Billie mused. "Better yet, maybe it's the Medicine Man. Wisdom hell; if I had any, I'd be at the hospital with my son."

Less than fifty yards away, Billie caught a glimpse of Jacob slithering through the trees like a snake. Spanish moss, hanging from the oaks in thick blankets, quickly obscured Billie's frontal view. The inside of the hammock was still and quiet, not even the animals were stirring. The lack of animal sounds confirmed Billie's suspicions. It was too quiet. Someone else was present.

Sweat began dripping from Billie's brow, running into his eyes, the saltiness burning them. It was so hot Billie felt like he was in an unventilated green house on a summer afternoon. But it wasn't the heat making Billie perspire, he was acclimated to that, it was the tension, it could be cut with a knife. Billie saw Jacob easing around a clump of palmettos. At the same instant, he saw Christina, her back to both of them, sitting in a small clearing. Peering intently, he could see no one else.

Billie couldn't see Monique positioning herself to fire at Jacob, who continuing through the trees, appeared a few yards away, directly in front of her. Jacob caught a glimpse of movement as Monique raised her gun and fired. He dove to the dirt behind some palmettos as the shot whizzed past his head. The sudden explosion startled Billie. Immediately ducking behind a tree, he peered in Jacob's direction. Billie could see Jacob start to run as another shot rang out, the bullet thudding into a tree next to Jacob. A third shot rang out; the bullet struck Jacob in the shoulder. Unable to see the attacker, Billie felt helpless, knowing that if he were spotted, they would both be caught.

Abruptly, the shooter approached Jacob. Billie was stunned to see it was Monique. Had she been in on this all along? "She played me for a sucker, and I fell for it, Billie thought to himself. "Of all the things that could happen, I am such a sap." He continued to watch as Monique reached Jacob.

"On your feet," Monique said, jabbing Jacob with her gun. "Move over to your friend."

Jacob, having difficulty walking, reached Christina and sat down on the ground beside her, his back to the log.

"Sorry Christina," Jacob wheezed. "My sneaky Injun' skills aren't up to par."

"Shut up," Monique said, obviously irritated and stressed. "You can reminisce later."

Certain where they were, Billie crept forward. After a short distance, he could see all three clearly. The only one missing was Paul. Where was he?

"As long as they don't have me, they won't kill them," Billie muttered to himself. The question is how do I get to them before I'm spotted?"

Billie continued to creep forward, keeping a sharp lookout. Without warning, an explosion ripped the air, the source of the sound whizzing past Billie's ear, scraping bark from a nearby tree. Billie dove to the dirt, bark showering him as he crawled forward and around the tree for more cover.

"Give it up Billie," Paul yelled. "I've beaten you again."

"Not until the tree frog croaks," Billie yelled back.

Billie crawled faster through the undergrowth, several bullets ripping into the ground about his feet.

"I'll make it easy on your friends if you give yourself up," Paul said. "I promise they'll die quickly."

"You're the one who will die Lorio," Billie said. "My son is near death because of you. If anyone deserves to die, it's you."

"Because of me?" Paul asked. "You wanted the deal as much as I did. You were just as greedy, you're just as responsible. Those kids are in the hospital as much due to you as to me."

"I did it for my own people, to make a living, not to pollute and poison our land," Billie yelled. "If you hadn't been doing illegal dumping, none of this would have happened."

Billie spotted Paul, too late, a bullet ripped through Billie's calf causing him to drop his gun. He quickly hobbled away into thicker cover. Paul could see the hit.

"Give it up Billie," Paul said. "You're mine now."

"Never!" Billie screamed as loud as he could, anger in his voice. "We've never lost a war to the white man. This won't be the first."

"If you're going to lose it might as well be to me," Paul yelled. "And you will lose this time. In a few minutes, you'll be gator bait. Without a body, there's no crime."

Paul walked over to Monique.

"I'm going after him," Paul said. "If they move, kill them."

"Don't worry, nothing will come between me and my money," Monique replied.

Paul hurried after Billie, trying to pick up the blood trail.

"I'm on your trail like a bloodhound, Billie," Paul yelled after him. "How long do you think you can hold out?"

"Long enough to see you dead."

Billie's calf was bleeding badly. He stopped long enough to stuff Spanish moss into his pants leg to stem the blood flow, then, used his belt as a tourniquet, tying it off just above the calf.

"I never lose Billie," Paul yelled again. "I thought that was clear to you. On the other hand, the Indian has always fought a losing battle. Just like this one."

"Our people have never been conquered," Billie yelled back.

Billie moved on, trying to keep ahead of Paul. Although the hammock was a large one, he wouldn't be able to hide from his pursuer for long. He would find where the blood trail stopped, but they were already nearing the end of the hammock. There would not be much room left to maneuver. If Paul trapped him in this small area, it would be life or death. As Billie hobbled along, he tried to remember all the lessons the Medicine Man had taught him about disappearing in the woods. The problem was they didn't consider a severe wound, just becoming one with the swamp. How the hell do you do that? Billie was frantic.

Paul's shouts to Billie had faded as Monique stood watching after him. She hoped this would be over soon. When the helicopter arrived, she would be free and even if they linked any of the crimes to Paul, she would be out of the picture, just an employee who served as an administrative assistant. Monique glanced over her shoulder at Christina and Jacob. They weren't going anywhere. Jacob was in bad shape. Monique turned back, canting her head to the side, trying to hear Paul and Billie. There were no sounds other than the rustling of leaves in the treetops from a gentle breeze that had begun blowing in from the gulf.

Monique was standing casually, her left hand across her waist as she rested the right elbow atop the left wrist to support the heavy weight of the revolver she held. The gun was extended in front of her in a relaxed position. Without warning, a muscular brown arm appeared over her shoulder. Startled, she began to turn as a hand jerked the revolver from her grasp and she was pushed violently forward. Monique landed on her back, several feet from where she had been standing.

Looking up, she saw an exceptionally large, muscular Indian standing over her. He was dressed in full Seminole battle regalia, wearing war paint, a red head band around his forehead. He looked like the pictures of Chief Osceola featured in history books. Looking about in bewilderment, Monique saw a dozen more Indians in a semi-circle behind the first. She was wide eyed, terrified. They carried a variety of weapons — bows and arrows, modern pistols, and 30/30 rifles, the old standby for hunters in the Everglades. Abruptly, the large Indian stepped to the side. Directly behind him was the Medicine Man, holding a spear in his right hand, his white hair falling about his shoulders in stark contrast to his dark skin and weather-beaten features. Suddenly, the large Indian bent forward, his face directly in front of Monique's, scant inches away. She swallowed hard, thinking this was the end as the Indian's eyes glared at her, a scowl on his face. As if she were a feather, the warrior yanked her onto both feet.

"Who, who are you?" Monique stuttered, frightened.

"We are the guardians of the Tribe," the Medicine Man replied. "We see all. We saw you this morning."

"Paul forced me to do this," Monique cried. "It wasn't my choice."

"A feather in the breeze requires little force," the Medicine Man said sternly. "Greed was yours. Bind her."

Two Indians stepped forward and bound Monique's hands behind her back. Christina had been untied from the log and Monique was placed in the same spot she had just vacated. As the two Indians began tying Monique to the log, Christina interrupted them.

"Here, let me do that," Christina said. The Indians backed away and began helping two others who were tending Jacob. Completing her task, Christina rose, looking down on Monique.

"I guess you're happy now," Monique said sarcastically. Christina looked at her, tears forming. Suddenly, she struck Monique across the jaw with a right cross.

"Yes, I am getting there, bitch," Christina replied, walking away.

"You really should choose better companions Christina," the Medicine Man said.

"I'll work harder at it next time," Christina answered. "Hurry, we must help Billie. Paul will kill him."

"If it is to be so," the Medicine Man said. "We will not interfere with his test of life."

"But..."

"They must pit their skills against each other. Billie cannot lead our people into the future without passing this test."

"Then, Billie is a dead man," Christina blurted out, tears welling in her eyes, beginning to run down her cheeks.

"If Billie links his mind with the swamp as I have taught him, he will win," the Medicine Man replied. Does not the sun rise and set each day? Has not the mighty Seminole survived all the white man could throw at us?"

"Yes," Christina replied impatiently. "But many have died, lost their livelihood, or been displaced from their homelands."

"Humphh!" the Medicine Man said in disgust. "We are still here. It will always be so. Come, we will watch the outcome. Have faith in the Great Spirit who watches over us all."

The group marched off in the direction that Paul and Billie had taken, moving through the undergrowth like ghosts. Jacob, having had a native poultice applied to his wound, remained behind, in the able care of two warriors. They formed a single line headed by the muscular Indian, followed by the Medicine Man, then Christina, and the rest of the group. After a few minutes they heard voices in the distance, an occasional shout followed by a reply. The group quickened their pace as they pressed forward.

Billie, having managed to elude Paul, was walking down a game trail. As he turned a corner, the trail disappeared into the swamp at the edge of the hammock. A small clearing lay before him. Looking around, Billie thought quickly, assessing the strategy of the moment. Careful to avoid leaving noticeable footprints in the soft, mucky soil, Billie slipped into undergrowth on the east side, picking up a dead branch in the process.

Paul appeared almost immediately in front of him, gun in hand. Having made it just in time, Billie's heart was pounding so hard he was sure Paul would hear it.

"End of the trail Billie," Paul yelled, not sure if Billie had stopped or gone on. "There's nowhere else to run. Come on out, I'll make it easy on you."

Paul walked back and forth looking at the ground for a sign of Billie's passing. At one point, he passed within two feet and still didn't see him. As Paul turned to retrace his steps, Billie sprang from his hiding place, knocking the gun from Paul's hand with the stick. It fell near the edge of the swamp, out of Paul's reach. In the same motion, Billie landed a solid right punch on Paul's jaw who sailed through the air, landing on his back.

"You shouldn't have done that Billie," Paul said, shaking his finger back and forth, rising to his feet. "I won't make it easy on you now."

"I'm real scared," Billie replied, hobbling toward the gun. Paul tripped him as he passed and retrieved the gun himself.

"It would be so painless and easy if I just squeezed the trigger, but I can't," Paul said. "You see, I have to make you feel the pain; all the millions that you cost me."

Paul put the gun in his belt, behind his back.

"At least I have a chance," Billie thought to himself.

"Aren't you getting a little cocky now?" Billie asked.

"On the contrary, it's you who has the wounds," Paul said. "Besides, I'm a former golden gloves boxer."

"Yeah," Billie muttered. "Well, let's see if you fight as well as you talk."

"Oh, but I assure you I do," Paul responded.

The two men closed on each other. Billie lashed out with a right punch and struck Paul across the forehead and then a left to his ribs. Paul countered with a kick to Billie's wounded calf, followed by a right to the side of the head. As Billie fell to his knees, he hissed in pain.

"How did I do?" Paul asked arrogantly.

"I've fought better," Billie retorted.

"And won?" Hah!

Paul approached Billie, letting him get up. Billie surprised him by driving forward and tackling him to the ground. As Billie fell on top, he managed to strike Paul several times in the face, breaking his nose. Paul angrily threw Billie off. Extremely pissed, he got up and kicked Billie in the ribs, then hauled him to his feet. Paul hit Billie in the ribs so hard it took his breath away. He was in a rage, like a mad bull.

"To hell with shooting you," Paul screamed. "I'm going to beat you to death." Paul threw a knee into Billie's ribs. "Even if you were---*Billie received an elbow to the head*---Beastmaster---*a left upper cut*---and could talk to animals---*right cross*---all your swamp creatures---*left jab*---couldn't help you now." Paul struck Billie with another knee to the stomach, dropping him to the ground, and then he kicked him again.

"Ten million dollars," Paul yelled. "That's what you cost me. Get up. I want every cent."

Paul helped Billie to his feet and knocked him down again.

269

"We could have made lots of money, but you care more about a few kids," Paul said. "So what if they die, they're going to die anyway."

"Children are our heritage," Billie said, wincing at the pain of talking. "You would kill them for money? You don't deserve to breathe."

"It's you who's having trouble breathing," Paul said. "And I have news for you. Money makes the world go round. Everything and everyone has a price."

"Our children and our land have no price," Billie said, "Nor does our love for them."

As they talked, they rested. Paul stood first and viciously kicked Billie in the ribs again, knocking the wind out of him. "It's good to know you love your land," Paul whispered in Billie's ear. "You're about to become part of it."

In the edge of the trees, unseen, the Medicine Man and his group stood as silent sentinels, witnesses to the scene before them. Two of them were restraining Christina. One had his hand over her mouth. Another Indian drew a bow and was about to release his deadly arrow, the Medicine Man raised his hand to stop him. The Indian slowly lowered his weapon to the ready, bewilderment on his face as he eyed the Medicine Man.

Paul walked into Billie, striking him several times, finishing with a fist to the face. The force of the blow propelled Billie backward. He tripped and fell face down upon the ground, half of his body in the swamp, the other half on the hammock.

"Any last words," Paul asked, his breath coming in heavy gulps as he drew his pistol?

"Yes," Billie hissed painfully. "They're for an unfinished conversation. Tell Christina I love her."

Paul thought about it for a moment then, he smiled down at Billie. Billie was desperately looking around, trying to find anything he could to use for a weapon. Directly in front of him lay a baby alligator. It was very still, trying to remain hidden from this creature with a round head who had just invaded its home. Cautiously looking about, Billie spotted the mother gator about eight feet away. It was one of the largest gator's Billie had ever seen, so large it frightened him to be so close. He estimated it at about thirteen feet. It would have to weigh close to fourteen hundred pounds or more. Sweat began trickling down Billie's forehead as he gingerly grasped the baby gator around the head and neck with his thumb and index finger.

"I'll tell her," Paul replied. "Just before Blayde kills her. You have a last request?"

"No, but I have a souvenir, compliments of the Seminole Tribe of Florida," Billie said as he tossed the baby gator to Paul.

"Catch," Billie whispered, the baby gator was now in midair.

"Thanks," Paul said, laughing. "I'll make a key chain out of it and have it monogrammed with your initials. It'll be great to remember you by."

No sooner had Paul caught the baby gator than it began squeaking. Paul had a puzzled look on his face, like he was trying to remember something. He started to open his mouth when a loud roar erupted from the swamp directly in front of Billie who threw himself to the side, barely escaping as the mother gator exploded out of the water toward Paul. Stepping back, Paul fired at the gator, his shot going wild. Panic stricken, he tried to fire again, but it was too late. The gator grasped him between the legs in its cavernous jaws and made several corkscrew-type turns, bouncing Paul against the ground like a rag doll. The screams Paul made were interrupted each time his body hit the ground.

The gator retreated into the water, hapless Paul still screaming in its mouth. The screams gurgled to an end as the gator pulled her victim beneath the black waters of the Florida Everglades. In great pain, Billie tried to push himself up when he noticed a pair of feet directly in front of his face. For a second he panicked, but then realized the moccasin clad feet were those of an Indian. A hand reached down to clasp his shoulder and help him up. Billie was able to stand as several more hands helped. He came face to face with the Medicine Man and Christina, the other Indians about them in a circle. Christina grabbed his right arm to help support him, intending never to let go.

"Your test is over Panther," the Medicine Man said.

"How did...?" Billie began to ask.

"Sharp eyes," the Medicine Man replied with a twinkle in his eyes as he pointed at them with two fingers.

"You were here?" Billie asked incredulously. "You heard?"

"I heard you Billie," Christina whispered softly, hugging his shoulder. "We all heard."

Dizziness overwhelming him, Billie's knees buckled. At that moment, the search teams arrived, roaring in on their airboats, a couple of helicopters hovering overhead, in a pincher movement of the helicopter that was to pick up Paul. With FBI choppers in front and armed officers in airboats surrounding it, the pilot cut the engine, nowhere to go. The officers jumped out like swat team members before they realized it was all over. Paramedics were directly on their heels. Genesis rammed the bow of his airboat into the shore of the hammock. Christina and the Medicine Man led Billie over to a log and sat him down. Two paramedics reached Billie and began dressing his wounds. The Indians with the Medicine Man, their purpose accomplished, silently filed away, seeming to vanish in an instant.

"Looks like you've been gator wrestling," Genesis said.

"I wish," Billie replied. "That would have been easier. Did we get them all?"

"Yeah," Genesis said. "Mike and Blayde dead, several deputies dead, and Jacob seriously wounded. He told us where to find you and is already on his way to the hospital." Genesis paused as several officers led Monique past them. She pulled away to confront Billie.

"This is only the beginning you know," Monique said. "The landfill was built with mob money. They'll want it back."

"Do you think they can take it back?" Billie asked. "They can't do anything to us the white man hasn't done before."

"I'll be sure to tell them," Monique said proudly.

"If you ever get out of jail," Christina chimed in.

"Tell them this," Billie said. "We own the site now. They forfeited it when Paul broke the law. It's Seminole business, upheld by Indian law."

They watched as Monique was led away and put in one of the choppers. The down draft from its blades pounding the sawgrass around them as it took flight.

"Why are people so greedy when they have so much?" Billie asked.

"That philosophical debate will need to wait until later," Genesis said. "Come on, I have a surprise for you."

Genesis and Christina helped Billie into his boat; a paramedic climbed in with them, checking Billie's wounds. The other search team members were already speeding away. Genesis cranked the boat and sped off across the sawgrass. Seeing that Billie was pretty banged up, he kept the speed slow. Genesis kept his eye on them as the breeze whipped his face. A smile appeared when Christina snuggled close to Billie, wrapping her arms around his neck and kissing him on the cheek while attempting to stay out of the paramedic's way. "There's hope for them," Genesis thought. "Yep, they'll make it just fine."

The gentle rocking of the boat as it bounced across the swamp had a calming effect on Christina. Sitting next to Billie, she mulled the last few days over in her mind. She had never understood how much Billie loved her. It had never been clear until she had heard him request that Paul tell her. It would have been Billie's last words had he not linked himself to the swamp. To think that his dying words would have been of her caused an indescribable emotion. It washed over Christina's entire body, like diving into warm water. She shuddered as if cold, but then bathed in the warmth of the beauty and depth of Billie's love. She looked at him, so tired he could barely sit up as she steadied him, Christina realized at that moment, she would never leave his side.

The sun was beginning to set when Genesis pulled the airboat up to the docks. The last of the search teams were leaving the parking lot. Billie wasn't paying much attention as a helicopter landed. Still a little unstable, Christina held tightly to his arm, not wanting to leave him, as she and Genesis helped him climb onto the dock. Unseen in the shadows, the Medicine Man observed. It was his nature. "Such heart I have never seen," he thought to himself. "Not in all my days. Panther is indeed special, like Chief Osceola in days long gone."

Billie was making his way along the dock. Now feeling a little better, he glanced toward the end. Spotting the doctor, he also noticed someone in a wheelchair beside him. Taking a second look, he recognized his son. A burst of energy seemed to explode from deep inside as Billie hurried faster, his face erupting into a smile as he saw James clearly. Billie reached him and bent down, his arms encircling the boy in a hearty embrace.

"Are you okay dad?" James asked. "You don't look so good."

"I'm fine," Billie said. "Nothing a little rest won't cure. It's great to see you son. How do you feel?"

"Better," James replied. "I can walk around, but the doctor won't let me."

"He needs to get some rest for the next few days," the doctor said as he stepped forward. "After that, he'll be fine, thanks to you Billie. Once we knew what the chemicals were, we were able to help all the children. They're safe and on their way to a speedy and full recovery."

"Thanks doc," Billie said. "Have you notified their parents?"

"Some," the doctor replied. "Genesis said he would take care of the rest."

"I'm going to take care of that now Billie," Genesis said, walking off.

"Wait up, I'll go with you," the doctor said. "Remember to make him rest Billie. Call me if you need anything."

Billie, Christina and James were finally alone on the dock. The sunset was a bright red orange as they faced each other. As Christina looked deep into Billie's eyes, she placed a quivering hand on his cheek, leaning forward to kiss him. She was interrupted by a tug at her jeans; James had his arms wrapped around both of their legs, not wanting to let go.

"Are you going to be my mom?" James asked innocently.

Before she could reply, the Medicine Man was by her side. He held up Billie's right hand and Christina's right hand, forearm to forearm.

Looking Billie directly in the eyes, with the most penetrating look Billie had ever seen the Medicine Man said, "I give you your new name; **Ga-lu-na-di A-danh-te-ha-e-sv**."

It was clear Billie did not understand. "You are Sky Thinker." Then, taking a small, colorfully beaded leather band from his pocket, the Medicine Man wrapped it around Billie and Christina's wrists.

"You have both decided?"

Billie nodded affirmatively.

"Yes!" Christina replied happily, tears streaming down her face.

The Medicine Man silently walked down the dock and climbed into his dugout; assisted by the young muscular Indian, who was ever at his side. Helping the Medicine Man into the boat, the young warrior gazed quickly and fiercely at Billie and Christina then, began poling the canoe across the swamp.

Billie, Christina, and James watched the two of them leave, in awe of the Medicine Mans' uncanny ability with people. Wondering how he knew. Billie pulled Christina toward him, looking into her eyes. As the sun's golden rays washed over her beautiful face, he kissed her passionately, their silhouettes framed against the glow of the setting Florida sun.

END

ABOUT THE AUTHOR

James Tindall is the author of Jagged Grass, Sun God's Treasure, Alas Omega, and other books, including two best-in-field textbooks. He grew up on a Florida reservation wrestling alligators and training horses to earn money. He is a U.S. Army veteran who served in intelligence and is an expert in sharpshooting and hand-to-hand combat. He has five martial-arts black belts of advanced rank including a 9th degree in Kenpo, as well as four college degrees. As a federal scientist, he specialized in water, energy, and food security, engaging him in the areas of homeland and international security and counterterrorism. His assignments have taken him from Latin America to Brazil, Mexico to Alaska, Turkey to China, and many points between. When not writing, he consults and helps solve tactical and strategic problems for international governments and SOGs.

www.ingramcontent.com/pod-product-compliance
Lightning Source LLC
Chambersburg PA
CBHW071128200626
46817CB00018B/2453